READER

CHIANTI SOULS

"Absolutely LOVED this book and made me feel
like I was back in Tuscany with my family in Lucca
near Florence!"
-Doranne Bendinelli-Christner

"Just finished your first novel and felt like I had a mini trip
to my absolute favorite place in the world! Brava! I really
looked forward to every chapter and will definitely await
the sequel. I am an Italophile, loving all things Italian which
led me to start my own villa rental company 13 yrs ago."

- Sheri Levitt, Owner, The Villa People
www.thevillapeople.com

"Be warned, Luca Rusconi is swoon-worthy, as are the
descriptions of my beloved Italy."

- Brenda Viola, Blogger, Speaker
www.brendaviola.com

Charmaine,

Dream of love and romance in Tuscany!
(or anywhere!)

CHIANTI SOULS

An Italian Love Story

Karen Ross

March 2016

Third edition 2015

Italian wine quotations from *Too Much Tuscan Wine*, by Dario Castagno
with Robert Rodi © Dario Castagno and Robert Rodi 2008. Used by
permission of Dario Castagno.

ISBN: 1491050756
ISBN-13:   978-1491050750

Printed by Create Space, An Amazon.com Company

Map and cover illustrations by Karen Ross
Photography by Jonathan Gibbs

To my husband Craig and our romantic days in Chianti...

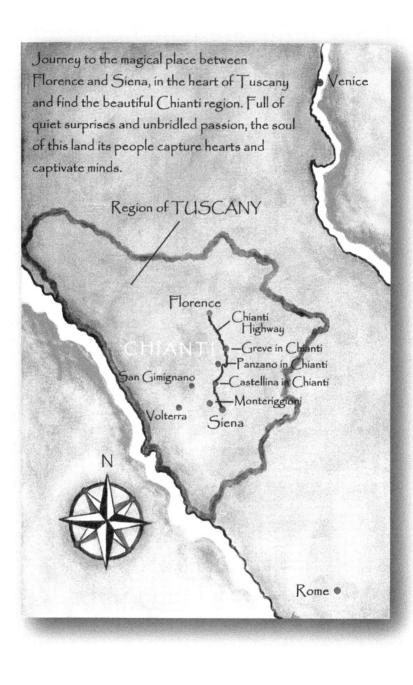

Journey to the magical place between Florence and Siena, in the heart of Tuscany and find the beautiful Chianti region. Full of quiet surprises and unbridled passion, the soul of this land its people capture hearts and captivate minds.

Venice

Region of TUSCANY

CHIANTI

Florence

Chianti Highway

Greve in Chianti

Panzano in Chianti

San Gimignano

Castellina in Chianti

Monteriggioni

Volterra

Siena

N

Rome

TO AWAKEN QUITE ALONE in a strange town is one of the pleasantest sensations in the world. You are surrounded by adventure. You have no idea of what is in store for you, but you will, if you are wise and know the art of travel, let yourself go on the stream of the unknown and accept whatever comes in the spirit in which the gods may offer it.

— *Freya Stark*

VENICE

Chapter 1

"THIS IS NOT A VALUABLE PIECE," the jeweler said as he inspected the etched swirls and silhouettes on the case of a silver pocket watch.

He scratched his thick gray beard before opening the cover to examine its face decorated with Roman numerals. He tried to wind it, but the dial wouldn't turn. The hands were stuck at 7:11.

"It is broken and cannot be repaired."

"No kidding," scoffed his female customer.

The short, stocky jeweler peered at her above his magnifying lenses, judging how desperate she was.

Gucci-donned customers like this beautiful, young lady usually entered his closet-sized jewelry store – Gioielli Antichi di Venezia – with a wealthy spouse, boyfriend or lover and departed with an expensive purchase. Not her. She was alone, impatient and angry in some way.

"Are you sure you want to sell?" he asked. "It's at least 50 years old and seems quite sentimental."

"Sentiment is for the weak. And for my peasant boyfriend."

She tapped her fingers on the glass counter then crossed her arms.

"And I have only 10 minutes until my train leaves for Florence."

The jeweler knew how to handle her. He'd bought and sold jewelry his entire life, like his father and every generation before him. So a kind of merchant's intuition rippled through his Venetian blood. Silence would make her nervous and press her deadline.

After a few minutes she spoke first.

"I'm running out of time. Are you going to give me a price?"

"Well," he paused and rubbed his brow. "It is not worth much since it is useless as a watch, but I might be able to sell it as a pendant. Let me think a little more."

His well-manicured fingers traveled over the circumference of the watch's scalloped edge. The watch felt light in his hand. He was sure all the mechanics were removed. It wasn't even worth taking the time to open the back of the case to confirm it.

"I'll give you 15 euros."

He knew he could resell it for 60.

"No more?"

She rubbed the arms of her tailored brown suede jacket.

"No, 15. Firm."

He didn't budge knowing she would accept it.

She pursed her lips and avoided making make eye contact.

"*Va bene*." – "Okay." She added, "I'm glad to be rid of it."

He began to write a receipt for the transaction.

"Your name?" he asked.

"Lia."

"Surname?"

"I don't have time for this. Just give me the cash so I may leave."

"*Va bene*."

As he handed cash to the Florence-bound traveler, she tossed her long dark hair over her shoulders and hurried outside into the cool April air, toward the Santa Lucia train station.

He shrugged his shoulders and chuckled as she left. Nothing surprised this old salty Venetian.

To create an attractive pendant with the watch, he rooted through a box of silver chains until he found one he liked. He threaded the chain through the loop of the watch. Then he strung a paper tag on it, marked the price at "€68" and hung it in his store window knowing it would appeal to a sentimental tourist.

He was right.

PHILADELPHIA

Chapter 2

SEVEN MONTHS HAD PASSED since graphic designer Mary Sarto had made a single brush stroke on canvas. It was exactly the number of months since Ian Copeland had broken up with her. But she had fresh inspiration to get back into her painting hobby, and not because of a new man in her life. It was much simpler than that – and definitely less painful.

It happened on an ordinary morning in early July when she went to the small advertising agency where she worked. She had been out since the end of June and when she flipped the page of the 1999 Tuscany-themed wall calendar to July, she found the much-needed inspiration.

A castle's medieval tower peeking above thick cypress trees was the monthly photograph and it tickled something deep inside her. It was as though she was being invited to enter the castle's fortified walls.

That very evening she began recreating the dreamy Tuscan scene on a large canvas that was five-feet wide and four-feet tall. She painted nearly every evening.

Chapter 3

A FEW WEEKS LATER, Mary was hours away from finishing the painting and could hardly wait to get home from work. She watched the clock all afternoon. At five, she changed from heels to her favorite worn flats. Then she shed her cropped linen jacket and stuffed the work clothes into her tote bag.

She hit the hot city streets of Philadelphia, heading to Moretti's Italian Market to buy groceries and her favorite red wine – Chianti. Her refrigerator was empty, and she wasn't sure what she would eat for dinner, but she knew her friend and market owner Enzo Moretti would have suggestions, as he always did. He loved food, and he enjoyed sharing it with her.

So her visits were frequent, not only for groceries and wine, but for the gentle way he warmed her heart and filled the shoes of her deceased father.

As she stepped into the tightly packed South Philly market, Mr. Moretti happily greeted her.

"*Buongiorno*, Mary! Beautiful day, like-a you, *cara mia*."

"Thank you, Signore Moretti."

They kissed each other's cheeks in the traditional European manner.

"How's business today?" Mary asked.

"On a sunny day like-a today everythin' eez-a good. The fruit eez-a sweeter and da people have more smiles, but you know your smile is my favorite always."

Mary loved listening to his thick Italian accent. It made English sound so lyrical and poetic. His words flowed and even bounced.

"If I didn't know better, I would think you were flirting," Mary teased.

She flashed a bright smile, showing off the dimples she'd inherited from her half-Italian father. She also had his dark hair and olive complexion.

"If I was a young man and single, I would ask-a you for a date." One of his deep-set brown eyes sent a wink her way.

"You're so sweet."

"No, not sweet am I. Gelato is sweet. What do you need today?" She giggled.

"I'm painting again, tonight, so I need a bottle of Chianti."

"Of course you need it!"

He laughed and continued.

"*Se berrai vino rosso rinnoverai il tuo sangue*...red wine renews your blood."

Mr. Moretti had many expressions about the importance of drinking wine, and his preference was Chianti. It reminded him of Tuscany, his home, which he called "the most beautiful place on earth."

Mr. Moretti had given Mary the wall calendar as a daily reminder that she needed to see Tuscany. She agreed, but she didn't know when she would go or who she would go with.

"I haven't decided what I'm having for dinner yet. Any suggestions?"

"These Roma tomatoes are ripe and *delizioso*, and perfect for *insalata caprese*."

"Good idea."

It was a favorite recipe of Mary's, just sliced tomatoes, buffalo mozzarella, fresh basil and olive oil nicely arranged on a plate. And it was equally as good chopped and tossed into a bowl.

"I'll take two."

While he carefully sorted through the produce basket for two perfect tomatoes, she asked him how his family was doing, and he gave her precisely the same answer he gave every time she asked. But she listened as though it was the first time she'd heard it. She adored him and didn't mind his repetition.

"*Dio mio*, my son Giovanni is gonna kill me," he sighed. "We fight every day and I'm gonna explode with a heart attack right here in this market, in this basket of tomatoes."

He gestured toward the produce and rubbed his deeply wrinkled brow and puffed more.

"Giovanni is lazy. He will never marry and never have sons who can run our family business. Ah, what does he know about la famiglia? And where is the crazy boy right now? I see him nowhere – he's always goofin' off and I have to watch him all-a the time. And I have to keep-a his hands out of the cash register – he steals money for cigarettes, you know? And his-a friends are no good, either!"

He took a breath, sighed, and shook his head.

"Mary, I wish he was a good worker, and I wish he would marry a nice girl, like you. He needs to have his own family by now."

"Don't give up. He's still young."

She knew Giovanni was only two years younger than she was, and she had just celebrated her 32nd birthday a week earlier, on July 11. She hoped they both still had plenty of time for families.

"How is Mrs. Moretti?"

She knew the answer to this, too.

"She eez-a good woman. She spends all day and all evening taking care of her sister. She comes home to sleep. I do not know how she does this every day. She eez-a saint."

"Yes, I agree. Tell her I miss her."

She wandered through the market, picking up her favorite Italian grocery items. She selected Lavazza coffee – the only variety that should ever be served, according to Mr. Moretti. She also chose a package of Perugina chocolates – the purest chocolate in the world with no fillers, Mr. Moretti frequently reminded her. She had learned early on that he had strong opinions about food and everything else, including the men Mary dated.

"I WILL KEEP MY EYES OPEN for a hard-a working man for you, but do not worry, it will not be my Giovanni or another Ian. You are too good for boys like them. You need a hardworking man like me."

Mr. Moretti firmly put his hand over his heart.

"I am sure your *papà* would-a want that, too."

Mary blushed at his comment about Ian, her most recent long-term boyfriend, if four months counted as long-term. Now all she had left of the aspiring songwriter and guitarist was "Titian Eyes," a beautiful love song he had written about her.

The relationship had started with that song, but had ended abruptly in early December with an awkward message on her answering machine. Ian had said that he was headed to Nashville "or someplace like that."

She hadn't heard from him since. He was a free-spirited musician who changed locations on a whim. She had admired his ability to pick-up and go wherever his heart desired, but he had been so tender and loving that it surprised her when he left in such a painful way. He didn't own a cell phone, so there was no way to reach him and say goodbye.

"You have fresh basil?" Mr. Moretti asked, ending her thoughts of Ian.

"Um, yeah. I have the plant you gave me. It's in my kitchen window, growing well."

"*Bene. Mozzarella?*"

"I need to buy some."

"No, no. I give to you. *Scusi.*"

He returned from the back of the store with homemade *mozzarella di bufala*. He didn't sell his own handcrafted cheese, but always gave some to Mary when he made it.

"For you. Take it. The freshest."

"*Grazie!* I will eat it tonight."

She gave him $20 and collected change from his thick, calloused hands.

"I'll be back in a few days," she said.

"*Ciao*, enjoy the *caprese*. I will have a new wheel of *Parmagiano-Reggiano* next time." He winked again.

Whenever a new shipment arrived from Emilia-Romagna, Italy – the only place in the world that could claim ownership of the king of Italian cheeses – he always gave her small wedges of it.

"Ciao," she said heading out the door.

As she walked toward her apartment, she smiled about seeing Mr. Moretti. Week after week, he had taught her basic Italian expressions and simple Italian cooking. He had given her old family recipes, insisting they be made only with the freshest ingredients. He explained that if she accepted the recipes she was also agreeing never to change them.

About three blocks away from the market, she remembered that she'd recently finished her bottle of olive oil and she needed some for the *insalata caprese*. Without hesitating she turned around to go back and buy his quality Italian oil.

As she walked into the market again, Enzo Moretti hurried toward her.

"*Dio mio, è il destino!*" – "My God, it is destiny!"

Mary was surprised by his dramatic greeting. Mr. Moretti's arms were outstretched and he was grinning from ear-to-ear.

"This eez-a the pretty girl I tell you about."

She looked toward the register, where a ruggedly handsome blonde man in a tailored charcoal gray suit stood with his hand on a bottle of Gabbiano Chianti Classico. His cheeks reddened, as did hers.

"This eez-a Garrett. Garrett Hansen."

Mr. Moretti made a long roll of the "r" and sharp staccato of the "t" each time he said "Garrett."

"Heez-a single businessman, new in Philadelphia."

Mr. Moretti particularly emphasized the word "businessman."

Mary swallowed hard and blushed harder. She felt her mouth going dry.

Mr. Moretti had more to say.

"He says he likes my store and the Chianti. I tell him he's family already if he likes this store and the best *vino* on earth. I tell him about you, *bella*, and tell him he should-a come sooner."

Garrett stepped toward Mary with a strong hand outreached, and she melted when she got a close-up of his cool, green eyes.

"It's a pleasure," she said as she took his hand.

She caught herself thinking that he probably wasn't the kind of guy who wrote love songs or stayed awake into the wee hours of morning making sweet love after singing in a bar. But he was just the kind of man she needed to date.

During the painful months after Ian's vanishing act, she decided it was time for a different type of guy. No more musicians, artists and carefree individuals who chased their dreams and soothed her romantic soul, because those guys kept breaking her heart.

Chapter 5

"How about dinner?" Garrett asked as they walked out of Mr. Moretti's market.

"Sure, I'd enjoy that."

"Is tonight possible? A client cancelled dinner at the last minute, so I'm free."

She considered the offer. She was intrigued by the fateful nature of their meeting and wanted to agree, but was planning to finish her painting. And she didn't want to seem too available. She hated dating games, but she knew they were real. Then she reminded herself that it was only dinner, not a marriage proposal, and she could test out her plan of dating different types of guys – ones who wore suits and had jobs and bank accounts and cell phones. She decided she could paint after dinner.

"That sounds fun," she said.

"How about Italian?" he said, smiling.

"Perfect!"

"It should be easy to get into nearly any restaurant since most everyone is at the Jersey Shore."

"They're the lucky ones," Mary said.

"Yeah, some friends rented a house there last week to hang out at the beach all week, but I wasn't able to go because things were busy at work. How about Cucina di Luna? I've heard it's good."

"It is. I've been a few times."

She had sampled all the Italian restaurants in town.

"Do you mind going again?"

"Not at all. I love it."

"Great. Is seven okay?"

"Yes, but I need to go home first, so I'll meet you there."

She played it safe by meeting at the restaurant since she knew nothing about him except that he was handsome and liked Chianti. He was off to a promising start.

She hurried to her apartment and stashed all her groceries for the following night. Then she freshened up her makeup adding more eyeliner and mascara to enhance her brown eyes. She changed to a flirty ruffled red dress and put on her favorite silver hoop earrings. She left her long, wavy hair down, giving it a quick brush.

Chapter 6

WHEN SHE ARRIVED at the family-owned restaurant, Garrett was already sitting at a candlelit table in a prime location by the front window with a bottle of Villa Antinori Chianti Classico and two glasses.

He stood up and greeted her with a friendly handshake.

"Glad you could come," he said.

"How could I say no to a delicious Italian dinner?"

And with a gorgeous guy, she thought.

Garrett poured wine into both glasses.

"*Salute!*"

"*Salute,*" she said.

After they both took a drink, Mary said, "This is excellent Chianti. Great choice."

"Thanks, I'm a big fan of Italian wine," he said. "Today was my first time in that market. I liked it, especially the wine selection."

"Oh, I love it," Mary said. "I love Mr. Moretti. He's like a father to me. He spoils me with wedges of cheese and basil plants."

She realized how silly it sounded to say she was spoiled with cheese and basil, but she kept talking, a bit nervously to keep the conversation from dying.

"After I moved downtown five years ago, I found the market when I was taking a walk. Mr. Moretti and I hit it off as soon as I walked in. He thought I was Italian."

"I can understand why," Garrett said.

"He said '*Buongiorno, come va?*' and all I could say back was, 'Um, *buongiorno*. That's the only Italian I know.' He told me I looked like *una italiana*. So, I explained that my dad's grandfather was an immigrant from southern Italy, but the rest of my ancestry was a bit of everything. Mr. Moretti laughed and called me a mutt."

"I guess you have a good sense of humor if a stranger can call you a mutt and you're still friends."

"Of course, and we are great friends. I love Italian food, so our bond could have been sealed for that reason alone, but our relationship is more special than that. When my dad died after my freshman year of college, Mr. Moretti was so nurturing. He's been like that ever since. You must have wondered why a market store owner worries about my love life."

"Now I know, and I'm sorry to hear about your dad."

"Thanks. I miss him terribly. It was 13 years ago, and some days it feels like yesterday. But Mr. Moretti keeps a close eye on me. He wants to meet everyone I date so he can give his seal of approval. So you must have already passed."

"Lucky me," he said.

His teeth were beautiful and the smile came with a long dimple as a bonus.

"He sounds like a good surrogate father," Garrett said.

"He is."

"You said you walk there?" he asked.

"Yeah. My apartment isn't far away, just off South Street."

"Do you have a roommate?"

"No, I have a small one-bedroom place, in building with only four units. I've lived there for a few years."

"I'm downtown, too. I live at –"

Garrett stopped when their waiter walked up.

"*Buona sera, signorina.* Welcome. I'm Nino."

"Could I interest you in an appetizer?"

"Is there something you want?" Garrett asked Mary.

"Their mixed crostini is excellent and they change the toppings daily."

"You talked me into it," Garrett said, and he nodded to Nino.

"Do you want to order anything else?" Garrett asked Mary.

"That should be plenty, especially if I order their homemade pasta, which I can never resist."

"Tonight's fresh pasta dish is pappardelle Bolognese," Nino said. "It is my grandmother's recipe."

He patted his chest and looked up to the ceiling.

"And from the grill, we have roasted rosemary chicken with steamed, herbed broccoli. I will give you time to decide."

They both reviewed the menu for a few minutes.

"What are you thinking of having?" Garrett asked.

"The pasta special. Have you ever eaten pappardelle - the long, wide, flat noodles?"

"I don't think so, and I only eat pasta when I know I'm going to do a long run or bike ride on the following day."

"Do you do that often?"

It sounded like he did.

"Yeah, I run long distance regularly, and right now, I'm training for another triathlon."

"Wow."

It explained his muscular physique and tanned skin, now shown off by a fitted black tee and jeans. She wouldn't have been surprised to learn that he was a model for a fitness company. He was that good-looking.

"So you moved here recently?" she asked as she put down the menu.

"Two months ago. I've been in Los Angeles for seven years, but decided to come back east."

"Philly's a great place and I love working and living in the city, especially after growing up out in West Chester."

"What do you do?" Garrett asked.

"I'm a graphic designer at a small advertising agency."

"That sounds interesting."

"It's not bad. I spend most of my time on packaging design, so it can be repetitive. I'd rather be doing projects that require more creativity."

"Like what?"

"Ones that require original painting and photography."

"Do you have art I could see?"

"Sure."

She blushed faintly and wanted to tell him about the nearly finished Tuscan castle painting, but she was shy about her creations.

"Would I find it in a gallery?" he asked.

She felt her stomach wrench. She wanted to create more art to display, with a goal of someday owning a gallery - maybe as a second career - but she'd taken no action to make it happen.

"I wish. How about you? Something where you have to wear a suit every day?"

"I work for an investment firm. My title is Investment Manager, but I'm really a relationship manager - a salesperson."

"I bet you're successful at it."

"I'm doing all right," he said.

She noticed him playing with his silver Rolex Submariner. She wore a Rolex most days, too, but hers wasn't a status symbol. It was her father's, an analog model from the early sixties on a dark brown leather band. She remembered him every time she had to wind it.

"You said you live downtown, too?" she asked.

"Yeah, I have a two-bedroom condo at Rittenhouse Square."

Mary nodded. She was familiar with the upscale area - a neighborhood out of her price range.

He shrugged and said, "But I'm not sure about downtown. In hindsight, I'd prefer being farther out, in someplace like Valley Forge. It would easier to head outdoors or to the mountains."

He clenched his square jaw.

"Really? I love living in the heart of the city. It's great to walk to work, restaurants, bars and the grocery store. I enjoy the diversity, too."

She thought she noticed a subtle smirk from him as she said the word diversity, so it could have been another reason why he would prefer a less urban neighborhood. But the topic didn't go further because Nino arrived with the crostini.

The three toppings of the day were black olive tapenade, chicken liver pâté and white beans drizzled with extra virgin olive oil. While at the table, Nino took their dinner order. Mary chose the pappardelle, and Garrett opted for the roasted chicken.

No run tomorrow, she thought.

Chapter 7

T HROUGHOUT DINNER, the conversation was easy. When Mary asked what he did during his free time, he talked at length, sharing his passion for physical fitness and outdoor sports. It seemed almost like a religion for him.

Virtually every weekend, he hiked, camped, backpacked, sailed, mountain biked or water-skied. In the winter, he went snow skiing, ice climbing and winter camping. And during the week, he trained daily, around a hectic work schedule. His discipline was impressive.

By the end of the meal, Garrett ventured where most first dates of 30-something singles did.

"There is one question I typically hear on a first date and I'm surprised you haven't asked it."

She knew where he was headed, and reluctantly rolled with it.

"Which question?"

"Have you ever been married? Aren't you always asked that?"

"Yeah, sometimes, but there are better things to talk about."

He laughed.

"True, but I'll go ahead and answer the question. I've never been married."

"Engaged?"

"No," he said. "I've been close, but never proposed. How about you?"

She hesitated.

"Engaged once. Married once."

He seemed surprised and looked to her left hand to make sure she wasn't wearing a wedding ring. All fingers were unadorned.

"It didn't last long," she said.

Every time someone asked, she wished she could lie and pretend it never happened. She still didn't like to talk about it.

"How did you stay single so long?" Mary asked.

"I've been building my career. After I graduated from Fordham, I worked at Vanguard here in Philly. My career wasn't ramping up as fast as I wanted, so I contacted my uncle who lives in Los Angeles. He is tremendously successful in commercial real estate. He had a few strong job leads, so he suggested I head out there. I thought, why not? So I left Philadelphia seven years ago and landed a position with a private investment firm. I worked hard and built a broad client base. I haven't had time for a relationship.

"And my uncle's on his third marriage and he's unsure if it's going to make it. He encouraged me to put off marriage until I was more mature – or at least 30 years old. He didn't want me to repeat his mistakes."

He stopped and chuckled a little.

"Now that I'm 33, I understand his advice."

"Makes sense," she said.

She understood the value of waiting.

Garrett took a drink, and his expression indicated he wanted to ask more about her personal life, but he was polite and refrained. He waited and let her make the decision to speak.

Obligated, she gave him the snapshot.

"I married my college sweetheart, and we were too young."

She stopped briefly, deciding how much to say.

"It only lasted two and half years and now I know I married for all the wrong reasons."

Since she didn't want to go deeper in the topic, she talked about her family's opinions.

"My divorced and single status makes my mom and sister Catherine crazy. My sister is a bit of a prima donna. She married a cardiovascular surgeon, plays tennis at their country club and has an adorable baby daughter. It's the life she wanted, and she made it happen. She went to college for an 'MRS' Degree and she succeeded."

Mary didn't say it, but their mother encouraged both daughters to take the "MRS" path – to find husbands in college and marry right away. Her widowed mother feared being unable to take care of the girls and pushed aggressively for sons-in-law. Looking back,

Mary recognized she didn't have the courage to resist or disappoint her mother, so the summer after graduation from Lehigh University she married Danny McGovern, who she met in Biology 101 their freshman year.

Mary continued.

"Now Catherine thinks I should want her same life, and my mom has a similar perspective, but it's because she's from an earlier generation. They think I'm 'rebellious and wild.' Would you believe Catherine is suggesting therapy?"

She chuckled, as did Garrett.

"But we rarely agree, and we don't look alike either. Catherine and mom are blonds with blue eyes, while I look like my dad."

"He must have been a handsome guy."

"He was, and thanks."

"Well, setbacks can make you rethink your goals, but it's important to remain strong and true to what you want. Maybe your sister just got lucky in finding love. It sounds like she has a good life."

She emptied her wine glass, knowing she had said enough, and she didn't want to debate whether Catherine's suburban life was "good" or not. She and her sister rarely saw eye-to-eye.

"So you're not dating anyone right now?" he asked.

"Nope, nothing serious."

She chose not to tell him she hadn't dated anyone since Ian. She already mentioned an ex-husband and didn't want to talk about ex-boyfriends, especially on a first date.

"Same here. And you didn't ask, but I'll answer anyway. I don't have any children."

She giggled to hide pain.

"No, me neither," she said.

The miscarriage with Danny was the demise of their young relationship. Both were unable to cope with the trauma and heartache after the unexpected pregnancy, and this wasn't the time to bring it up. There was no good time for that topic.

Garrett must have sensed it was time to lighten the dialogue, so he mentioned his weekend backpacking plans. She listened and thought his life was interesting, but at the same time she knew dating him would be challenging. Even though she was genuinely ready for a more stable guy, Garrett didn't seem like the right fit. She felt immature thinking it, but he seemed too driven. He clearly had a Type A personality, and it was a turn off for her. But he was exceptionally charming, and she was glad for a date since her breakup with Ian. Like her desire to paint, this was another sign she was moving on.

Garrett paid for dinner, although she offered to split it, and they exchanged phone numbers, but didn't make plans to see each other again.

At home, she called her best friend Stella and proudly shared the news that she finally had a date with someone who was nothing like her ex-boyfriends.

"So, you're not going out with him again, are you?"

Stella's feisty tone was one that only good friends were permitted to use with each other.

"You know me too well." Mary laughed. "I told you I need a new approach so I gave it a shot. But I don't think Garrett's the right guy for me."

"Your mother would love him, I bet."

"Of course she would. He's nothing like Ian."

"Or Ricky, or Jon or Dylan."

"Enough," Mary said, giggling.

She didn't want to be reminded of the rest of the list.

"Would I like him?" Stella asked.

"Of course you wouldn't. He has a job and wouldn't try to clean out your bank account like Trevor did."

Stella laughed at the sarcasm.

"Touché! We're such hopeless romantics, aren't we?"

"Yeah, hopefully our luck changes soon."

"No kidding. Want to grab margaritas tomorrow night?"

"Sure," Mary said. "Same time. Same place."

They would meet at six at their favorite Mexican cantina – the place where they often solved life's problems with margaritas unless the problems were exceptionally bad. Then the medicine would be straight tequila shots. No salt. No lime.

The cantina happened to be where Mary met Ian who had been hired to bartend and sing. She and Stella frequented the bar long before Ian, but now it always reminded her of him. So many things did.

"I'll be there," Stella said.

After hanging up, Mary moved to her bedroom where her painting waited on its easel. She stayed up until the early morning hours finishing the mystical Tuscan scene that soon occupied the empty wall space above her bed.

Chapter 8

A FEW DAYS AFTER THE DINNER at Cucina di Luna, Garrett called and invited Mary out for another dinner, but she politely declined. She wasn't interested and didn't believe she needed to explain.

The following week he called, again. This time, for lunch. Same as before, she said no and hoped he would get the hint, but the rejection didn't dissuade him. He tried a new approach a week later on a Wednesday afternoon.

As soon as she heard his voice on the telephone, she shook her head in frustration. She would have to be direct this time.

"Hey, Mary! I have unexpected free time this weekend. My buddy Brad can't go on our mountain biking trip, so I want to see if you're interested in going to Bucks County. We could have lunch in Newtown or New Hope and walk around for the afternoon. The weather is supposed to be nice, so you could bring your camera or a sketchbook, since they're such artsy towns."

She was surprised by this invitation, because she thought he wouldn't enjoy doing something that didn't require any athletic ability or technical gear.

She found herself thinking she should give him a chance. He was interested and making more effort than most guys – and she wasn't meeting any other guys. She liked Newtown and New Hope and hadn't been since the previous summer. And it was possible she could like him more after another date.

"Sure," she said.

Chapter 9

On SATURDAY, it was sunny and gorgeous. Garrett picked her up at noon in his shiny, silver 528 BMW. She found out he already cycled at dawn and worked a few hours before picking her up. All she had done in the same amount of time was sleep, drink coffee, and wash two loads of laundry.

During the drive north on I-95, they decided to have lunch and craft beers at Isaac Newton's, in Newtown. The place was packed, as always, and they dined in the cozy bar area. She couldn't refuse the burger and fries, but Garrett ate healthy food, again.

They explored Newtown for about an hour, and stopped in a couple of small shops before taking the narrow back roads to New Hope.

They weren't surprised to find the eclectic town swimming with visitors, and eventually had to park on the other side of the Delaware River tin Lambertville. Instead of hurrying to walk the bridge back to New Hope, they lingered in Lambertville, strolling its friendly streets and canal path.

While they were in a small gallery admiring some black-and-white photography of Prague and Venice, Mary said, "I'd love to be a travel photographer and own a gallery like this someday."

"Here in Lambertville?"

"Oh, I don't care where."

"Then you need a plan to ensure it happens," he said without any hesitation. "I can help you figure it out, if you want."

His comment made her realize how much she'd dreamt about doing this - and other things - without ever taking serious steps to achieve them.

He's not a dreamer, she thought. He's a doer, and could be a good influence.

"Thanks," she said. "I could probably use the help."

They finally crossed the bridge to New Hope and wandered more, peeking in a boutiques and galleries. After a few blocks, Garrett asked if she wanted to stop for another beer.

"Sure," she said before seeing the Bow Wow dog boutique ahead of them. "Mind if I run in here? I want to buy treat for my dog."

"Dog?"

"Yeah, Mr. Dolittle, a beagle. He lives with my mom, since I can't have pets in my apartment – and she likes his company. Do you like dogs?"

"Love them, but I'm not home enough to have one."

That's a good sign, she thought.

Chapter 10

AFTER BUYING TREATS and chatting with the store's friendly clerk they crossed the street to the Havana Bar. As they entered the patio, a loud group of women exited. Each one had her hair dyed a bright color, and they all wore numerous strands of rainbow-themed Mardi Gras beads, which reminded Mary of trips to New Orleans.

As they waited for a pair of Yuenglings at the outside bar Mary asked Garrett if he'd ever been to New Orleans."

"No, never have, but I want to go."

"I have a college friend who lives there now, and I've gone to Mardi Gras and Jazz Fest a few times with her. I love the city."

"Is one event better than the other? I know a lot of guys who went to Mardi Gras during college and they had wild times."

"They're very different, but I like them both. Mardi Gras can be a huge drinking party - not that I don't like to drink - but it's crazy and crowded with college kids. So I prefer Jazz Fest for the great music and food. It takes place at the New Orleans fairgrounds and there's jazz, blues, R&B, rock, gospel and almost anything else you want to hear. There are big name performers, but some of the best music is from the local musicians. Ever heard of Cowboy Mouth or Marcia Ball?"

"Nope, not familiar with them," he said.

"Cowboy Mouth's lead singer is also the band's drummer and they're fun. Marcia Ball is an incredible piano player, with saucy, soulful music. I'll have to let you hear the CDs I have."

"Okay, I'd like that."

Another good sign - he likes music.

Mary continued.

"As good as the music is, the food matches it. Caterers set up booths and they sell delicious stuff like crawfish sacks and meat pies. And the crawfish bread is to die for - the butter runs down your arms."

"I need to add it to my destination list."

She wondered if he really had a piece of paper with destinations listed on it. She imagined he did. Successful people always seemed to be list-makers.

"You should. It's hard not to love, especially if you see more than Bourbon Street."

The only fact about New Orleans she didn't mention was the ex-boyfriends who had gone with her.

She wondered if Italy was on his list. It was on the top of hers. So she asked.

"How about Italy? Ever been?"

"Nope, only to France, Germany, and Switzerland. I've skied and mountain climbed in the Alps. That was a rush. But I still want to visit Italy."

"Me too. During college, I had hoped to study art in Florence, but it never worked out. Now, I'd like to take a romantic trip there with someone special."

She giggled nervously and realizing what she'd said, she spoke again.

"Wishful thinking, huh?"

"I don't think so," he said, and winked. "Anything is possible, if you want it."

When they ordered their second round, the bartender asked if they were staying for the live southern rock band performance.

She had no evening plans but waited for Garrett to answer, unsure of when he wanted to head home.

"Not tonight," he said. "I have a 20-mile run tomorrow morning. So, I'd like to head back soon, if you don't mind."

"No problem."

She'd never run more than the 3.1 miles of a 5K road race, so couldn't imagine running 20 miles.

They talked the entire drive home, and she found herself scrutinizing their compatibility. She liked his confidence and polished presence, although formal, and she admired his discipline, knowing he could positively influence her. She was definitely attracted to his looks and strong body.

Only one thing lacked - there was no sizzling chemistry. She didn't melt with an accidental touch, or a revealing look, and she wished she did. But as she considered this last point, she reminded herself that earthshaking attraction hadn't led her to successful relationships. In fact, it had brought nothing but heartache.

She also reminded herself that she shouldn't worry if sparks weren't flying like a wildfire out of control.

It wasn't long until they arrived at her apartment.

"I enjoyed our afternoon," Garrett said. Thanks for going with me."

He lightly kissed her cheek as he said goodbye.

When he pulled away, she realized she wanted to know more. So in the upcoming weeks, she did agree to more dates. They went out for dinner. They cooked Italian at home - after shopping at Mr. Moretti's market. And they went for long walks in the city. He never swept her off her feet, but won her slowly and smoothly. However, he held back physically. After a couple of months, they'd never stayed at each other's places or been to bed. They had heavy make out sessions, but that was it. One night, he finally approached the delicate topic.

"Mary, you are incredibly sexy and desirable - it's all I can do to control myself. I imagine us together all the time, but sex has complicated some relationships in the past and before we go down that path, I want to know that we truly like each other. I'm 33, and I'm not looking for a casual relationship. I want to get to know you - the real you."

She couldn't deny similar experiences - more than she wanted to admit - and she liked that he wanted a meaningful partnership. His honesty was heartwarming, so she took a deep breath and flirted.

"Fair enough, but you better be worth the wait."

He laughed and promised he would.

Later, before heading home, he said he was going sailing in Newport, Rhode Island the following weekend with friends.

"Want to join us?"

"I've never sailed, but I've always wanted to. Is that a problem?"

"No worries. My friends and their wives have sailed all their lives. We can teach you."

"Well, then, sure! Sounds fun!"

Chapter 11

"BUONGIORNO, MARY!"

Mr. Moretti greeted her with hugs and kisses.

"How are you?" he asked.

"Good, and guess what? I'm going sailing this weekend with Garrett and some of his friends."

"I think Garrett is a good man. Tell me, is he?"

Mr. Moretti smiled proudly.

"He sure is," Mary said. "He works hard and plays hard, too."

"I am so glad he is a good worker. Some of the young men like-a my son are so lazy. I don't know what's wrong with them. A man must-a work! He must make money to provide for his family. Tell me more about his job. What does he do?"

"He works for an investment company that finances other businesses. It's mostly commercial real estate, and Garrett is a relationship manager. He helps his company decide who to fund."

"Hmmm. Sounds like something I would not know how to do."

"No, me neither," she said and giggled. "I don't know if I understand everything. He spends a lot of time working, but tries to keep it separate from his personal life. He says he doesn't like when people talk endlessly about their jobs."

"He seems to treat-a you well, and I am so glad you like-a him."

"Thank you."

"I hope you enjoy the boat trip. Are you are a good swimmer?"

"I am, and I'm sure I'll be safe."

"Okay, you know I always worry about you."

This warmed her heart.

"What do you need today?" he asked. "Chianti?"

"Of course! And I need to take antipasto for the weekend trip."

"You have come to the right place," he said. "Let's start with the *formaggio...*"

Chapter 12

JAMES AND HIS FRIEND DREW were former college room-mates. Now they worked in finance and banking. Their wives, Beka and Candice, worked as interior designers, and were business partners.

The men stood on the dock and debated the Y2K challenges that were predicted to affect their businesses at the turn of the century.

Mary sat with the wives in the cockpit, chatting. She told them she was an artist, making a living as a graphic designer in the underpaid advertising world.

"Advertising is alluring," Beka said. "But there are better ways to make money as an artist."

"No doubt," Candice said. "We cater to high-end clients who are willing to pay well for our services. We have a decent-sized staff, so now that we both have young children, we don't have to spend as much time in the office. You might want to think about something similar, because I'm sure you want to have kids yourself someday."

"Sure," Mary said.

She didn't tell them she almost did have a baby once. Mary felt a punch in her gut, though she knew that wasn't Candice's intention. The ladies were friendly, but she hoped when she had kids she wouldn't talk about them as incessantly as these women did.

After knowing them just a couple hours, she knew about their kids' ballet lessons and soccer games, private school teachers and homework assignments, and their eating and pooping habits. But Mary just politely smiled and listened with the help of a few glasses of wine.

"You two would have gorgeous children," Candice said, looking at Mary while pointing at Garrett.

Beka jumped in.

"Candi, that's presumptuous of you. But I agree! You seem like a great couple, and we'd love to see Garrett settle down with someone. He's a good guy, and he works too hard."

Mary demurely grinned because she still wasn't entirely sure about Garrett. There was a lot she liked, but she still wondered about their long-term compatibility – and their sexual chemistry.

"Yeah, he is a good guy," Mary said. "Maybe too good for me."

Candice and Beka laughed and Mary did, too. But she was serious.

The group sailed all day Saturday, and Mary found she loved the sport. She quickly picked up the lingo and learned when she needed to move to prevent the mainsail's boom from hitting her head or knocking her overboard. She even took the rudder once. The fresh air, wind and sun were invigorating.

Chapter 13

ON SATURDAY NIGHT at a local pub, the three couples emptied a full bottle of tequila, and Garrett's friends were jazzed for a night of karaoke.

Garrett told Mary he didn't care to sing in public and wanted to take her back to the boat. He had thrown back several shots, and feeling the liquor's effect, he surprised Mary with some newly relaxed inhibition.

Back at the boat Mary and Garrett lay on the bow enjoying the starry night. Holding hands, Garrett talked about how much he wanted to own a sailboat himself, at least the same size as the boat they were on, maybe larger.

"Imagine sailing in remote places where we could swim and sunbathe nude - no tan lines for us!"

"Garrett! I didn't think that was your style."

He laughed.

"You must not know me."

"So get naked now," she said.

The tequila relaxed his need to be in control. He stripped and stood naked in the bow's pulpit.

"I'm king of the world!" he shouted.

They both started laughing like it was one of the funniest things they'd ever heard.

He shouted again.

"Hey world, I'm naked! Why is Mary still wearing all her clothes?"

She kept laughing. She couldn't believe he had done this.

"Your turn," he said.

He impatiently undressed her and grabbed her hand.

"Let's go below," he said. "We don't want anyone to see what we're about to do."

She felt a surge of excitement as they hurried down the ladder into the cabin.

Naked and alone, he pulled her close and kissed her wildly while he put his hands on the small of her back. But he didn't leave them there long. He gripped her fleshy butt and pulled her hips into his with a forceful rhythm. Fully naked for the first time, body pressed to body, they rocked like a boat adrift at sea.

He was strong and athletic and easily lifted her, nudging her to wrap her legs around his hips. They moved in harmony as she molded her body into his chiseled one. He was hungry for her, and she loved this newly discovered fire he possessed. He lifted her body higher to devour her breasts. But he stopped, and looked at her with an expression that was nothing but desire. He wanted her and he slowly lowered and guided her hips so he could slide inside her warm body.

"Ohhh," she cried out.

He felt incredible and powerful. She figured they would move to the cramped bed where they'd slept the night before. But he had other ideas. He took a couple of small steps and rotated their joined bodies, so his back was aligned along the cabin's ladder. She instinctively reached behind him and grabbed a step.

"That's what I want you to do," he said. "Show me how much you want me."

She slid up and down, while her long, wavy locks fell in her face. She breathed heavily and couldn't get enough. Up and down. Up and down. She arched her back and her hair fell behind her, swaying as their bodies pulsed on the buoyant sailboat.

Minutes later, he held her hips to slow her, and he pulled her close to him. He lightly nibbled on her ear, then whispered.

"Climb up a couple of steps."

She let out another heavy breath, knowing exactly what he planned. As she climbed up, his tongue went down. His mouth followed her torso until his face reached the delicate cleft between her legs. He tenderly kissed and licked the soft, swollen flesh, making her gasp and shake, and he didn't stop until her hips rocked and her body shuddered with a powerful orgasm. She breathed heavily and barely stifled any moans or cries, with her head now at deck level.

It was his turn, and she looked around the dock to make sure his friends weren't on the way back. The coast was clear so she slithered down the steps, and easily slipped onto his commanding erection. Up and down. Up and down. Faster and faster, like the boat hit a turbulent storm. He exploded inside her, and gripped her hips like he never wanted to let go.

As soon as he caught his breath, she wrapped her damp body tightly around his, and they giggled and kissed.

"Was it worth the wait?" he asked.

"Better than I could have dreamed."

She meant it. He was sexy and strong, and she was completely enamored. The rest of the night she was intrigued with his every move. She wanted more. And after that weekend, without talking about it, they began to see each other regularly and exclusively.

In the upcoming months he treated her to new experiences, most of which were outdoor adventures, and she gradually adjusted to his rigidly scheduled life. He was organized and disciplined about work, fitness and fun. He clearly knew what he wanted and how to get it. And he helped teach her the same.

She increased her frequency of running and exercising under his influence, and he encouraged her to build her art portfolio. She decided to focus on paintings of Italy.

Undoubtedly different from Ian and other ex-boyfriends, his strengths offset his pragmatic nature. He knew how to enjoy himself, but he was responsible. He was consistent and did what he said he would do. And he lived a comfortable lifestyle. He made hefty commissions, and he paid for everything. It was the most grown-up relationship she'd ever had, and not surprisingly, her mom and sister loved him.

When her mom met Garrett for the first time she said, "Thank goodness he's not another long-haired guitar player."

Chapter 14

Two days before Thanksgiving, Mary visited Mr. Moretti. She wanted to buy coffee, chocolate and Chianti to take to her mom's for the holiday weekend, where she planned to stay for a few days. She had a small gift for him, too.

"*Buongiorno*, Mary, *come va?*"

Mr. Moretti greeted her with a big hug and kisses.

"*Bene, molto bene*," she said.

"You look good. Garrett *è buono?*"

"Yes, he's good. He's in California now. He went for work and decided to stay with his uncle for the holiday weekend. I'm going to my mom's."

"*Va bene*," he said. "It is important to be with your mother. You will have the big American dinner for Thanksgiving?"

He asked in spite of already knowing the answer.

"Of course, my mom will roast a turkey, and she'll make mashed potatoes, gravy and stuffing - my favorites."

Mr. Moretti laughed in delight.

"*Perfetto!* I am glad you will be with your family for the big dinner. It eez-a the best way to eat."

"I always enjoy it."

"I have a treat for you and your family. Here are fresh persimmons. You know, they are ripe in Toscana now, and it makes me think of home. The large fruit is the only color in the countryside. These orange persimmons hang on the tree branches when all the leaves are gone."

"I've never eaten one."

"All you do is slice and eat-a fresh. They are sweet and juicy."

"Thank you, I look forward to trying them. And I have a gift for you, too."

She pulled a small four-inch-by-four-inch canvas painting from her bag, a smaller less-detailed version of the Tuscan tower scene. She painted it just for him.

"Ah, Mary, this eez-a *bello* like Toscana! Talented you are!"

He perched it on the shelf behind his register so all his customers could see it.

"*Grazie, grazie,*" he said.

"*Prego.*" – "You're welcome."

"Is Garrett treating you well?"

It was Mr. Moretti's self-designated job to ask her about him.

"Yes, but he's the busiest guy I know. He works and travels so much, mostly to California. And when he's in town, he's always doing something outdoors or training for a race. But I am enjoying some new sports with him. He takes me along when he can."

"Well, you sound happy. He takes good-a care of you."

"He does. How about you? What will you do on Thanksgiving?"

"The same thing I always do. I will rest at home, because I can close the store for a day."

"You deserve it. I hope you enjoy your quiet time."

"Yes, it will be very quiet. My wife will be with her sister and who knows where Giovanni will be. Quiet will be good-a."

He nodded his head as she paid for the groceries.

As she walked out the door she said, "A *presto*" – "See you soon."

"*Stai bene,*" he said. "Be well."

After she left, Mr. Moretti pulled a bottle of grappa from under the counter, poured a shot and looked to the heavens.

"*Dio mio, grazie.* She is the daughter I had never," he said out loud in the empty store.

His eyes welled with tears as he drank the grappa. He never told Mary about his baby girl Isabella who died immediately after birth.

Mary filled the empty hole in his heart, like he filled the one in hers.

Chapter 15

MARY AND GARRETT STAYED in town on a wintry December weekend to go to Garrett's office holiday party. Mary knew Garrett didn't want to miss the Friday night event since he was a rising star at the privately owned investment firm M.L. Graham, Inc. As the only single employee in the group, the owner, Maxwell Graham, had made it clear to Garrett he should show up with a date. Max valued marriage and family. And Max valued appearances, as did Garrett, who was always impeccably dressed in custom suits and tailored shirts. These were expenses Garrett believed were necessary for a job focused on client relationships with the wealthy.

As they rode the elevator to the top floor of the office building, Mary wanted to make sure her appearance was flawless, too. She checked her hair in the smoky glass mirror, making sure it was tucked in place. She wore it up for the special event, but her natural curls didn't always cooperate. She tried taming a wisp.

"Leave it alone," Garrett said. "It's sexy against your neck, especially with those impressive diamond earrings. I can't wait to take you back to my place tonight."

Mary grinned and stopped fooling with her hair. She was glad she'd borrowed the diamonds from Stella's amazing collection of vintage jewelry.

"That can't happen soon enough."

She was flirting, but she was serious too. She was always craving more time in bed with him.

He lightly kissed her cheek.

"You look so sexy tonight. You should wear short skirts like that all the time."

He looked like he wanted to devour her.

"I'm sure all the other men will be envious of me," he said.

He slipped his hand under her sweater of soft, black cashmere – another vintage item she had borrowed from Stella. It was Chanel, one of many pieces by the French designer in Stella's collection. His hands were warm against her skin and she felt a little tremor of excitement with the touch. She savored this moment because they had dated long enough for her to know he wasn't often expressive like this, especially in public – unless he was tequila-drunk on a sailboat – so she loved it when he was.

What a difference from last year, she thought. She remembered crying through most of the holidays because of Ian's abrupt departure. She still wondered where he was and what he was doing, but she was glad she was in a solid relationship now.

The elevator arrived at the 52nd floor and they easily found the banquet room by following the noise. When they walked in, a spectacular panoramic view of Philadelphia's night sky greeted them. Garrett offered to check Mary's black velvet coat and get wine.

As Mary surveyed the room, Garrett's company president and owner spotted her, walked over and kissed her on the cheek.

"You look as lovely as ever, Mary. Happy holidays!"

"Thank you, Max," she said loudly, to be heard above the crowd. "I'm glad to be here. What a great location for the party. Everyone seems to be enjoying themselves."

"Yes, we are all happy, healthy and wealthy. It's been a successful year with reason to celebrate, and we still have three more weeks to close sales."

"That's great!"

"It is. It is. Thanks to the hard work of the employees here, our growth over the last year was significant. But I especially have to recognize Garrett's accomplishments. He's a top gun! In only six months, he saved two large accounts that were ready to axe us. And he's already brought in several new West Coast accounts. Not little ones either. You must be so proud."

"Yes, I am." She really was.

"Garrett's a dedicated employee with the work ethic of the men of my generation."

He paused, took a sip of his single-malt scotch-on-the-rocks and leaned close as if he were divulging a secret.

"Right now, Mary, his work may keep him from spending time with you, but it'll be worth it. Trust me."

He rubbed his thumb over his index and middle finger, implying there was money in it for Garrett. Then he raised his eyebrows and dropped his chin. It was a disturbing look, which she interpreted as "ask no questions because you have no choice."

Mary graciously smiled, but was annoyed by Max's materialistic and chauvinistic attitude. She searched for the right words to say.

"Yes, he works heavy hours, but I know he loves it."

"You know, you might want to talk to my wife Susanne. She's near the window over there, in the red suit. Susanne sacrificed so much for me, but she did a magnificent job managing our family. Now we're empty nesters, and we're reaping the rewards of my business success. I still put in way too many hours here, but not as many as I did when I was Garrett's age. We're able to travel frequently now, and as I'm sure Garrett told you, we're both avid golfers and scuba divers."

"Speak of the devil, here he is," Mary said.

Garrett handed her a glass of Cabernet Sauvignon and she eagerly accepted it, giving him a "save me" look.

"Garrett, I was just telling Mary about how instrumental you've been to our financial success this year, and how I appreciate all of your hard work."

Max raised his glass.

"Cheers! To Garrett Hansen!"

After they drank, Max continued.

"I hope you're taking your girl out on the town tonight after the party."

Mary shuddered at being called a girl.

"Well, yes, I am, and I have a little surprise for her, too."

Garrett winked a twinkling green eye at Mary.

"But I'm not saying another word. I don't want to ruin it."

He winked again.

She couldn't wait to find out what it was. She loved surprises.

Mary found Susanne and they talked at length before rejoining Garrett and Tom Hiatt, his manager. "Y2K" was the talk of the party for most of the employees, since there was no certainty their computer systems would be working at the upcoming turn of the millennium.

Mary and Garrett mingled for about an hour and a half and drank a couple of glasses of wine before saying their goodbyes. They grabbed a taxi, and Garrett gave the driver their destination without Mary hearing him.

Chapter 16

"MAX SURE IS PLEASED WITH YOU," Mary said, in the car.

"I like working for his company, and I'm making heaps of money for him. He's a strong leader, if a bit chauvinistic."

He added this last comment for Mary's benefit, knowing she didn't care for him.

"But Max rewards me well for my work. I make the clients feel good about doing business with us. That's all I do."

"Do you think his wife is happy? Because I think Susanne's bitter, like she regrets sacrificing her goals for him. Did you know she wanted to be a journalist and worked as a copyeditor at a newspaper in Trenton? She told me that when Max's career took off, he insisted she quit her 'meager job' in favor of managing the household and helping him entertain clients."

"I don't know what happened in their past, Mare, but I know she enjoys the life he provides now. He's made a boatload of money, and she has everything she wants. How could she not be happy?"

Money isn't everything, she thought. But she knew Garrett was wired to succeed financially, and it drove his life. During the party, Garrett, Max and Tom continually one-upped each other about their cars, boats, clubs and vacations. Garrett didn't own a boat yet, but tonight she learned there was pressure for him to buy one since Max and Tom had boats.

This intense financial drive wasn't a surprise. It was one thing that made her somewhat nervous about ever making a long-term commitment with Garrett, because her financial goals weren't the same.

Just as she was about to say that Susanne clearly didn't have everything because she had given up a personal dream, Garrett slipped his hand under the short wool skirt.

"You look great tonight," he said.

She beamed and nudged his hand a little farther up, but the taxi stopped in front of Cucina di Luna, the wonderful Italian restaurant they had gone on their first date.

"Is this where we're having dinner tonight? This is so romantic!"

"I'm not finished yet."

She was surprised because he said so often he wasn't a romantic kind of guy. More than a few times he'd told her he showed his love by his actions and commitment. According to him, flowers and candlelit dinners didn't prove love. So, she was thrilled when his romantic side came out. She knew it was in him, he just didn't show it very often.

As soon as the restaurant door opened, the aroma of fresh bread, garlic and basil sent Mary to a heavenly state. The host took them to the same window table they had shared on their first date. Soft candlelight illuminated the table, and the flames' reflection danced in the glass window, just like the last time they'd been there. From this spot, they could see the restaurant's charming interior and the city street scenes, but it was still a quiet spot for intimate conversations.

"This is so perfect," she said. "Pinch me so I know I'm not dreaming."

Garrett flashed his big, bright smile that always made her melt. She felt like a character in a romance movie.

They started dinner by ordering a bottle of Villa Antinori Chianti Classico and a plate of mixed crostini from Nino – the same thing they ordered on their first date. But tonight's toppings were roasted tomato and ricotta, *bistecca tartara* with olive paste, and goat cheese with figs and balsamic vinaigrette.

"Think about the day we met each other in Mr. Moretti's market," Mary said. "It's like it happened only yesterday. I still can't believe the timing. If I hadn't forgotten to buy olive oil, I would have never met you."

"It's been fantastic! *Salute!*"

He lifted his glass.

Nino didn't rush them to place an order, giving them time to talk and drink. They were deep into a conversation about Mary considering a training program for a spring half-marathon. Garrett was explaining the 16-week training schedule when Nino walked up, both hands behind him.

Nino raised his eyebrows toward Garrett but didn't say a word. Garrett stopped talking and nodded.

"Impeccable timing, Nino, thank you."

Instead of dinner menus, Nino presented Mary with a tidy package wrapped in gold paper with a gold bow.

"For the lady, *la bella donna*."

"I didn't want to wait another minute," Garrett said. "I know it's still two weeks until Christmas, but I wanted to give you my present tonight."

Mary blushed.

"But I didn't bring anything for –"

"Shh," Garrett interrupted. "I know we didn't talk about this, but I thought this would be the right moment. Please, open it."

Mary's hands trembled as she held the package. Her mom and sister had already expressed their hopes of a marriage proposal, but this didn't seem to be jewelry disguised in a small shirt box. It was too heavy. Regardless, she wasn't ready for a proposal, having dated for only six months. She knew Garrett wasn't either.

She peeled away the metallic paper and lifted the box lid to find a handbook – *Frommer's Guide to Italy 2000*.

"Thank you, Garrett. You know how much I dream about going there."

He laughed.

"Yes, I do. There's more, though. Open the cover."

Inside, Mary found a small gold envelope. She opened it and read the handwritten card.

Dear Mary,

We met in a little Italian market in South Philly, and this year I want to take you to a "real" Italian market on the romantic vacation of your dreams. Let's go to Italy!

Merry Christmas,
Garrett

"Garrett, really?"

"Yes, really! I'm thinking we might want to wait until spring when the weather is better – and after you do your first half-marathon – but we can start planning now. I'll pay for it all."

He smiled and even glowed.

Mary knew he was proud to be able to offer this. His hard work was paying off. She held the book to her chest.

"I can hardly wait," she said.

She got up to hug him.

"This will be so wonderful," she said. "And it will help me through the rest of winter."

"Merry Christmas, Mary. I've been so happy with you these last six months. I look forward to our next six."

The rest of the night, Mary was moonstruck. The wine flowed from a bottomless bottle. The homemade pasta dishes were delicious. And Garrett's handsome face glowed in the candlelight. It felt like she was in a dream. He always had a way of surprising her when she least expected it or when twinges of doubt about their compatibility surfaced.

Chapter 17

AFTER DINNER, they took a taxi to Garrett's condo and her hands were all over him, but he kept telling her to slow down. In the hallway of his building she tried to slip her hands into his pants, but he asked her to wait until they were inside his condo. She bit her lip and told him to hurry as he unlocked the door. Once behind closed doors, she wrapped her arms around him, not noticing the trail of rose petals on the floor leading to the bedroom.

Garrett drew her attention to the floral path, and she followed it to his bedroom, where he lit candles and turned on the radio. He searched the stations to find light, romantic music, but the first one he found was playing Christina Aguilera's "Genie in a Bottle," so he quickly changed it.

"Wait! Go back."

It wasn't a favorite song, but she knew all the words since the radio stations were playing it nonstop and right now it fueled her sensuality. She began to sing the flirtatious lyrics while she danced provocatively, taunting Garrett like a striptease dancer.

She unbuttoned and stripped off her sweater, followed by her skirt, while she sashayed before him and erotically slid her hands up and down her own body.

Sitting on the edge of the bed, he watched and enjoyed, until she removed his tie and lassoed it around his neck pulling his face into her chest. As he closed his eyes and moaned, she climbed on the bed and straddled his lap to begin a night of untamed sex.

But on Saturday morning, a loud buzzing alarm clock ended their intimate weekend.

She sat up, looked over Garrett's shoulder and saw it was 7 a.m.

"Oh no, you must have forgotten to turn that thing off. It's Saturday."

"No, I didn't forget," he said.

He pushed back the covers and sat up.

She recalled the romantic dinner and wild night in bed. Now, it was the weekend, and she wanted more lovemaking followed by sipping Lavazza coffee curled up on his sofa.

She tried to sit up and ask him where he was going, but her throbbing head quickly reminded her of the overindulgence of the night before and she groaned instead.

"I need to head to the office," Garrett said. "I have to get caught up on some work before I go to Los Angeles next week. But I need to run first."

She fell back into the pillows, closed her eyes and sighed. She felt the pain of too many glasses of wine blend in with the pain of wanting him to stay in bed and be the amorous man of the night before. But the more she thought about it, the more she realized she should have been able to predict this morning's events.

He had eaten pasta for dinner.

Chapter 18

MARY SPENT MOST OF SATURDAY lying on her sofa nursing a headache and an upset stomach. She ignored two phone calls from her sister Catherine, since a conversation with her would worsen the clanging in her head.

In the early afternoon, though, she called Stella and invited her to dinner. It was time for girl talk, and she could return the borrowed sweater and diamonds.

Around eight, Stella knocked on the door of Mary's apartment. She looked frenzied and her long, red hair was pulled into a ponytail on the top of her head.

"Sorry, I'm late!"

"There's no schedule, Stella. You know me, any time is fine. I'm just beginning to feel like a real person, again. I had way too much wine last night."

"You sounded horrible on the phone, but I was afraid to ask why. I should've known."

"When will I learn?"

"I hope I'm not making your day worse, but I ran out of time to bake the brownies I promised. Sorry."

Stella's favorite food was brownies, but it didn't show. There wasn't an ounce of fat on her slim five-nine frame.

She scrunched her face to show her disappointment in herself.

"No problem," Mary said.

"But I stopped at the store around the corner and picked up some bakery brownies. I'm sure they're not undercooked and ooey-gooey like the ones I bake."

"As long as they were made with sugar and chocolate, I'm in."

Stella's blue eyes brightened.

"You know, we could eat the brownies first..."

"You're right, let's do it!"

Mary grabbed two cans of Diet Coke and they sat down on her butterscotch leather sofa with the box of brownies on the cushion between them.

"How's life with Garrett?" Stella asked after a couple of bites.

"Good. His job is going well, and guess what? Last night, he offered to take me on a romantic trip to Italy with him next year!"

"Wow, you must be thrilled! You've always wanted to go."

"I can't believe it's going to happen."

Stella scowled at her brownie.

"These definitely aren't chewy enough. I'll bet Garrett wouldn't touch this brownie or any brownie for that matter. Is he still training for another triathlon?"

"Nope, he gave it up for now because work is too busy. He's still running almost every day, though. Even this morning at seven, after an incredibly romantic night."

Mary rolled her eyes in disgust.

"He must not have had as much wine as you did."

"I think he did, but he has an unbelievable level of discipline."

"I guess the world needs people like that, but that won't be me any time soon."

"No, me neither, but we're running a 5K road race on Friday night – the Reindeer Dash. It's a fundraiser with free beer and live music after the race. Why don't you come to the post-race party?"

"I might. But I have my final December shipment coming in on Friday morning, so I should unpack it and organize the store."

Stella was one of those lucky people who always knew what she wanted to do after high school. Her goal was to own a vintage clothing business, so she studied fashion design and merchandising in college. And she had an amazing personal collection of vintage designer clothes, accessories and jewelry that she began collecting in high school.

After a few years of working in boutiques and learning the business, she opened her own vintage clothing boutique specializing in formalwear.

"My inventory is low. You were there, you saw how busy it was during the fall show with everyone looking for something unique for Christmas and the Millennial New Year's Eve."

Her boutique - Stellar! - was well known for the eclectic fashion shows Stella held twice a year. She had one in September for the holidays and one in February for summer weddings. The turn of the century was fueling sales this season.

Mary tried to entice her.

"You might meet someone new at the party."

"Meet him, sure, but that would be it. As soon as he finds out I live with my parents, he'll never call back. They're all the same. They figure I'm looking for a husband, or someone to save me from my despair, but I'm just broke. Trevor ruined me. I can't believe I got involved with another loser. It's killing me to live with my parents again."

They chuckled about Stella's extremely bad luck with jobless, money-sucking guys, one right after another. Just like Mary's bad luck with musicians.

"Well, you might be better off without a guy. And don't you think a scoop of ice cream would be good with these brownies?"

Mary went to the kitchen for two bowls of French vanilla.

Stella became more serious.

"Are you and Garrett doing okay?"

"Mostly."

"What happened? You're upset, aren't you?"

"Um, sort of. Maybe. But I feel dumb complaining about him because he's a great guy. He's smart. He's handsome. He's athletic. He's successful at work. And I knew he was a full-throttle Type A personality when we started dating."

"Perhaps the problem is that he doesn't play a guitar or write you love songs?"

"No kidding!"

Mary laughed about her unsuccessful dating history with musicians. She tried to imagine Garrett with a guitar, but it was impossible.

"He sure is different," Mary said. "It's not as romantic, but calmer and more mature."

Stella smirked.

"You like that?"

"Well, most of the time."

"Oh, come on, tell me the truth. This is about sex, isn't it? He must be awesome in bed, because he is not your type otherwise. I'm surprised it's lasted this long, no offense to Garrett. He's just so different than you are."

Mary cringed. Romantic and erotic nights like the previous one were not all that common. In fact, they were increasingly rare and she could be open with Stella.

"Last night he was so charming. Then it got really hot back at his condo. Dates like that don't happen often and I loved it. Lately we've only been doing it on the weekends and he's not been very impulsive or creative."

"Really? You're accepting of that? You?"

Mary giggled.

"I think so, but I don't know anymore. I keep reminding myself there's more to a relationship than sex. Remember Dylan, the drummer? That's all we ever did. We had nothing else in common. Relationships based on sex can't last."

Stella tilted her head and raised her eyebrows.

"I never thought I'd hear you say anything like that. Being a hot lover was always at the top of your list. Along with must have teeth, must play guitar and must not be on an America's Most Wanted poster."

Mary giggled again.

"You know me better than I know myself. I'm surprised I'm saying this, but one attractive thing about Garrett is the security, which seems to make me overlook the lack of romance. He's so responsible and predictable."

"That's new for both of us."

"He's the perfect guy."

Mary's voice faded off and she stopped talking.

"Maybe you're bored?" Stella asked.

"Hmmm."

"I've seen you like this before. The newness is over and the sizzle is gone. It's not exciting enough anymore."

Mary could tell Stella the truth.

"There's never been any real sizzle, but we're always busy, and I do a lot of great outdoors stuff with him. And just when I least expect it, he surprises me with interesting dates, like taking me to see a Marcia Ball concert after I mentioned once that I liked her. And he rents Fellini films I've never seen."

"Fellini? Garrett?"

"Yeah, I was surprised, too. He said he took an Italian Cinema course as an elective in college, thinking it would be easy, but it wasn't. He enjoyed it, though, and Fellini's *La Dolce Vita* was his favorite along with others I'd never heard of until we watched them, like *The White Sheik* and *Amarcord*."

"That all sounds nice, but I'm going to be honest, I don't hear passion when you talk about him."

Stella was correct, and Mary knew it.

"You're right, but it's hard to be passionate, because Garrett is such a taskmaster, marching through his life with a regimented plan. I call it his 'Master Plan.' Not to his face, of course."

Stella laughed.

"He's motivated by achievement, and he defines most of it by financial success, like driving a BMW. He already owns one, but wants it to have a bigger engine. Or owning a Rolex at an age younger than his father. He did that too. Now he wants to buy a 40-foot sailboat. The list goes on, and sometimes, I feel like I'm just another task on his Plan. 'Find a wife and start a family.' Sometimes it feels that sterile and predictable."

Mary had her own goals, too, but they were more fluid. After her divorce, she vowed to experience life wide-eyed and passionately, and she knew Stella was trying to remind her about this. She never described her relationship with Garrett as dreamy or soulful, and she was wise enough to know Garrett would never change.

"I'm sure you care about him," Stella said. "But it seems like you're talking yourself into this relationship. I'm curious, has marriage come up?"

"Not really. We agree it's not something to rush into."

Mary paused for a few moments.

"I keep thinking it's me. I think I need to be less romantic and more realistic. There was a line in Sleepless in Seattle I keep thinking about. It's when Rosie O'Donnell says to Meg Ryan, 'You don't want to just fall in love. You want to fall in love in a movie.' Do you remember that scene? I think that's me. I want something that only happens in movies, not real life."

She sighed before continuing.

"Sometimes, I think I'm afraid of getting married again, but more than anything, I think it's time to grow up. I dated Danny all through college, then we got married and I got pregnant so quickly. None of it worked out, and I missed all the fun in college. Ever since I moved downtown, I've been making up for lost time."

"I hear you, but don't forget who Meg Ryan ended up with. It wasn't the predictable guy. You know, it's possible there's someone who's both responsible and fun."

Stella was candid with Mary. They'd been close friends since junior high school, by now able to read each other's minds and finish each other's sentences.

Mary heard Stella's message loud and clear, but it seemed like an impossible task to find "Mr. Right." She wanted to believe in romantic love, but doubt was moving in.

"Well, I don't think we'll solve it tonight," Stella said. "But time holds the answer. You've only dated Garrett about six months and in another six months you'll go to Italy. It's not much time to spend getting to know him better. See what happens. I'll bet your relationship will be either much better or much worse after the trip."

"You're right. I don't want to make any decisions right now. I'm too confused. Anyway, he's in the middle of an important negotiation with a company in Los Angeles, and he's under a lot of pressure. Maybe I'm craving more attention from him, which should happen when this deal is done."

"Are you thinking he might have planned the trip to propose? Like a year of dating is the milestone?" Stella asked.

"I don't know, but if he does propose, I doubt I'll be ready for it."

"You'll figure it out and make the right choice. I'm sure of it."

"Thanks. It helps to talk about it. Enough about stupid boys. How about eating rigatoni? I can put it in the oven now."

"Let's wait. I want to savor this chocolate buzz."

Mary laughed about how Stella lived to eat sugar.

Chapter 19

Most of the snow had melted, and signs of spring were appearing. Dogwood trees sprouted March blooms, and thawed bulbs peeked above ground.

Mary was enjoying nature's rebirth as she walked to Mr. Moretti's market. It had been weeks since she had visited him, because she hadn't been home much.

She and Garrett skied most weekends, but this weekend Garrett was camping with friends in the White Mountains of New Hampshire. It was an excursion beyond Mary's ability because the group planned to hike up the snowy, icy mountain carrying their equipment and then camp overnight to ski the fresh morning snow in the mountains' bowls.

So she stayed at home for the weekend intending to paint, but today's weather was sunny and crisp – nicer than forecasted. It was an easy decision to make the six-block walk to see her Italian buddy and share her ideas for her summer vacation in Italy.

She opened the door to the aromatic market and Mr. Moretti lit up with delight. He hurried from behind the refrigerated deli case to greet her.

"*Buongiorno*, Mary! Beautiful spring day, like you, *bella*."

He kissed her cheeks.

"Thank you, Mr. Moretti. How's business today?"

"Good, the sun makes people come outside. Tell me about Italia. How are the plans?"

He was so happy she would have the opportunity to see his home country.

"Well, we've decided to go in early June. It works out better for Garrett. He's in the middle of a huge negotiation that should close by then."

"June will be nice, but there might be many *turisti*. And it might be hot. But not like July and *Agosto*."

He shook his head thinking of the heat.

"Where are you goin'?"

"I think I've talked Garrett into renting an apartment in the heart of Tuscany, in Chianti. In the beginning, he suggested we find an organized tour with a small group or do a biking tour. But I didn't want to do that. I don't particularly like tours because we'd be on a structured schedule. And what if we didn't like the other people? And a biking trip? Who wants to bike every day on vacation? I think we should go to relax and drink bottles and bottles of wine!"

Mr. Moretti nodded in agreement with everything she said, especially the "drink bottles and bottles of wine" part. He pulled a loaf of bread from a deep wooden bin behind the register and prepared to slice it.

"I showed Garrett an article I found in a travel magazine about the benefits of renting an apartment at a working Tuscan farmhouse – an agriturismo."

She stopped and asked Mr. Moretti if she pronounced the word correctly.

"Sì," Mr. Moretti said.

"Good, thank you. I like the idea of staying in the same place all week and not having to check in and out of hotels. From a base at the farmhouse, we could take day trips to the cities and towns we want to visit, like Florence, Siena and the Cinque Terre. And it's reasonably priced, too. We could add a couple of days at the end to see Venice or Rome. I want to see Venice, but Garrett is pushing for Rome. I guess we'll decide eventually."

"That sounds wonderful. Toscana is beautiful – the most beautiful place on earth, like heaven. You know, I still have family there. But I will never see them again since I can never leave this place."

Mr. Moretti shook his head.

"My Giovanni is so lazy. You know he is a bad son. I cannot believe we have the same blood."

"He'll grow up. I'm sure he will."

"Ah, forget him. You are goin' to Toscana, so you should-a visit *mia famiglia*. My sister, her children and her grandchildren will treat you like family. I tell them you are comin'. You go? Of course. I will tell them the next time I call. And here, eat this."

He handed her a slice of bread.

Mary took a bite, nodded in approval and continued to talk about the trip.

"I'd love to meet them, and I think Garrett would, too."

Garrett didn't have time to help her organize the vacation, but she knew he liked Mr. Moretti so he'd surely enjoy meeting his family.

"How is Garrett? I never see him. What have you been doin'?"

"Oh, we've been out of town a lot, mostly skiing. But during the week, Garrett has been going to Los Angeles because he has several accounts there, and he's trying to get more."

"Mary, I know I introduced you to Garrett, but I worry. Every time I see you, you say he is in California or he is about to close a deal. What about his pretty girlfriend? You know, he is not *un italiano*, and maybe I made a mistake-a when I introduced you."

"Oh, no, Mr. Moretti. He's wonderful – he's responsible and hardworking. He likes to keep a busy schedule."

"Okay, I believe you. I will say no more, but he should adore you. Do not accept less. Okay?"

"I promise."

She didn't want to break this vow.

"I will contact *mia famiglia*. They live in Greve in Chianti, a small town. You will go to their big Sunday dinner, and they will give you Chianti they make on their farm."

"Thank you. That would be wonderful."

She loved his passion for food and family.

"And they make olive oil, too. I can taste it now."

He closed his eyes and pinched the fingers and thumb of his right hand in front of his lips.

"It smells like-a grass and tastes like-a nut. It is the best in Toscana."

"I love how you describe food. Americans should be so passionate."

"Food is everything. You must eat to live. And you should eat with your family and friends. It tastes better when you share. And fresh only. You see no frozen food here, do you?"

He handed her another slice of bread and took a slice for himself.

"No frozen food," she said as she bit into the crusty bread.

"Never."

He shook his head with his lips tightened.

"Only fresh. And no ketchup."

She laughed at his comment.

"You need this."

He handed her a bottle of olive oil.

"It is from Italia but it is not as tasty as my family oil. And here eez-a bread from the Caruso bakery."

He pulled another loaf from the wooden bin, scrutinized its color and tapped it.

"It might be a little over-cooked. *Giudica il vino al sapore ed il pane al colore.*"

"What?"

"Judge the wine by its taste and the bread by its color." He paused a moment. "I should-a make my own bread."

He huffed as he put it into a brown paper bag.

Mary grinned and thanked him as he bagged her groceries. He grabbed a small basil plant and held it out for her.

"This is new. I grow from seeds in the back."

"*Mille grazie.*"

She loved the aroma of basil, so she took the pot and held it to her nose. It smelled wonderful.

"You are so sweet."

"No, gelato is sweet, not me. I do not want to be sweet."

Then he began grumbling about Giovanni and predicting he would die over the basket of tomatoes.

Mary smiled as he ranted and walked out of the store, thanking him again over her shoulder as she left.

Chapter 20

THE JUNE AFTERNOON was hot and muggy, feeling more like late July. And the antiquated air-conditioning of Mary's historic office building barely kept up with the tropical conditions. But it was better than being outdoors. And only three days remained until she and Garrett left for Italy, so she decided it was best to eat a Lean Cuisine at her air-conditioned desk and finish last-minute work.

She needed to complete design revisions for a client and deliver camera-ready art to the printer for another. She needed to cross off several other items on her list, but the most annoying one was unrelated to work.

She picked up the phone and dialed her sister, thinking she had to get it over with. They had little in common other than their biological parents.

"Hi, Catherine."

"Hey, Mary! I wondered when you were going to call. I hardly ever hear from you. Are you ready for your trip?"

"I've been busy, and I still have a few little things left to do. Only three more days until we leave. I'm so excited."

"Did you send me the e-mail with the contact info?"

"Not yet, but I will as soon as we hang up."

"Don't forget."

"Okay."

Mary rolled her eyes, and wondered when her older sister would stop telling her what to do.

"Do you think this will be it?"

"It?"

Mary knew exactly what Catherine meant, but didn't feel like playing along.

"Mary, I'm sure he'll propose. Don't worry and don't act like you don't know what I'm talking about."

"Catherine, I'm not worried and I wish you wouldn't either."

"He's the greatest guy you've ever dated. He's perfect, and I'd hate for you to ruin this. Do you know how happy mom would be if you came home engaged?"

"Catherine!"

Mary started to defend herself, but stopped. She didn't have the energy today.

"We'll see," Mary said.

"Call me as soon as you're home."

"I will, but I need to get back to work now."

"Bon voyage! Or however you say it in Italian. And good luck!"

"Bye."

Mary hung up. Her sister could get under her skin like no one else, and had done so her entire life. She found it hard to believe they were siblings.

She diverted her attention to this year's Tuscany calendar. The June photo featured a rustic farmhouse surrounded by olive trees and vineyards. She could hardly wait to go.

ITALY

Chapter 21

MARY SAT ALONE in the tattered back seat of a taxi approaching the Philadelphia airport when her cell phone rang. She quickly hit the talk button.

"Hey!"

Garrett let out a lengthy sigh.

"I'm so glad you have your phone with you."

"I almost didn't bring it since I can't use it in Italy. Where are you? Near the airport?"

"No, not yet. I, I –"

He stammered.

"I haven't left the office yet."

She couldn't believe it. He should have been on his way to the airport by now.

"What? Are you serious? You'll miss the flight."

"I won't miss it. I'll make it. I'm just cutting it close."

He heaved another sigh and she knew he was speaking with his jaw clenched, as he always did when he was stressed.

"It's the Palmer deal. It didn't close today like we thought it would, so the meetings and teleconferences with their L.A. team haven't stopped."

"So when are you leaving?"

She didn't care about the Palmer deal right now. Her concern was Garrett getting to the airport on time.

"In a few minutes. I need to have a quick talk with Max, and then I'm on my way. Go ahead and check in, get your boarding pass and go through security. Then you won't have to rush with me."

"This is cutting it way too close."

He barely had enough time if he left the office immediately, and she knew his conversation with Max would exceed five minutes. Max couldn't even say hello in five minutes because he needed time to boast about his financial success.

"I'll make it, I'll make it!"

He was shouting. This wasn't his typical controlled demeanor.

"Sorry," he said, "But please keep your cell phone on, and I'll let you know where I am."

She sat and stared at her dad's watch on her wrist. In less than two hours, their flight to Rome would leave, so it was going to be tight. She wondered if they would have any other options, like going through New York City on another Rome-bound flight, but it was unlikely. Garrett needed to leave the office right away.

"Mary, are you still there?"

"I am. Hurry! Don't miss the flight. We have to go tonight. I can already hear the cork of a Chianti bottle popping."

"I know. I know, I know, I know. I should already be on the road. I'll call after I've parked the car, so keep your phone on. Sorry, Mare, I didn't mean for this to happen."

He hung up without saying goodbye, as he always did.

Mary's taxi arrived at the departure terminal. She hopped out and threw her carry-on over her shoulder with her tote bag. After paying the driver, she grabbed her suitcase and trudged into the airport where she joined a long international check-in line. She waited impatiently, constantly looking over her shoulder for Garrett to walk in, knowing it would be at least 45 minutes before he arrived.

After she went through check-in and security, she walked to Gate A24 and sat down in an uncomfortable chair. She tried to read but she couldn't focus. Her mind was whirling, teetering between being nervous and angry. She fidgeted with her silver hoop earrings and watched as the other people on her flight gathered nearby.

A young Italian couple sat across from her, infatuated with each other. Their bodies touched everywhere possible and they never took their eyes off each other. Their conversation was quiet and personal, impossible to hear, and she envied their intimacy.

Her phone rang.

"Garrett?"

"Where are you?" he asked.

"At the gate. You?"

"I'm in line for security. I'll be at the gate soon, but since I was so late they gave away my seat, so I'm on the wait list now."

"You're kidding."

"You know how flights are, always overbooked. But the agent said I shouldn't have problems getting cleared."

"I hope so."

Stella had predicted Italy might be the test of their future. Right now, it wasn't looking good since Mary was thinking she would go alone if he didn't make it.

"I'll be on the flight," he said and hung up.

Several minutes later, he arrived at the gate and after another nerve-wracking wait, he received a seat assignment 21 rows behind her. She was in 22A and he in 43B. They pinned their hopes on someone agreeing to switch after boarding.

Chapter 22

ONCE ON THE PLANE, Mary took her window seat and pulled her hair into a ponytail.

"Hi!"

A forty-something bleach-blonde dropped her large fake-leather purse onto the aisle seat.

"Looks like I'm going to be your neighbor for the next seven or eight hours. I'm Rae. Rae Lynn, really, but most people call me Rae. What's your name?"

"I'm Mary."

Garrett's late arrival meant that now Mary would have to listen to this chatterbox all the way to Rome.

"Mary, it's real nice to meet you."

Rae had a strong Southern drawl.

"Is this your first time to Italy?" Rae asked.

"Yes."

"You'll love it. It's my second. I'm takin' a vacation with my mama, daddy and little brother. We go somewhere every year."

She stuffed a black-and-white polka-dot bag into the overhead bin.

"They're all right over there, in the middle section of Row 21."

Mary bit her lip to keep from chuckling. It was the poodle family. They all sported the same over-permed, over-bleached blonde hair. Mary guessed someone in the family was the hairdresser, maybe Rae herself.

"Mama and daddy take me and Jimmy on vacation every summer. This year we're goin' back to Rome for a week."

Rae kept looking up the aisle.

"Mary, if the person in front of me will switch, I'm goin' to try to move. No offense to you, but I'd like to sit next to my family. We had a big fat screw-up with our seats, and the ticket lady moved me to this row so I could be near them, but I'm still going to try to move to their same row."

"I understand."

This would complicate the switch to sit next to Garrett.

"Are you travelin' alone?" Rae asked.

"No, my boyfriend's on the flight, but we don't have seats together."

"Oh, he shouldn't be worried about not sittin' next to you on the flight, but when you're in Italy he better stay by your side. Those Italian Romeos are going to think you're an Italian yourself, with your pretty dark skin and dark hair. They're all going to like you, and they're so handsome, let me tell you, you will be tempted!"

Rae laughed at her own comment.

Meeting an Italian man was not in the plans this week, she thought. She didn't know what to do with the relationship she already had.

Rae Lynn was still laughing when the occupant of 21B arrived. He didn't mind switching with Rae, so Mary had a new quiet neighbor, which was good if she stayed in this seat. But she still hoped the passenger in the seat next to Garrett would switch. Fortunately that switch was made too.

Once they were settled, Garrett immersed himself in reviewing work documents. For some reason, the Palmer deal his company was working on made him uneasy. He scribbled notes and made calculations feverishly, and when she asked what was wrong, he told her not to worry about it. He isolated himself, so she flipped through a magazine. After a preservative-filled dinner and two airline-sized bottles of Cabernet Sauvignon, she fell asleep until the flight attendants served breakfast.

When she woke up, she was tired and stiff from the cramped, uncomfortable seat. Her mouth was dry and her lips felt like they were glued together, but she greeted him anyway.

"Good morning," she said.

He didn't reply. He looked exhausted and miserable.

"Did you sleep at all?"

"Maybe 40 minutes."

"Too noisy and uncomfortable?"

"No, it's the Palmer deal. Something's not adding up. But I don't know what it is."

He was still in his own world and kept running his fingers through his thick, dark-blond hair.

She knew it was best to leave him alone.

They ate breakfast while flying over the Alps, and the plane began its descent toward Rome. It was dawn and the bright sunrise illuminated the airplane's engines in a mellow orange glow. There were a few white wisps of clouds, and the landscape was rural, more so than she expected. She scanned the peaceful horizon for Rome's skyline or signs of urban sprawl, like in the U.S., but never found it. All she saw were miles and miles of rolling hills and farms.

At last, she thought. She was in Italy.

After going through passport control, she and Garrett went to baggage claim. Mary saw Rae Lynn and her blond-haired clan with piles of colorful, mismatched luggage. She told them she hoped they enjoyed their trip.

Rae checked out Garrett and winked at Mary.

"He's a hunk, honey. I wish I met someone like him when I was your age. Now I'm too old for anyone to want to marry my sorry butt. Don't let him get away and remember what I told you. He better keep a close eye on you, cuz you ain't seen nothin' until you have seen those Italian men. Umm-ummm. And they are gonna love you."

Rae let out a hearty hoot and flashed a cheesy smile.

Chapter 23

"WHAT IS THAT?" Garrett asked as they approached their assigned rental car.

Cars were squeezed into every imaginable space in the cramped garage.

"Um...a very little car."

Mary laughed as she checked out the tiny burgundy Opel Corsa with dark gray interior.

"Well, maybe it's not a car, it might be a roller skate," she said.

There was only enough room for two people and two medium-sized suitcases.

They agreed Garrett would drive and she would navigate. Once out of the airport, he tried to pick up speed on the highway, but the car had little power, especially compared to his BMW. The performance frustrated him, and the bright sunshine exacerbated their jet lag. The lack of air conditioning in the car didn't help either. Mary tried to read the road signs and a map, but navigating in this rural area outside of Rome was more difficult than she anticipated. After a short distance, she asked him to stop at a gas station to buy a better map. Hers didn't have enough detail and she was sure they'd missed their turn.

She gasped as she walked into the small store at the gas station. The attendant at the register was about six feet tall with dark hair, dark skin and chiseled features. A perfectly tailored yellow shirt with fine red pinstripes sculpted his body, like a second layer of skin.

This must be one of the Romeos who Rae warned me about, Mary thought.

"*Parla inglese?*" she asked.

She'd practiced basic expressions with Mr. Moretti.

Romeo shook his head no, but it didn't matter that he didn't speak her language. With hand gestures and broken Italian by Mary, he understood the young American needed a *mappa* and he sold her one for approximately a dollar. It probably wasn't meant to be sold, since he peeled it off the wall, tape and all. He only wanted to help and flirt with her as long as possible.

Leaving the gas station, they needed to turn left, but a right turn was their only option.

"Let's drive until we find a place to turn around," Mary said.

Garrett pulled into the nearest parking lot. It seemed like a good idea until they realized they had entered a church's parking lot where a wedding had just taken place.

Mary spotted the bride and groom who were riding in a horse-drawn carriage. Each car in the procession that followed the couple had enormous white bows on their hoods, which were quickly getting covered with dust. A closer look at the couple revealed the distinguished groom was in his forties or fifties and the petite bride in her early twenties.

This is like a scene in a *Godfather* movie, Mary thought.

Garrett had to move their car so the procession could continue on its route, which forced them directly into the Saturday morning wedding parade.

Mary smiled as she remembered a similar experience in Rosarito Beach, Mexico, on a trip with her dad. He was going to a conference for work in San Diego, and he asked Mary to join him to see southern California before she started her first year of college. As part of the trip, they were invited to his colleague's vacation house just south of the border in Rosarito Beach.

Mary had no way of knowing it would be the last trip she and her dad would take together. He died the following summer and now she cherished the memory of that trip, just like she cherished the silver hoop earrings he bought her in a small jewelry store near the famous Rosarito Beach Hotel.

She decided to tell Garrett about the trip.

"The summer before I started college, I went to Mexico with my dad. One morning, we left the beach house where we were staying to buy pastries, and we drove onto the main road into town. There was no traffic, which seemed odd for a Saturday morning. Then we noticed a crowd by the side of the road, and we realized the road was closed for a parade. When we looked out our rear window, the head of the parade was behind us, which meant we were leading the parade. We almost pulled over, we were laughing so hard. Dad told me to wave to the crowds, because they might think we were important."

Mary laughed, but Garrett just let out a little charity chuckle. He was frustrated about being lost and wasting time, unlike her dad who would have seen getting lost as an adventure.

She grimaced at his seriousness and went back to reading the map.

Once on the right road again, they easily found the entrance to the highway, called the Autostrada, where they quickly learned the left lane was for fast – very fast – traffic only. In their powerless little roller skate – like the majority of cars on the highway – they stayed in the right lane with the windows rolled down.

Garrett seemed miserable. Every time a BMW flew by them, Garrett sighed. Then he asked why she didn't rent a performance car with air conditioning.

"Well, I read parking is difficult so I thought we'd be better off with a small car. There weren't very many available with air conditioning and the ones that had AC were expensive."

"Money's not a problem," he said. "You know that."

He wiped the sweat from his forehead with the back of his hand.

His criticism offended her, especially because he did little to participate in the planning, and she wasn't comfortable spending his money. He was generous, but that didn't make things easier. She bit her tongue, and changed the subject by commenting on the new sights they were seeing.

There were mountains on the horizon and the landscape was dry and brown, similar to southern California or Mexico. The occasional exit had a gas station with an Auto-Grill instead of a McDonald's or another American fast food restaurant. Mary

wondered what an Auto-Grill was like, and she figured they would
find out when they stopped for gas.

As they drove northwest, the roads became hillier and there
was an occasional olive grove, vineyard or line of cypress trees
along a property's border. Perched atop hills she saw large castle-
like structures and small villages that looked ancient, as if pictures
in history books had come to life. The vegetation was lush and
overgrown. By U.S. standards it would be considered messy, but
here it looked rustic.

Mary eventually figured out the road sign system. There
weren't prominent route numbers displayed. Instead, signs were
marked with the name of the destination city. So they followed all
signs to "Siena."

Once in the Siena area, they watched for an exit on the north
side to access SS222, the Chianti Highway, and easily found it.
With only 10 kilometers to go, the route seemed simple, and
Mary shifted attention to the owners' directions, which had been
faxed to her. There were no street names, only landmarks.

Take SS222 north. Drive 4 km. At San Giorgio Church turn
right. Drive 4 km and turn left at sign Cielo. Drive through
Terzano and watch for another sign for Cielo.

They drove in circles trying to find the San Giorgio Church.
They knew they were close, but couldn't find it. Hot and sleep-
deprived, their patience was quickly running out – Garrett's faster
than Mary's. Mary asked him to stop at a gas station, where she
asked for help from a young Italian man who knew some English.
But instead of trying to verbalize the directions, he offered to lead
them there in his dusty little Volkswagen. He said he would take
them to the place where they needed to turn.

The church hadn't been easy to find because giant cypress trees
surrounded it and hid it from view. Once they turned right at the
church, the serene Tuscan countryside stretched out before them.
They passed orderly vineyards with weathered farmhouses nestled
among the hills. Cypress trees and olive orchards accented the

landscape, like all the pictures Mary had seen in guidebooks, magazines and her calendar. But reality was even more incredible because she could feel it, smell it and be part of it.

The vineyard-lined roads curved and climbed a hill for a couple of kilometers. They almost missed the small, craggy sign with hand-painted black letters on pine proclaiming "Cielo," the name of the *agriturismo* that would be their home for the next week. As soon as Garrett turned left onto a narrow road, Mary saw it. Not the farmhouse, but the tower of a majestic hilltop castle that captured her imagination and reminded her of the painting she created about a year earlier.

"Garrett, look!"

"What?"

"A castle," she said. "Like the painting above my bed."

He missed it since he was closely watching the narrow, winding road. Then within seconds, it was out of sight for her, too. But she didn't stop thinking about it. She wanted an up-close view.

The paved road kept ascending until they reached Terzano. As pretty as a picture in an Italian guidebook, it was a small, hillside hamlet of about thirty apricot-colored stucco homes, accented by exposed bricks, fieldstones and wood. Several were hidden by privacy fences, and a cat was perched on one for a midday nap. Each home had a hand-painted tile next to the door identifying the house number. Young boys played in the street, kicking a ball. They moved to the side so Mary and Garrett's car could pass through. Mary waved to them, but they didn't really notice or care.

The road through Terzano appeared to come to a dead end in front of a house, but in fact made a sharp left turn uphill between two houses. There was scarcely enough room for their car, even one this small.

"I've never seen such narrow roads in my life," Garrett said.

He seemed agitated as he made another hard right turn to keep from hitting another house.

After this turn, they were out of the hamlet and out of pavement. As the road surface changed to gravel, it became a dusty uphill path through an olive grove with trees stationed in grassy fields on their left and right.

Garrett stopped the car. His patience was running thin.

"Are you sure we're going the right way?"

"You know as much as I do," Mary said. "And even if it's the wrong way, it's beautiful."

"Mary, I'm tired of driving and –"

Before he finished, she spotted another hand-painted "Cielo" sign. An arrow directed them to the left.

"Keep going," she said, pointing to the sign. "I think we're close."

In a short distance, a majestic 15th-century villa appeared at the end of a long cypress-lined gravel driveway. Their home for the next week was even prettier than the photos online.

Chapter 24

GARRETT PARKED and Mary offered to take care of the registration. She grabbed their passports, while Garrett reclined his seat and closed his eyes to rest for a few minutes.

As she approached the main entrance of double wooden doors outlined with ivy, a mature and proper Italian lady in a colorful print dress rushed out to greet her.

"Mary Sarto?" she asked.

"Yes, I'm Mary."

"Mary, *piacere*. I am Lucia, and I'm sorry, but I have bad news."

Her English was easy to understand, but she was clearly angry and upset.

"What?" Mary asked.

"I apologize, but your apartment is not available. We have a problem with the ancient pipes. We have a leak, and I cannot let you in the room."

Mary was shocked. She wondered where they would stay now.

"All week, the pipe is broken, and all week the worker promise to come. When he arrives, he will be lucky if I don't break his neck."

Lucia shook her head and pursed her lips.

"So –" Mary said.

She started to ask for a suggestion, but Lucia interrupted her.

"Since I have no more rooms, I make an arrangement with my neighbor."

"Oh?"

"There is another rental property. It is close. And they promise a good apartment for you. It is bigger and nicer. But you pay no more. I give you directions, and I give you wine. Follow me."

Mary entered the old building and walked into a small foyer. At a round wooden table, Lucia showed her a hand-drawn map. If it was to scale, the new property named I Ribelli was close. Lucia explained the simple directions and gave Mary a bottle of their own farm's Chianti. She apologized repeatedly as she walked Mary outside.

Mary relayed the situation to Garrett, and he sighed a few times as he put the car in reverse. They retraced their route, and just before they hit the paved road, they spied a gravel road they hadn't noticed the first time they drove through. This road led them to I Ribelli, and it wasn't out of their way at all, as Lucia promised.

Up a small hill and through another field of olive trees, they arrived in the small gravel courtyard of a sprawling rustic farmhouse. The complex had numerous buildings of brick, fieldstone and stucco. Abundant flowers splashed color against the earthy tones of the buildings and landscape. In a small corner of the main building, Mary spotted a sign reading "L'Ufficio," with its entrance marked by a collection of red geranium-filled terracotta pots and urns.

"We're in the right place. There's the office."

Chapter 25

GARRETT PARKED THE CAR AGAIN and this time it was in a gravel lot next to a large terracotta olive-oil cask. Two large dogs warmly welcomed them - a black lab and a yellow hound dog mix.

Mary grabbed their passports for registration, and Garrett got out of the car this time, too. He stood up and stretched, then played with the friendly dogs.

Mary entered the small office that barely had enough room for a desk and chair.

"*Buongiorno,*" she said.

A tired woman with a round flushed face grinned nervously. She wore a simple, cotton print dress and apron, like Mary remembered her grandmother wearing when she cooked for endless hours on Easter and other holidays.

"*Buongiorno,*" the lady said while making little eye contact, flipping through papers and notebooks on her desk.

"*Parla inglese?*" Mary asked.

"No, no."

The woman shook her head and waved her hand side to side.

Mary handed her the note from Lucia, written in Italian. The lady nodded her head in acknowledgment and pointed to a sign-in sheet for Mary to document their names and passport numbers.

Mary finished the registration process.

"*Come si chiama?*" – "What is your name?" Mary asked.

"Rossana," she replied.

Rossana picked up a key and gestured for Mary to follow her.

Garrett and the dogs joined them and they traversed the gravel terrace to a first floor entrance, also marked by geranium-filled pots. A stout, elderly man wearing a fishing hat sat quietly at a white plastic table near the door, smoking Lucky Strikes and watching their every move. Rossana ignored him, unlocked the door and entered. Mary and Garrett followed her, leaving the dogs outside.

They entered a foyer with a staircase to the right, its floors covered with terracotta stone. Rossana climbed the worn tile steps and they followed. Every step was bowed in the center and Mary fancied the number of feet that had trod on them over the hundreds of years. Historically, in a Tuscan farmhouse, the people lived on the top floor and their animals lived on the ground floor, she had learned in her research.

At the top of the staircase to the right was the door to their one-bedroom apartment. Rossana unlocked it and they entered. The windows and shutters were already open and fresh air filled the rooms. The simple Tuscan apartment was illuminated with natural light and furnished with simple antiques. The stucco walls were painted a warm white and tile covered the floor.

Rossana showed them the bedroom and the bath. In the kitchen, she opened all the dark wood cabinets. She showed them there were plenty of cooking utensils, including pots, pans, a colander and a cheese grater. On the tiled kitchen counter was a bottle of red wine - Chianti. Rossana handed it to Mary and pointed to its simple label - "*I Ribelli, Chianti, Terzano, Siena, Italy.*" It was this working farm's production.

"*Per Lei.*" - "For you." Rossana said.

"*Grazie,*" Mary said.

She wanted to ask more about the property, but she didn't speak enough Italian to know what words to use.

Rossana pointed to a narrow stairway leading to the rooftop balcony, and then left, smiling and closing the door to the apartment behind her.

Mary went to a bedroom window to look outside.

There were no screens, only small, white, lace-edged curtains pulled to the side of the window. The sill was the thickness of the stucco wall, about fifteen inches, and there were solid wooden shutters outside.

The view was a valley with orderly rows of grapevines and olive trees peppering the landscape. Mary heard children playing and splashing in the pool nearby, but she couldn't see them.

"This view is incredible - like a painting. I think we'll like it here as much as the other place."

"Yeah," Garrett said. "We're isolated in the country, aren't we? I don't think we'll hear traffic noise tonight like we do in the city."

He stood next to the window, checking out the windows and shutters.

"Are there no screens on the windows here?" he asked.

She ignored his question and walked to another window for a different view and she saw it again - the castle tower on the hill above them.

"Garrett, come and look at this! It's the same castle I saw on the way here!"

She wanted to him to come quickly, like it might disappear.

"That's cool, must be really old," he said.

"I wonder if anyone lives in it. I would love to explore it."

He turned away and looked around the interior.

"What is the chance there's a computer and Internet connection in this place?"

"Internet? We're here to get away from the Internet."

"But Mare -"

Garrett had more to say, but she interrupted him.

"I know. I know. You need to stay in touch about the Palmer deal. We'll probably have to go back to Siena to find an Internet café."

Garrett smirked, but didn't say anything else. He unzipped his suitcase and put on a fresh t-shirt.

"Let's check out the rooftop," she said. "That's a lucky upgrade for us."

They climbed ten steps to a door that opened to another set of steps.

The private rooftop terrace was open on all four sides and had a vaulted wooden roof. A wrought-iron chandelier hung from the roof and a mosaic-tiled table was centered underneath it.

Mary looked around at the panoramic view.

"Oh, my God," she said. "This is gorgeous! Look at the vineyards and the farms. And there's the castle again!"

It was mystically perched on an adjacent hill, surrounded by large cypress trees. She was able to see more of it, but still not enough to satisfy her curiosity.

"We were lucky that we were moved here," she said. "This is perfect!"

She hugged Garrett and kissed him. It was one of the most exciting moments of her life.

"Thank you, Garrett. I'm so thrilled to be here!"

"You're welcome," he said. "I know it means a lot to you. Hopefully I'll resolve the work issues by tomorrow."

He kissed her forehead and looked at the Tuscan horizon, not yet able to relax.

She put her hand on his chest, but he slightly flinched, so she backed off, giving him space. She knew his body language and he didn't want to be touched. But she yearned for his mood to be different and she fantasized about making love on the rooftop balcony.

"Want to go back in?" he asked.

"Sure," she said slipping back to reality.

They finished unpacking, and Mary asked Garrett if he wanted to open the Chianti, pour two glasses and look around the property. She was ready to see more.

"If you don't mind, I'd like to take a nap. I didn't sleep on the flight, and the driving was exhausting. Jet lag is getting the best of me."

"That's a good idea. I'll wait to open the wine with you, but I'm going to walk around, and probably sit by the pool. I'll come back in an hour."

"I know I haven't been much fun today. Hopefully sleep will help."

She hoped so, too.

As she closed the shutters in their bedroom she watched him undress down to his navy-blue tartan boxers. He climbed his sexy body into bed and she wished he wanted her by his side. She grabbed her travel journal and left.

Chapter 26

OUTSIDE, SHE STOPPED and took in the sights. Everything was weathered, but welcoming. She knew she would create many paintings from these landscape scenes when she returned home.

She began her exploration by heading around the corner of the main building and as she did, she heard a lively group of Italians nearby. She sauntered in the direction of their laughing and chatter while admiring a rambling rose vine with bright red blossoms on a faded yellow stucco wall. It outlined a door and several windows, and was as much a part of the house as the walls themselves. She made a mental note to take pictures of it later.

She turned another corner and discovered the noisy group - all men - gathered around a white plastic patio table. Some were seated, some were standing. But they all drank red wine from short glasses they filled from clear plastic liter bottles that looked like recycled water bottles. She assumed the deeply tanned men were workers from the farm because their clothing was soiled and they glistened with perspiration. It was possible that they had stopped for a late lunch or maybe they had finished for the day since it was Saturday.

A man with leathery skin approached after he put out his cigarette. He tipped his frayed straw hat and spoke very slowly with a thick accent.

"Ciao, I am Giovanni. Welcome to my farm."

Ah, Rossana's husband. She'd seen his name on the rental agreement. He had probably been a handsome young man, but now, like his wife, he was worn. His body was still lean and muscular, but his teeth were stained from red wine and tobacco.

"Ciao. I am Mary, and thank you, *grazie*. The farm is wonderful, *molto bello*."

As she finished speaking, a young farmer who had his back to her turned around. His soft blue eyes met hers and their gazes froze. It was impossible to look away. The attraction was breathtaking, and in an instant, she recognized him. She remembered him. From where or when she didn't know, but she felt like he remembered her, too.

His eyes spoke her very thoughts. There you are, at last. I've been looking for you, searching everywhere. I never gave up, and I'm glad I didn't. I've finally found you. Look at you. You're radiant. And still so beautiful.

Their connection seemed like it was from another lifetime or another world.

His eyes kept speaking. Life is good to you this time, and I'm so relieved to know you're okay. I've been worried about you, but now I can stop worrying. At last, you are here, and we are united again.

As clear as the sky was blue, she understood their souls had been restlessly struggling to find each other, not even knowing they were searching. She had never experienced such a powerful and mesmerizing emotion, but it was undeniably real, and she had no doubt who he was. They had already loved each other, and they had been waiting to meet again.

He gently smiled, shaking her from the riveting moment.

She smiled, too, feeling her face flush. How much time lapsed during their encounter, she didn't know. It may have been seconds. It may have been minutes. But she quickly remembered she was standing in front of a group of men. She recovered and said "*ciao*" before turning away and hurrying to find the pool. She needed to sit down before her knees buckled.

Around the corner, she discovered an empty lounge chair next to the pool. She hurried to it and sat, trembling.

She scanned her surroundings, before looking over her shoulder to where she'd been. She replayed the incident repeatedly, trying to determine if she'd imagined the whole incident or if she'd really just encountered a lost soul mate. She had never felt anything so strong or so moving in her life, but she was quick to chide herself.

She realized she was living in the movie in her head and dreaming about love across time with an alluring Italian farm worker. She laughed at herself, but she found she still believed it was possible. Rae Lynn hadn't warned her about this kind of Romeo.

The setting was serene and the view helped calm her down. There were huge pots of geraniums along the pool's perimeter, rows of vineyards down the valley and forest-covered hills in the distance.

But the pool itself was noisy with other renters.

There was a German family with a brood of five children swimming, jumping, running and screaming.

The same older man she'd seen when they arrived now reclined in a lounge chair wearing his fishing hat and dark sunglasses, reading a novel supported by his large, furry belly. But she noticed he never turned the page.

There was a pretty Italian lady with her teenage son. They sat silently, not speaking to each other. The woman paged through an Italian fashion magazine while her son listened to his Sony Walkman.

Mary didn't talk to any of them. She quietly observed and wondered if the mysterious man was still nearby and if she'd ever see him again. And if she did, would the same feeling come over them? And what would they say to each other?

She pulled out the journal and decided to use it to record what she was feeling.

I'm such a dreamer and here I am in an artist's and dreamer's paradise with rows of vineyards in front of me, olive trees only steps away and a rustic farmhouse behind me. It's unbelievably enchanting in its simplicity and naturalness, as though I've stepped into an ancient world that was waiting for my return. I feel like I belong here, as though something pulled me to this very farmhouse.

She loosely sketched the view and she wanted to write more, but all she could do was bask in the landscape, with unrelenting thoughts about the startling encounter with the Italian man.

Who is he?

After she wrote the question, she sketched a large question mark on the opposite page and drew grape vines wrapping around it.

An hour later, she followed the same path back to the apartment, but the group was gone. She wanted to see the man again, and at the same time, she was a bit relieved he wasn't there. She had no idea what to say or do with him.

Inside, she found Garrett still sleeping soundly. Instead of waking him, she left a note on the kitchen table and headed out to the supermarket she had seen on their way in.

She found it with no trouble.

Chapter 27

THE COOP, as it was called, was a mega-sized version of Mr. Moretti's market, full of her favorite foods. There was fresh produce, abundant pasta choices, deli meats, local cheese and crusty bread.

She chose big green grapes, Pecorino cheese, Parmigiano-Reggiano cheese, Barilla boxed pasta, jarred tomato sauce, rosemary-spiced crackers, Sienese almond cookies called ricciarelli, Lavazza espresso, Perugina cream-filled chocolate and milk. She also selected fresh bread and cinnamon pastries in the large bakery section of the store.

With all of this food, she and Garrett were prepared for at least one light dinner in their apartment and for breakfast for a couple of days.

At the register, she learned plastic grocery bags were available to purchase for an equivalent of five cents each. It was a simple idea to promote reusing bags, and she liked it. It also helped her understand why she'd seen a man in the parking lot emptying all his groceries from his cart directly into the car's hatchback without any bags.

Mary drove back to the Ribelli farmhouse with the windows rolled down. The sun was descending, and she eagerly anticipated her first Tuscan sunset from the rooftop. Now that she'd seen it in person, she understood why this idyllic land inspired so many contemporary and historical artists.

She approached the area where she had seen the castle earlier. This time she noticed a dusty, gravel road that looked like it might lead to it. On an impulse, she turned off the paved road and drove along the gravel path.

On one side of the road there was a pasture of large white cows unlike any she'd ever seen at home. She later learned they were the Chianina, some of the biggest cows in the world, with a long tradition of breeding in Italy. They were known for their tenderness and flavor and were the source for the famous Bistecca Fiorentina – Steak Florentine. These were large-boned tenderloin steaks, cooked rare to medium rare, and seasoned with olive oil, salt, pepper and sometimes rosemary. Mr. Moretti had told her about this dish, and she promised to try it while she was in Tuscany.

On the other side of the road was a vineyard.

She kept climbing toward the castle tower, and towering cypress trees soon flanked the road. It was breathtaking.

She drove cautiously, feeling every little bump in the road while watching for potholes and ruts. A huge dust plume was billowing up behind her car.

The farther uphill she drove, the denser and more overgrown the vegetation became. She lost her view of the castle tower, but she kept going, and the narrow dusty path continued through another large, orderly vineyard.

The castle tower came back in sight and her excitement grew.

She made yet another long curve to the right where an old stone wall followed the road, then she passed through a thick copse of oak trees before finding a small driveway leading to the castle.

The large stone-and-stucco fortification looked abandoned, and she tried to picture it in its former glory. She looked upward at the tower and imagined the view of the countryside from its lookouts. It had to be spectacular.

She decided she would see more of the property, but not tonight. She'd have to come back another day with Garrett.

Chapter 28

WHEN SHE ARRIVED back at their apartment, Garrett was awake and in a better mood. They went to the rooftop to watch the sunset and sat at the tiled table, eating cheese, crackers and grapes and drinking the exceptionally good Ribelli Chianti. The golden sky, scintillating vistas and earthy wine were intoxicating, and in this perfect setting, they quickly emptied the complimentary bottle from Rossana and then opened the Cielo bottle.

As they ate and drank, the sky changed from golden yellow to amber and cast an ethereal glow on the landscape and on them.

Garrett seemed loose and relaxed.

"You were right about renting an apartment here," he said. "This is a beautiful, quiet place. I have to admit I wasn't sure about it while we were driving here, but I like it, and this rooftop is wonderful."

He flashed a smile and raised his glass.

"And you look so pretty tonight."

"Thank you."

He took a drink, then stood up and moved behind her. He smoothly leaned over her shoulders to wrap his strong arms around her and he nuzzled his face into her neck. A quick chill ran along her spine as she felt his warm breath.

"Thanks for everything you did to plan this trip," he said. "I want it to be special for us."

He pushed her hair aside and softly pressed his lips right below her ear, knowing it would make her crazy. It always did.

He slid his left hand over her shoulder beneath her soft cotton shirt and inside her bra.

"You taste good, and you feel good," he whispered. "I need more."

He paused for a moment to make sure they had privacy, then pulled off her shirt and bra and moved both hands over her breasts.

She gasped.

The light breeze of the evening air made her skin more sensitive, heightened by the sun's warm glow and the scents of nature. He hungrily kissed her neck and nibbled her ears and shoulders. They had nowhere to go and no one to interrupt them. She arched her back against the chair, inviting him to devour her. She wanted him. On the balcony. In the chair. Right there. And that's exactly what happened. They made love on the balcony at sunset, an exciting way to begin the romantic week in Tuscany.

Chapter 29

Early rays of sunshine poked through the open windows, roosters crowed on a nearby farm and dogs barked as they patrolled their vineyards - a Tuscan alarm clock.

Mary was thrilled to wake up in Italy with an easy day of touring ahead. She rested her chin on Garrett's chest.

"Good morning, handsome."

He grinned.

"We're naked and we have nowhere to go. Ready for more?"

Her hands moved slowly down his torso.

"Maybe after I go for a run. My muscles feel tight from all the traveling."

"Okay."

She didn't try to change his mind. She knew she couldn't.

While Garrett was gone, Mary lay in bed and heard another calming sound - the distant ring of church bells. She opened her travel journal and started writing about her sense of peace at this farmhouse.

Then she picked up the large sketchbook she'd hesitated to bring. She drew the architecture in their apartment - the ceiling timbers, the tile floor pattern and the thick, solid wood doors and shutters. Everything was centuries old, made to last.

She stopped drawing and before taking a shower she took a moment to peek out each window to see if there were workers in the vineyards. Not today, it was Sunday.

Wonder if I'll ever see the farmer again? She thought.

She didn't know if she could ever stop thinking of him. He had a powerful hold on her.

Garrett returned precisely 45 minutes after he left, and went directly to the bathroom to shower. Then he dressed and sat down at the kitchen table to eat breakfast and drink the coffee

Mary made with the little stovetop coffeemaker, just as Mr. Moretti had taught her. She was glad for his lesson because she wouldn't have figured out where to put the grounds or the water in the little two-compartment appliance that looked like a tall, skinny teapot. They never went back to bed and started to discuss plans for the day instead.

"Where do you want to go today?" she asked.

"What do you recommend? You've done more research than I have."

She opened the map and pointed out the areas she thought they should see. They settled on first visiting San Gimignano, "a place not to be missed," she had heard.

In the car, she read the guidebook and paraphrased for Garrett.

"San Gimignano is described as the 'Manhattan of Italy' with its famous medieval towers, fourteen of them in all, forming an actual skyline. In the middle ages, there were 72 towers."

She paused, thinking about what she'd read.

"It must have been an incredible sight," she said.

She snapped pictures of the scenic landscape from the car window while Garrett mastered the curvy and narrow roads, dodging numerous cyclists. As the driver, he was a bit annoyed, but Mary was enjoying the "rear" view of the fit male athletes in their colorful Spandex racing clothes.

When the "Manhattan of Italy" first came into sight, the towers looked like American skyscrapers, almost out of place and out of time. She snapped more pictures from the car, eager to explore this medieval town where tower construction dated back to the eleventh and thirteenth centuries.

The narrow streets inside the thick city walls were crowded with tourists as expected, but they managed to navigate their way up the cobblestone paths toward the town's apex, where they found interesting historic sites like the thirteenth-century cistern in Piazza della Cisterna. People gathered around the historic water source to meet and talk, with many sitting on its steps to enjoy a gelato. They visited the Collegiata Church with its faded but stunning frescoes and the regal Palazzo del Popolo, the town hall.

They planned to climb the Torre Grossa, the tallest tower in San Gimignano, at about two hundred feet high. But before they started up the tower, Mary insisted they have gelato.

They found a *gelateria*, and Mary was much more excited than Garrett. The stainless steel tubs were filled with colorful towers of *gelati* in several flavors. Each tower was embellished with the berries, chocolate, cinnamon sticks, coconut wedges, pistachios and other visual aids to convey the flavor to tourists. Mary decided on *limone* in a medium cup. In her first bite with the teensy plastic spoon, she fell in love. The smooth ice cream was as sweet as it was tart.

Garrett didn't order any for himself, commenting about the pastry he'd eaten for breakfast, but he tried a bite of hers.

"It tastes like it has less fat than our ice cream," he said.

When she finished, Mary wished she'd ordered a larger cup.

They climbed the Torre Grossa for a panoramic view of the patchwork landscape, as well as a bird's-eye view of the Piazza della Cisterna below them. The views were breathtaking, but the lookout was crowded with tourists. Mary and Garrett had to wait for people to move before the view was clear and they could take pictures. It was worth the wait.

After reading the guidebook again, Mary suggested lunch at Ristorante La Terrazze where they ate regional specialties like stewed boar and gnocchi in pecorino cheese sauce. They drank San Gimignano's own white wine, Vernaccia.

From their table by the window, they had a view of the town's tiled rooftops with the hilly countryside as a backdrop. The scene was worthy of a painting, and the meal was exceptional. Mary savored it all, but she felt like she enjoyed it more than Garrett did. Consumed with work again, he busily scribbled numbers on a piece of paper Mary had ripped from her journal at his request. She couldn't understand why other people at the office couldn't take care of this issue, but she was respectful of his job, and hoped it would be resolved soon. She read her guidebook, planning their next stop and learning more about this old world, a place that had already captured her heart.

Chapter 30

From San Gimignano, they drove to Volterra, an area rich in Etruscan remains. On the ride, Mary delved into her books and read about the Etruscans.

"They were among the earliest inhabitants of Italy," she told Garrett. "Even before the Romans. And enough images have been discovered that we know they liked music, dancing and richly colored clothing and jewelry."

She paused.

"Oh my gosh, you're not going to believe this. Historians think the Etruscans introduced grapes to Italy around the ninth century B.C."

She turned toward Garrett.

"Can you believe that? The ninth century B.C.?"

"Wow," he said. "That's a long time ago. Who did you say lived then?"

It was clear he was only half listening to her.

When they arrived at the hilltop town, Mary suggested visiting the Guarnacci Museum, which had a large collection of Etruscan art. After touring the museum, they went in search of more Etruscan artifacts and found their way to the Porta dell'Arco, the oldest gated entrance to the walled city. Built by the Etruscans in the fourth century B.C., the gate was made of volcanic stone. On the arch, three stone balls protruded. Originally carved heads, they had eroded to smooth surfaces since they had been erected thousands of years earlier.

Mary continued to find herself dumbfounded by the relics and was glad to have references to draw her attention to them. Without guidance, many remnants would have been an easy oversight. But countless things were like this in Italy - old and unassuming. The people here lived close to antiquity every day of their lives.

They continued to explore and saw the first-century Roman amphitheater and historic Parco Arceologico, where remains of an ancient acropolis were excavated, including the foundations of two temples from the second century B.C.

Volterra, known for its alabaster, had numerous workshops and retail stores filled with everything made of that beautiful stone, in all imaginable colors. Mary chose the impractical souvenir - alabaster grapes. Each yellow fruit was about two inches in diameter and wired to a thick grapevine. They weighed at least 10 pounds and would undoubtedly need to be a carry-on item.

"What in the world will you do with these?" Garrett asked.

"Look at them and remember Italy. I've always dreamed of being here."

Mary was happier than she ever remembered, as if she was under a spell.

They took the faster highway route home and made plans to eat dinner on the rooftop. This time they agreed to cook the pasta before they drank too much Chianti.

They were on their last leg of the drive to the apartment when Mary suggested they look at the castle.

"I think you would enjoy it," she said.

"I'd like to, but how about tomorrow? Jetlag and driving have done me in."

"Okay."

They still had a week ahead of them, so Mary agreed, but she didn't want to leave Italy without exploring it.

As they pulled into the farm's parking area, a group people were getting into their cars. As the cars rolled past them, Mary saw Rossana in the doorway, waving goodbye. She figured friends or family who had been visiting were leaving. After the last car drove away, she saw the back of a lean, muscular man in faded jeans and a black leather jacket. He put on a motorcycle helmet and straddled his bike. A few seconds later, a woman came out of the house and jumped on the bike behind him.

To leave the parking area, the motorcyclist had to turn around and drive past Mary and Garrett. As he slowly cruised by, Mary caught his eyes, and she realized it was the farm worker, the same mysterious man she'd seen the day before.

Her eyes locked on his, and as before, the glance was brief, but it felt like time had stopped. His baby blue eyes spoke untold volumes.

Then the cyclist shifted his look to Garrett and quickly checked him out before revving his motorcycle and taking off.

Garrett looked toward Mary.

"Who was he?"

"Huh?"

"The guy on the bike. He looked at you like he knew you."

"Knew me? How is that possible?"

"Well, I don't know. It was like...like...never mind."

This was the first time she'd seen Garrett act insecure or jealous.

"Garrett, I've never been to Italy. How would I know him?"

"Forget it."

"I've never seen you stressed like this."

"I'm all right."

He refused to admit weakness.

As planned, they stayed at the villa, ate dinner on the rooftop and drank more of the Ribelli Chianti that Mary purchased from Rossana for about $5 per bottle.

After dinner, Garrett buried himself in work. He sat at the kitchen table and crunched numbers, scratching his head and sighing.

Mary looked over guidebooks and took notes in her journal.

"Hey Garrett, how about leaving early tomorrow morning and driving to the Cinque Terre. It's a cluster of five fishing villages along the sea. Remember me telling you about them? Only one has road access, but footpaths connect them all. The southernmost town is Riomaggiore with a path called La Strada di Amore, or the Lovers' Road, connecting it to the next town of Manarola. We could hike to three more villages from there. It sounds like such a romantic place."

He looked up at her without making eye contact.

"That sounds interesting," he said. "And we could get some exercise by hiking."

He went back to his work.

Mary stared out the window, disappointed by his lack of interest. What she didn't know was that while he was working, he was also thinking that the Lovers' Road would be ideal for his surprise proposal. There hadn't been enough privacy atop San Gimignano's bell tower earlier that day, and he was determined to find the perfect place.

Chapter 31

M ARY WOKE ON MONDAY morning to an empty bed. She jumped up and padded across the cool tile floor to the kitchen, where she found Garrett. He was seated at the table, pen and paper in hand, rubbing his forehead, shaking his head. It was almost the same scene as the night before, but now he wore nothing but boxers.

"How long have you been awake?"

"I don't know," he said. "I was tossing and turning, and I didn't want to bother you."

She put her arm around him and struggled to show concern rather than her more pressing frustration and budding anger.

"Are you going to be able to have a vacation?" she asked.

"I don't know."

He rubbed his chin and upper lip.

"This is the biggest deal we've ever landed, and I brought in the account. Some of the numbers aren't right, so I'm responsible. I could cost my company millions if we don't get this business. Seriously, millions. It goes without saying that I'll lose a huge commission, but this will likely weaken Max's confidence in me, too. It could limit my opportunities."

Mary didn't say anything. It didn't seem she could say or do anything to help, so she turned to the stovetop coffeemaker.

"If you have to be awake, Lavazza will help."

Garrett slightly nodded his head, but was already deep in thought again.

After she served him the coffee, she climbed back into bed. She gazed at the view of the bright blue morning sky, seeing an occasional bird fly by, and watched the white lace curtains lightly stir in the breeze. While troubled by Garrett's work demands, she was still living a dream just by being in Italy. She easily dozed off.

Not too much later, Garrett rubbed her shoulder gently to wake her.

"Mary, sweetie, I need to find an Internet connection."

"All right."

"Is there an Internet café near the supermarket?"

"Yes, I meant to tell you. It's next to the Coop off the main road we came in on. You can't miss it."

"What time do you think they open?"

"Probably nine."

"Well, it's almost nine now, so I'm going to head down there. I need to email Tom so he'll see my message as soon as he's in the office. I'm sorry to do this, but I have to. Wherever we go today, I need to have Internet, so we have to stay in a city. We can do the fishing villages tomorrow."

"That's fine, if it means you can wrap everything up."

He needed to get work out of the way.

"Do you want to stay at the farmhouse today?" she asked. "Then you can easily go back and forth to the Internet café. I wouldn't mind a day here."

"I know, but -"

"We're in the heart of Tuscany," she said, interrupting him. "We're in Chianti, one of the most enchanting places on earth. I love this farmhouse and everything around it. I wanted to take photos and sketch the vineyards. I can do that today and relax by the pool. I'd prefer you finish your work so you can enjoy our time here, too."

He clenched his jaw.

"Thanks for understanding. I'm sorry to do this to you."

"It's okay. I'm not suffering. Like I said, we're in Italy at a 15th-century farmhouse. It's gorgeous, and I love being here."

She meant it. And she didn't mind being alone. She never did.

"Okay. I'll probably be gone for a couple of hours, but I'll be back before lunch."

Garrett hugged her and left the apartment.

Chapter 32

Mary made more Lavazza espresso and ate the remaining pastry, which was beginning to get stale.

No preservatives, she thought. What a nice change.

She took a quick shower, pulled her hair into a ponytail and dressed in a white cotton skirt that hit above her knees, a pale pink tank top and flip-flops. When she did a quick appearance check in the mirror, she felt like she was glowing in the Italian sunlight. From the moment they had arrived, she felt at home and inspired. Now she was ready to explore.

Everywhere she looked, the scenes were picturesque. She meandered, taking photos or sketching her favorites, and found her way to the vineyards, walking slowly, breathing deeply and taking in the fresh air and the earthy aroma. Feeling its history, she tried to comprehend the generations of workers who had toiled on this land. Life couldn't have been easy for those who had lived and worked here, but she respected the way they'd lived in harmony with the seasons, eating what the earth produced. It would have been a hard life, and she had no way to fathom the stamina and endurance it would've taken, but it appealed to her more than the fast-paced, technology-driven life she was living. She thought about how all the modern world's conveniences stripped away the splendor and rhythm of life, and its balance with the land. She didn't recognize how much this mattered to her until now.

She strolled along the rocky soil, admiring the thick, knotty trunks of the vines and their unpredictable gnarly bends. It was as if they had minds of their own and changed their growth direction based on a whim, only to change it again and again, reaching for the sun. She took photos of the rows of strong-willed vines and close-ups of tight bundles of small grapes not ready for harvest until the end of summer.

Occasionally she would see a worker, and she had to admit she was keeping her eyes peeled for the mysterious man. She still wondered if she'd feel the same way she did before in his presence or if she had imagined those intense feelings.

Using her camera's zoom feature, she took a shot of an older farmer, of his calloused hands pruning a vine and his furrowed brow beneath a worn straw hat. She wanted to capture the intensity and stamina needed to grow and harvest grapes.

As she stepped out of the vineyard, she saw Rossana near the main house and hurried to catch her so she could stock up on Chianti.

Mary felt a little braver speaking Italian and asked Rossana how she was doing.

"*Come va?*"

Rossana smiled, seeming to appreciate Mary's attempt at speaking Italian.

"*Bene,*" Rossana said. "*E Lei?*" – "And you?"

"*Bene. Vorrei due bottiglie di vini.*"

"*Rosso?*"

"*Si.*"

Rossana went into the storeroom and came out with two bottles of red wine.

"*Grazie,*" Mary said.

"*Prego.*"

Mary took the wine to the apartment, but had more time until Garrett was due back, so she went outside again and walked along the driveway to where it passed through the shimmering olive grove.

She held her camera still and zoomed in on the silvery foliage and tiny green olives, now the size of peas. The smell of manure in the field was so strong she had to hold her breath.

As she was focusing a wider shot, she noticed a narrow dirt path along the grove's edge that looked like an access road for small vehicles. She walked over to it and looked down the stretch to where it led. About 50 yards on, there was a large altar. She'd seen these field altars as they'd driven the country roads, and this was a chance to see one up close.

She was surprised by the sturdiness of the structure. It was at least six feet tall and its bottom half was constructed of large mortar-filled stones. In the top half, there was an arched alcove with a large relief of the Madonna. The tiled roof protected the relief and the offerings of dried flowers and rocks left by those who'd visited the altar. On either side of the altar's base were terracotta pots filled with scraggly aloe. She noticed a plaque on the side of the altar and couldn't translate all the words, but she recognized the word "*castello*" – castle. She realized she was on the castle's perimeter and had unintentionally found a shortcut to the castle. But from this angle she couldn't see the building or its tower.

She decided to follow the trail, passing an overgrown vineyard with wildflowers and sturdy grapevines fighting through weeds.

In a few more steps, she could see the chipped stucco and stone accents of the *castello*. Scrappy remnants of earlier landscaping survived on a trail that led to the building, including roses growing wild along a trellis, tufts of lavender and scruffy white oleander bushes.

She climbed tentatively, feeling like she was trespassing, but also feeling like she was being drawn by a strong magnetism. At the top she stopped to take photos of the distressed architecture and as she was zooming in on a shot she heard someone walking nearby. She peeked around the corner, and on a gravel path next to the castle, she saw a motorcycle. Her first instinct was to turn around, but before she could retreat, a man appeared. Her mouth dropped and her body froze.

It was him.

Chapter 33

SHE MUSTERED UP a weak "hi" but was too stunned to smile.

"I mean, um, *buongiorno.*"

She bit her bottom lip.

He smiled as if he'd run into an old friend.

"Good morning. Don't worry, I speak English, American English."

His voice was warm and kind, and he had a nearly indiscernible Italian accent. His faded jeans were covered with dirt and paint smudges, and there was a tear above his left knee. A soft white t-shirt with similar stains hugged his trim, fit body and contrasted well against his dark skin.

"That's good," she said through nervous laughter.

She forced herself to think of small talk so she could ease into a conversation with this person about whom she wanted to know everything.

"Do you work here?"

"Yes."

He grinned as he ran his fingers through his long, tangled dark hair. He obviously hadn't prepared himself for a visitor, but it didn't matter, he still looked stunning.

"I most certainly work here if you can't tell."

He gestured to his dirty clothes then looked at her, noticing her sketchbook and the camera around her neck.

"And you?" he asked. "What are you doing here?"

"I'm just exploring. I'm staying at the Ribelli *agriturismo.*"

She paused for a second and thought that more specifically she was a visitor whose boyfriend had run off to work, giving her the perfect opportunity to meet a gorgeous Italian man.

"Maybe I've wandered too far from the property," Mary said.

She created an opportunity to politely exit although she badly wanted to stay.

"I don't want to intrude. I'll turn back."

"No, no. Please stay. You're welcome to tour this empty ruin. No one lives here. Come in."

"My name is Luca. And yours?"

He looked directly into and through her eyes, as if he could read her every thought.

"Mary."

"*Piacere*, Mary."

He warmly took her hand. His grip was strong and firm, but it wasn't calloused like she thought a laborer's hand would be.

For a moment she wasn't sure where her arm ended and where his began. She delicately pulled her hand away while reminding herself to look around the room and keep her composure.

The floor was covered with large square tiles and the stucco walls were painted a calm and soothing robin's egg blue. But there was no furniture. Carpentry equipment and lumber cluttered the room, which she assumed was the foyer.

"The house is being renovated. See? Here's the wall color on my shirt," he said, pointing to the edge of his shirt and laughing.

"You're doing all the work by yourself?"

"Yes."

His eyes told her there was more to the story, but he stopped.

"It looks like an interesting place," she said.

This was a complete understatement. She really wanted to say, "I feel like I belong here," but she didn't. She kept looking around, and on a small wooden table by the window she noticed a glass stuffed with lavender sprigs. That's an unexpected touch in a construction zone, she thought, then stepped a little closer to capture the fragrant scent.

"There's more to see," he said. "Come with me."

Without hesitating, she followed him, drawn to him in a way she couldn't rationally explain.

A tiled staircase led to the second floor, and she followed him up.

From this floor, she saw that the building was rectangular and open in the middle. Columns supported the second floor and were now visible in the open-air courtyard below them. As they moved along the upper-level corridor, she took quick peeks into the empty rooms and saw they all needed renovation and repair.

"When do the owners expect you to have all this work done?"

"There is much to do, but hopefully by the spring it will at least be ready for a summer residence."

"This is only a summer home for the owners?"

Luca stopped walking.

"The 'owners' you mention are my family and me."

Mary gasped.

"You? But I thought. Oh, I'm sorry. I thought you were just working here. I didn't know you owned it. Sorry."

She was truly embarrassed, and she wondered if he was married and had kids, since he mentioned a family.

"It's okay."

His eyes became larger, softer puddles of blue, as if he wanted to make sure she knew he wasn't offended.

"It's not a problem," he said. "Truly."

The corners of his lips turned up and he lightly laughed to assure her he wasn't insulted.

"I am doing all the work, and I am taking great pleasure in doing it myself. But it's slow since I am only typically here on the weekends. Today is an exception."

He looked around the room, seeming to assess his task list.

"By the time the weather cools, after the grape harvest, I'll get help from my brother, Giovanni. He and his wife operate the *agriturismo* and they manage the farm's production of wine and olive oil."

"Rossana? She's your sister-in-law? I had no idea."

"It's a long story. I live in Firenze, or Florence, and work for our father at the family's small leather factory. Giovanni lives in the farmhouse and takes care of it. In fact, the farmhouse is filled with all the furniture that used to be in this house. Maybe I can tell you the whole story when we have more time."

Mary had no idea when, where or how the next meeting would take place, but she loved imagining it.

"That would be interesting," she said.

"Do you want to climb up the tower? The views are spectacular."

"I'd love to."

"It's very dusty and there are spiders, but it is worth it."

He winked.

"I'm not afraid of spiders."

"Perfect."

She followed him up the steep stairs, taking the opportunity to check him out as they climbed. His faded jeans wrapped around muscular legs, and he had well-shaped calves. She could tell by the outline of the pant leg.

She wondered why she was always so intolerant of skinny legs on guys.

His butt was tight, like his waist, and his shoulders were broad. She liked the way his long, dark hair hit the top of his shirt, too. She didn't know what he did at the leather factory, but she imagined his hair smoothly combed back in the morning when he arrived at work, only to unravel by the day's end, tumbling in every direction, as it was now. Long hair on guys was something she'd always loved.

In seconds, they reached the top of the steps, and in that brief time, she had memorized his body.

They stepped onto wide wooden slats that were serving as a floor. He didn't seem nervous to be standing on a floor with gaping holes between the boards, so she wasn't either. Now they had access to the lookouts facing north, south, east and west. The openings were wide enough for them to share.

"Here, have a look," he said.

She stepped next to him at the north lookout, and her arm slightly brushed against his. Even though they had barely touched, she felt an overwhelming wave of electricity run through her body. She looked toward him and his gaze was locked on her. She knew he felt the attraction, too. But they said nothing and turned back to survey the view.

The vista of rolling hills covered with dense forests, rustic farms, orderly vineyards and olive groves was magnificent. Everything was so harmonious, like there had been a master design to the scene before her. Not only was the view perfect but standing next to him was, too.

"On the clearest days you can see San Gimignano, but today it is too hazy," he said.

She lifted the camera to take a shot.

"I'll just have to come back another day then."

She focused the camera and just before snapping the shot, her eyes veered right to peek at him. He was watching her every move. She went back to taking the shot and asked about the history of the *castello*.

He ran a hand though his hair.

"Well, *castello* is a little bit of an incorrect term. This is really a fortified villa, a home strengthened for protection during the frequent battles between Siena and Florence throughout history. But la torre, the tower, is a distinctive feature making it easily mistaken for a castle. It is named Castello di Rondinara, even though it is not really a castle. We don't know the true origins of the name because records are lost, but our family chose not to change it, so we still call it 'the castle.'"

"It's hard to imagine all that's taken place here."

Luca nodded his head but didn't say anything because he was now gazing at the same view Mary was looking at. He seemed to be enjoying the beauty surrounding the home as much as she was, as if this was his first time seeing it, too.

Mary took pictures from each opening, including close-ups of the farmhouse where she and Garrett were staying. As she framed a landscape shot, she saw their little roller skate-sized rental car heading uphill. Garrett.

"Oh, my God! Time has flown. My boyfriend is back, so I better go."

"Too bad. I have enjoyed every minute."

"Me, too."

They had more to say, but neither spoke. They didn't have to. Their eyes said it all.

They walked down the stairs to the foyer.

"Thank you for visiting," Luca said. "Please come back. There's more to show you, like the chapel."

"A chapel? I'd love to see it."

"You may bring your boyfriend, too. What is his name?"

"Garrett."

She walked to the front door. As she stepped outside, he pulled the lavender she admired earlier from its vase.

"Take these with you. They were my mother's favorite. She liked to put the blossoms in her pillow for its soothing scent. She said it made her sleep well. Maybe you will want to do the same."

Mary's heart skipped a beat. As she took the lavender, their hands lightly touched and her every nerve tingled.

"Sounds lovely. I'll do it. Thank you so much. Thanks for everything."

Reluctantly, she left.

She followed the same overgrown path back, her camera bouncing on her neck, the lavender clutched in one hand and her sketchbook in the other. She was stunned by the last thirty minutes. As she approached the farmhouse, the two dogs greeted her as if they'd known her all their lives.

"Hey Mare, there you are. Where have you been?" Garrett asked as she entered their apartment.

"Exploring the property, getting great shots."

"Did you get lost?"

He seemed a little agitated.

"No, I found a shortcut to the castle - I mean the fortified villa - on the hill."

"The castle we can see from here?"

"Yes, it's called Castello di Rondinara. The owner happened to be home, so he gave me a tour."

"A tour? Really?"

"Yes, he's renovating it himself. He's the brother of Rossana's husband, and he invited us to come back. He speaks English."

She didn't mention he was the same guy they'd seen on the motorcycle a day earlier. She knew it was best not to reveal that.

"Interesting. How about the flowers?"

"Oh the lavender? I found it in an abandoned garden. I need to put the stems in a glass."

She opened the cabinet doors, looking for a vase or glass for the lavender. Her face was flushed, so she kept her back to Garrett as she looked. It wasn't her nature to lie.

"Are you ready for lunch?" Garrett asked.

He didn't seem too interested in learning more about her adventure.

"Sure. Just let me freshen up a bit."

She put the lavender in a drinking glass and set it on the kitchen table. Then she went to their bedroom and stuffed some lavender blossoms in her pillow before heading to the bathroom to splash cold water on her warm face.

Chapter 34

THEY DROVE TO A NEARBY TRATTORIA and had wood-fired pizza for lunch. Made with a paper-thin crust and slightly bitter tomato sauce, fresh basil and melted buffalo mozzarella, the Margherita pizza was a fantastic treat, especially with the *vino rosso della casa* – Chianti.

As they ate, Mary asked Garrett if work was getting better. His answer was 'no.'

"If you could eat only one food for the rest of your life, what would it be?" she asked, trying to lighten the mood.

"I don't know."

"There's an easy answer."

"I don't know, Mary, and I really don't care. I don't like hypothetical questions."

He shrugged his shoulders and shook his head.

She fidgeted a little but didn't succumb.

"It's just something fun to think about. My answer is in front of us right now. I could eat thin-crust pizza like this every day. It's crispy on the outside but somehow still soft on the inside. I wish we could find it at home."

"It's is healthier with less cheese."

Mary stopped herself from rolling her eyes.

"I think pizza is the perfect choice because there is endless variety. Think about all the possible toppings – meat, vegetables, tomato sauce, olive oil, cheese – with thick or thin crust. And then there's dessert pizza!"

Garrett didn't respond because once again he was in another world. Mary dropped the topic.

Their handsome young server checked on them frequently, and in spite of not speaking English, he managed to flirt nonstop.

Mary remembered Rae's comment and chuckled about another young Romeo.

Garrett continued to sit in silence, and Mary began to entertain herself with flashbacks from her time earlier that day with Luca. She recreated their entire conversation and his every movement. She pictured his tousled curls falling in his face, his arm muscles flexing as he gestured, his unshaven face and his kind blue eyes.

She reminded herself she was in Italy with Garrett, graciously on his dime. But they were having different experiences. She'd never loved a place so much, but she felt alone in her joy. She wanted to say something, but couldn't. The tension was too thick.

Before they left, Garrett used the trattoria's payphone to make a collect call to his boss, Tom. Mary tried to listen to the conversation, but Garrett spoke softly as if he didn't want her to hear. He was always private about his business affairs, so she watched his body language. His jaw and fists were clenched. He tapped his foot and shook his head. He looked like a caged animal.

When he hung up, he couldn't hide his frustration.

"This is impossible. I can't work from here. I have to be there or this will become a disaster."

"What are you going to do?"

She didn't want to hear the answer.

"I don't know, because they absolutely can't do it without me."

"Garrett, this is ridiculous. You should be able to take a vacation."

"I don't quite think you understand," he said. "This is the biggest deal in our company's history. I probably shouldn't have left the country, but I didn't want to disappoint you."

He had never talked to her in such a condescending manner.

Back in the car, they went straight to the Ribelli without saying another word to each other.

When they got back to the apartment, Garrett immediately changed into his running clothes.

"I'll be back. I need to clear my head and burn off all that cheese I just ate."

With her back to him, she rolled her eyes and sighed. She didn't understand this situation at all. He'd done other deals, and it always sounded like he and Tom worked as a team, so Tom should have been able to cover for him while he was gone.

After he left, Mary grabbed her travel journal and towel and headed to the pool, thinking about Stella's comment that by the end of the trip her relationship with Garrett would be either much better or much worse. Right now the odds weren't on much better, especially since it looked like the vacation might not last. She thought he would decide they needed to go home early, and she didn't know what she'd say or do. She didn't want to leave.

The noisy German family played in the pool, so she sat in a chaise lounge facing the countryside as far away from them as she could get.

She wanted to write in her travel journal, but she was too upset, so she just sat and absorbed the scenery. She loved this place and she thought her dad would have loved it, too. She was sad he never visited Italy. His time was too brief, and she began to miss him intensely. He always encouraged her to live life fully by discovering and exploring instead of sitting back and watching life pass by. She wiped away tears and sunk into her chair, imagining what this trip would have been like with him. She tried to think of what advice he would give her now.

A plane flew overhead and she watched its path across the sky. She was glad she wasn't on it. She didn't want to board one sooner than she had to.

She closed her eyes and when she opened them, she spied someone walking up the hillside. It was the older scruffy man in his fishing hat with the dogs at his heels. When he got to the pool, he stopped and sat down in the chair next to her. The dogs nudged her to pet them and she did.

"*Buongiorno*," Mary said.

The man pulled out a pack of Lucky Strike cigarettes from his shirt pocket.

"Hello, how are you, young lady?"

His accent was thick.

"Let me guess...Boston?"

He hoarsely chuckled, then lit his cigarette and took a deep puff.

"Yes, pretty distinguishable, isn't it?"

"Sure is. Are you on vacation?"

"Yes. I come here every year I can afford it."

"Lucky you, it's a beautiful place. This is my first time here. Do you have a family with you?"

"A family? Ha! No! I started coming to Italy years ago to visit my father's grave at the Florence-American cemetery. He served in World War II."

He took another puff.

"The country grew on me. So I try to visit the cemetery as often as possible, and several years ago, I found this place. The owners are friendly and the price is fair. Now I'm retired, and I stay three or four weeks in the summer."

She thought it was ironic that she'd been thinking of her own deceased father only moments ago.

"You must be proud of your father."

"Yes. And now it's virtually a reunion here at the Ribelli, because there are several of us who are regulars."

"I'd like to start a similar tradition."

"I enjoy it, unless an unfriendly group of Germans shows up, which happens more often than I care for."

He rolled his eyes and shook his head in disgust.

"Some are so damn arrogant..."

She could tell he intentionally stopped himself from a tirade by changing the subject.

"For the most part, though, it's a good place to slow down."

"What did you do before you retired?"

"Detective. Boston PD."

"Very interesting. You're lucky you can spend so much time here. I'd have to win the lottery if I wanted to come every year," Mary said with a little laugh.

"Or maybe you could figure out how to get someone else to pay for your trip every year, like the Fishers."

"Who?"

"Oh, you haven't met them? The mother and son from New Jersey? I'm surprised you haven't heard them arguing."

"No, but maybe I've seen them."

She remembered noticing the mother and son once at the pool and another time with Giovanni. She'd assumed they were Italian.

"Well, I need to head to the Coop for groceries," she said.

As she stood up, he extended his hand.

"I'm Patrick Sullivan, Boston born and raised as you guessed. And yes, I'm Irish and Catholic, too. But you'll never catch me in a church."

He let out a hoarse, rolling chuckle that sounded more like a cough.

"I'm Mary Sarto from Philadelphia, and I'm here with my boyfriend. Speaking of names, what are the dogs called?"

"No fucking clue," he said and laughed. "I call them Blackie and Blondie and they must not mind. Why would they? I keep treats for them in my pockets."

He laughed again.

"Good to meet you," she said.

He nodded then puffed on his Lucky Strike, getting up and walking away with the dogs in tow. They followed him everywhere and she found it adorable.

Chapter 35

A̲ₙ HOUR LATER Garrett returned from his run. Standing in the apartment, glistening with perspiration and breathing hard, he had a look in his eyes she'd never seen. This wasn't the confident, controlled Garrett she'd known for the last year. He seemed possessed.

"We have to go home. It's our only choice."

Mary raised her eyebrows.

"Both of us?"

"Of course."

He looked surprised and almost annoyed she would ask.

"I'm not ready to go home."

While at the pool, she had decided not to let go of this potentially once-in-a-lifetime experience. She could hear her father and Mr. Moretti telling her to stay.

"What? You'd stay here alone?"

He acted like he couldn't believe she would do this and that her boldness was complicating his plans.

"Yes."

"That's an irresponsible decision, Mary. You should –"

She cut him off.

"Garrett, I'm staying. There's still so much to see and explore. And we haven't made it to Florence yet. It's only an hour away, and I want to see the Uffizi Gallery, the statue of David and the Pitti Palace. I want to visit Siena and some wineries. I want more gelato and wood-fired pizza. I want to experience this country. I'm not ready, and who knows when I'll ever come back?"

"I'll bring you back another time."

He crossed his arms over his chest.

She wondered if there would be another time.

"I'm already here," she said. "And it would be a waste to lose all the money on this apartment and the rental car."

"The money we'll lose from the trip is inconsequential to what I'll lose if I don't go home."

"I'm sorry, Garrett, but I'm not ready to go. I'll be okay alone."

"You're seriously considering staying? You think you'll be all right in a foreign country by yourself?"

Now he was patronizing her.

She cut him off, surprised by his attitude.

"You don't think I can do it?"

Now she was angry. She wasn't helpless and she didn't want to be told what to do.

She had a sudden memory of Garrett's holiday party at work and Susanne's story about Max forcing her give up her job at the newspaper. She wasn't going to do the same. She wasn't going to be bought or controlled by Garrett or any man. She turned away from him so he wouldn't see her tears. This isn't how she wanted to live, and she knew she wasn't only refusing to go back to Philly with him, she was expressing uncertainty about their future.

She went to the rooftop and stared off at the castle.

Garrett joined her in minutes. His posture was still rigid and his jaw was clenched.

"Mary, I have to change my flight, and I'm going to advise you to come with me. I don't want to go either, but I have to."

She realized their routine in Italy had been no different than it was at home. Work dominated his life in both places. And it was becoming clearer to Mary that it would always be like this.

"I can't go with you, Garrett. I don't understand the work issues, and I find it hard to believe that someone else like Tom can't manage them. Why can't we have a vacation?"

He looked away.

"It's more complicated than I am at liberty to explain. The consequences of not going back are serious."

He almost seemed frightened. This was another new emotion coming from him, but she didn't fold.

"I'm sorry, Garrett, but I've always dreamed about coming here, and I'll only be alone a few days. I'll pay you."

He interrupted.

"Mary, this isn't about the money. I want you to come home with me. I don't want to leave you here alone."

"I'm not ready. I can't leave yet."

She sounded cold and knew she did. But this wasn't about him or anyone else. It was about doing what she needed to do for herself. Spending time alone in Italy could be liberating. She'd never done anything like it.

He turned away and didn't ask another question or say another word about it. He spent the rest of the afternoon making travel arrangements.

The change of plans created even more tension between them, so to avoid arguing they only talked about travel logistics.

Mary knew she was able to take care of herself. She would stay in the apartment the rest of the week, meet the Morettis on Sunday and go to Venice on Monday.

She would keep the car, and she had maps, guidebooks, money, and credit cards. Most importantly, she had the passion for it.

Chapter 36

THE ALARM CLOCK buzzed at 4 a.m., an early wake-up so they had ample time to make the three-hour drive to Rome. Garrett's direct flight to Philadelphia was taking off at 10:05 a.m.

They rolled out of bed and dressed without speaking. Fifteen minutes later, they were outside.

Garrett put his suitcase and heavy carry-on in the backseat. He'd kindly offered to lug the alabaster grapes home for her.

As he started to get in the driver's seat, Mary said, "I'd like to drive so I'm more familiar with the road for the return trip."

Garrett sighed.

"Are you sure? I don't mean about driving to Rome. Are you absolutely sure you want to stay here alone?"

"Yes, Garrett. My mind is made up."

"I can't believe you want to be here by yourself."

"Then maybe you don't know me as well as you think you do," she said.

They barely talked all the way to the departure terminal of Rome's Leonardo da Vinci airport. Mary stopped at the passenger drop-off area, and they sat in silence in the car for several minutes. Garrett finally spoke.

"You know I'm upset about this."

"Garrett, why should I go home? You'll be working all day and night and most likely heading back to Los Angeles. The apartment rental is non-refundable, so –"

"Mary, this is not about the money. How many times do I have to say that? We can come back later this year."

"If we can't do the trip now, how is it going to be better later? How do you know you're not going to have another big negotiation?"

He didn't answer, so she continued.

"If you could stay –"

Garrett interrupted, nearly shouting.

"I can't stay Mary! I can't! Do you know how hard this is? Do you know how much I love you and want to be with you?"

"Garrett, do you realize how much I take a backseat to your job? I sometimes think you enjoy working more than being with me. You hardly know me. You're too busy to get to know the real me. I'm just another task on your Master Plan."

She said it. She'd been thinking it for months and it finally came out.

"Everything I plan and do is for our future," he said. "I'm making money for us to have a great home and to have a family and take care of them. I want the best for the people I love and that's my priority. It's all that matters. Our kids will go to private schools, and you can have the gallery you've always wanted."

Mary's eyes filled with tears. She knew this was Garrett's way of showing his love, by providing for her and helping make her dreams come true. He had just said he planned to spend the rest of his life with her, but she wanted something else from him that he was unable to give. She craved love and an intimate emotional relationship. There was nothing wrong with him. He just wasn't what she needed.

She sat quietly while the tears streamed because she didn't know what else to say. She didn't want to risk saying something that might insult him.

Her silence intensified his frustration and he spoke up.

"I have to go. Have to. I have no choice, and I feel irresponsible leaving you here. You know your mom and Catherine will be furious with both you and me."

"I don't care if they're furious. They're never happy with me, anyway. So don't tell them. I'll explain it when I get back."

"I never meant for this to happen."

Her voice was almost a whisper. "I didn't either."

They were quiet and still as cars in front of them in the drop-off line continued to let out travelers. Mary watched other people say tearful goodbyes, but she doubted they were for the same reason as theirs.

Finally, Garrett let out another sigh and broke their silence.

"Mary, you don't know everything that's going on, nor do you know what I planned for this trip. I wanted it to be special for us, too. I mean it when I say that everything I do is for us."

He reached into his jeans pocket and pulled out a small, black velvet box. He opened it. Inside was a sparkling two-carat princess-cut solitaire ring.

"I want you to marry me, and I wanted to propose in Italy, but I never found the right time. What's going on at work is such a distraction and for that I'm sorry. But I want to marry you. I love you. Will you marry me?"

"What?"

Tears rushed down her face.

"You're proposing?"

"A simple 'yes' would be nice. I love you and want to be with you. The past year has been fantastic."

"Garrett, I don't know. This is so..."

Her voice trailed off.

This was another example of how separated they were emotionally. If he believed offering her a ring would fix things, he didn't understand. She wasn't worried about not getting married. She was worried about not being in love.

"I thought this is what you wanted."

He had exposed his emotional vulnerability, and he didn't like losing control. He snapped the box closed and tossed it in her lap.

"You have the rest of the week. Alone. In Italy. Think about what you want, and if you want me, I'm yours when you come home."

He looked away.

"I have a plane to catch."

She reached over to hug him, but his body went rigid.

"I'm so confused right now," she said. "Let's talk when we're both home."

She leaned in to kiss his lips, but he turned his face and all she got was stubble.

He opened the car door, grabbed his bags and walked away, never looking back.

Chapter 37

MARY'S DRIVE BACK felt much longer than the one to the airport. As she drove, she cried about her frustrations with herself, with Garrett and with the situation. He was a wonderful guy, but she didn't think she marry him.

She put the ring on, took the ring off, then put the ring on and took the ring off again.

Her life was crashing around her, and she was losing all confidence in herself. She couldn't get it right when it came to relationships, and now she was alone in Italy. She had to face herself – and her weaknesses. She hoped the time alone would help her sort through her emotions.

Tired from getting up early and the heavy emotions, she stopped at an Auto-Grill.

Italy's version of a fast-food joint was both a café and convenience store. She joined the line to order a cappuccino, enjoyed only as a breakfast drink in Italy. She had once read that Italians know if someone is a tourist if they order cappuccino after 10 a.m.

In line, she admired a display case full of panini ready to be grilled. She decided to have a prosciutto and mozzarella panini instead of a typical morning pastry.

While waiting for the thin sandwich to be grilled, she drank the cappuccino at the bar, acting like the locals. She gazed around at the displays of snacks, wine, cheese, salami, books, magazines, toys and candy. She eyed Perugina chocolates, and when the warm panini was ready, she bought chocolates and a bottle of water and headed to the car to eat as she drove.

On her way out, several young soccer players in their early twenties were heading in. They were singing their team song and wearing uniforms. She smiled at the lively group, and several winked back while checking her out.

More young Romeos, she thought. This country is full of them. Rae Lynn was right.

It was late morning when she arrived back at the farmhouse, but she didn't have the energy or desire to go anywhere. She was emotionally and physically drained.

As she parked the car, she saw Patrick Sullivan seated at the table near the door. The dogs were curled up next to him.

"You were up early today," he said as she approached the building.

"What?"

Mary was in her own world.

"I can never sleep through the night, and I saw you leave before sunrise. Everything okay?"

"Yeah, fine. Garrett had to go home."

"Is he coming back?"

"Nope."

She felt rude, but she walked away without saying any more, entering the foyer and taking the steps up to her apartment. She didn't feel like talking, and it was becoming clear he was the neighborhood gossip.

She went straight to the bedroom, setting the little black velvet box on the bedside table, then closing the shutters and crying herself to sleep.

A few hours later, she woke to the sight of the ring box next to her and groaned. The ring was forcing her to face her future with Garrett, and she was burdened by its value. She didn't want to wear the ring, but she didn't want to risk losing it either.

She headed to the vineyards for some fresh air. Here, she felt life was at its simplest, where the earth produced a divine fruit that weathered time and elements. In the vineyard, the grapevines dug deeply into the rocky soil, danced with the wind and drank the rain. This was where ancient secrets lived and where Mary felt most in harmony with the natural world. She wished she had the same passion for Garrett as the grapevine clinging to the earth.

She strolled up and down each row, thinking about how messy everything had become. Garrett was everything she should have wanted, and he was everything her failed relationships were not. He was responsible and smart. He would provide a comfortable life for them. He worked hard. He was handsome and athletic. Her family loved him. He loved her. But there was something missing. Something important. Something she couldn't ignore.

She left the vineyard and walked around the farmhouse. She ran into Rossana and she was sweeping the sidewalk.

Mary practiced making comments by talking about the weather.

"*Fa caldo.*" – "It's hot."

"*Sì, troppo caldo,*" Rossana said.

Rossana fanned her face and nodded her head, agreeing that it was hot. She was warming up to Mary, but the language barrier made it difficult.

After she finished her conversation with Rossana, Mary decided to go back up to the apartment.

She walked up to the rooftop balcony with a half-filled bottle of Chianti and the large sketchbook that she almost left at home.

As she gazed at the castle tower, she thought about her encounters with Luca and their startling connection. The feelings were real, but their timing was bad. She had a boyfriend, and now he had just proposed to her. She had to figure out what to do about Garrett before she got involved with anyone else. Her melancholy thoughts fed her frustration and she wondered why she couldn't have met Luca before Garrett.

Exasperation fermented into anger, and the more wine she drank the more it surfaced. She couldn't understand why she had failed time and time again.

Mary poured out her feelings into her journal, her handwriting swooping and curving wildly. The words were big and the writing was as coarse as the emotions. Then she sketched. The views from the balcony became her subject and with expressive, gesturing strokes, she drew the hillsides and vineyards, the villas and farms in the distance and the cypress trees with the castle tower peeking above it. She was glad she'd brought the large sketchbook – she filled page after page in an emotional frenzy. Time passed quickly into sunset.

Ready for more wine, she started to open a new bottle and then realized how hungry she was. She hadn't eaten since the Auto-Grill. She remembered the delicious Margherita pizza she had the day before. The pizza she told Garrett she could eat every day for the rest of her life. She decided not to drink more wine, but to return to the same trattoria for dinner.

Chapter 38

SHE SHOULDN'T HAVE DRIVEN after drinking on an empty stomach, but she got to the trattoria safely and walked in, passing two tables with diners and taking a table by the wall.

Roberto, the same flirtatious young waiter from the day before, greeted her.

"*Buona sera,*" he said.

"*Buona sera.*"

"*Due?*" he asked.

He must have remembered Garrett.

"*No, solo io.*"

She was feeling more confident speaking Italian after drinking half a bottle of wine.

"*Va bene,*" he said. "*Vino rosso della casa?*"

"*Sì, grazie. Vino rosso e una pizza Margherita.*"

"*Prego.*"

Roberto returned in a few minutes with the house wine and set down the glass.

"*Parla italiano molto bene.*" – "You speak Italian very well."

Mary laughed.

"*No, non è vero, ma grazie!*" – "No, it's not true, but thanks."

He smiled and lingered.

"*Come si chiama?*" – "What is your name?"

"Mary."

This guy was turning on the charm, Mary thought, exactly like the day before. But she didn't mind. She liked the distraction from thinking about her own failing relationship.

"*Ah, Maria in italiano. È bella!*"

"*Grazie.*"

She liked his flirtatiousness.

"*Mi chiamo Roberto.*"

"*Piacere. È Robert, o Bob, in inglese.*" – "Pleased to meet you. It is Robert, or Bob, in English."

"Bob?" he asked.

He sounded like he was from New Jersey as he rounded the "O" and made a big "B" sound at the end – "Bwob-a."

He repeated it a few times, making both of them laugh.

He is so adorable, she thought.

He was another of Rae Lynn's Romeos and she wondered how often single American women came to this trattoria alone. Probably not frequently.

Roberto kept a watchful eye on her and soon brought another glass of wine.

"*Un regalo della casa.*" – "A gift from the house."

"*Grazie!*"

She thanked the big flirter.

The freshly prepared wood-fired pizza took about thirty minutes to arrive, so she flipped through the pages of her journal.

She read her entry from the day she met Luca and laughed at how gushy and silly it sounded. What a hopeless romantic, she thought. She turned to the next blank page and started a list of all the failed relationships in her life. She added Garrett's name to the end of the list and put a question mark next to it. Then she wrote Luca's and put a question mark next to his name, too. She smirked as she wrote the last one, knowing it wasn't possible, but she could fantasize.

Roberto delivered the pizza and it tasted even better than she remembered. She devoured it all, and after the final bite, she gulped the last of the wine and asked him for the bill, *il conto.*

"*No dolce?*"

"*No, no grazie.*"

Roberto pouted as if he was sincerely heartbroken. He brought the check and from behind his back, he revealed a small plate with almond cookies on it.

"*Un regalo,*" he said, and he winked as he delivered her gift.

Mary giggled and thanked him. Romeo strikes again, she thought.

She ate the cookies and paid for dinner, but when she stood up and began to walk, she tripped over the chair at the adjacent table and almost fell to the ground.

Roberto hurried to help.

"I'm okay, I'm okay," she said.

She was embarrassed more than anything, realizing she shouldn't have had the last glass of *vino*.

"No," he said and shook his finger at the door.

He didn't want her to drive, and he pulled out a chair, encouraging her to sit and wait. He went to the kitchen, returning with a double shot of espresso.

He watched over her as she drank it, and she chatted away.

"I am so angry, and I know you don't understand me, but my boyfriend proposed to me today before he went home to work. He said he loves me, but don't you think our relationship should be more important than a job right now?"

Roberto had no idea what she was saying, but he offered a tender look and nodded his head to show his support.

"See, you know how to treat a lady," she slurred. "You gave me wine, cookies and coffee, and now you're listening when you don't even understand what I'm saying. That's the problem with Garrett. He rarely listens to me and doesn't truly know me or understand my heart. I'm sure you take care of your girlfriends."

She sighed and decided she wanted to go home and go to bed.

"I have to go now."

She headed toward the door, still a little unsteady.

Roberto shouted something to his kitchen coworkers that Mary didn't understand, and he walked with her, holding her arm to keep her stable.

"You are such a gentleman," she said as she opened her car door.

She turned toward him to shake his hand and instead she surprised herself by hugging him.

He hugged her back.

His body was warm, and his flesh smelled salty.

She looked up at his face and impulsively kissed him.

He kissed her back.

This feels so good, she thought.

She put a hand on his chest, then wrapped it around his ribcage. His body wasn't rock-solid like Garrett's, and she found herself incredibly attracted to it. He felt like a real person, not a training machine obsessed with triathlons. Roberto could probably spend a day in bed and not have to get up and go on a morning run. She wanted more of him and didn't stop kissing him.

"*Vieni.*" – "Come with me," he said.

He pointed toward a desolate path bordering a vineyard.

Mary looked at the secluded area. She was ready to go.

"*Sì?*" he asked while kissing her.

She wanted to. He was so delectable, but she stopped.

"No, no, I can't. Um, *non puedo.*"

She shook her head. It was a Spanish verb conjugation she remembered from high school. She tried again in Italian.

"*Non posso.*"

She didn't know what else to say. She didn't know how to translate, "I think you're sexy and would love to take off all my clothes and make love in a vineyard, but I have a boyfriend who I need to break up with before I do something like that. Then again, if I'm going to break up with him I should just go with you, but I still can't."

He kissed her again.

"*Buona notte, bella Maria.*"

Then he gently caressed her face with the back of his hand and said something melodic in Italian she didn't understand. His gesture was tender, and she adored him.

"*Buona notte,* Bob."

She winked and headed for her car.

Driving down the road back to the apartment, she rolled down the windows and fantasized about Roberto's offer. Somehow, she knew one night with Roberto would have given her the thrilling experience Garrett couldn't deliver. She considered turning back, but talked herself out of it. Her frustration with Garrett grew.

When she arrived at the apartment, she staggered up the stairs, fumbled to insert the key into the door lock and went straight to the bedroom. On the bedside table, the little velvet box was open, revealing the sparkling gem. The sight of the diamond stirred her.

Breaking up with Garrett will be so hard, Mary thought.

The ring was too valuable to leave out, so she put it on the top shelf of the wooden armoire in the bedroom. She tucked it into the front corner. Out of sight, out of mind, she thought, wishing she could make the same emotional dismissal of Garrett. All she felt was anger and vengeance toward him.

She went to the kitchen, poured a glass of wine, took a sip and toasted herself.

"*Salute*, Mary, *bella Maria*. Welcome to your new life alone in Italy."

She took another sip and had a sudden impulse to take off all her clothes and go outside. Naked, she grabbed the wine bottle and headed upstairs to the rooftop to enjoy the warm night. No one could tell her not to, and she loved how independent she felt.

She leaned against the balcony, looking at the night sky, the moon, the dimly illuminated landscape and the castle tower on the horizon. The scenery was as intoxicating as the wine, and her skin glowed in the moonlight. The entire inebriated experience, accented by her nudity, made her feel exotic and rare. She skimmed her right hand over her naked breasts and circled her puckered nipples. She dipped her finger into the wine and dabbed the nectar on them, intensifying their sensitivity. She dipped her fingers again, swirling the wine on her stomach, hips, arms, legs and face, painting herself like a warrior, preparing for the battles ahead.

Chapter 39

Alone and naked, Mary awoke in the farmhouse bedroom. The shutters were open and it was bright, so she knew she'd slept late. She squinted at her watch, still on her wrist. It was 12:15 p.m. Her head throbbed and her mouth felt as though it was stuffed with cotton balls.

She pieced together the prior evening – the wine, the trattoria, the pizza and Roberto. She closed her eyes and shook her head, thankful she hadn't gone down to the vineyard with him.

She wanted to cry, but her head hurt too much and she knew crying would only make the pain worse.

Her left ear throbbed, too, because she fell asleep wearing her silver hoop earrings. Her earlobe was folded in half against the pillow and the earring was pressed into her face. She sat up slowly, rubbing her tender ear and cheek.

Her skin felt crusty, and then she remembered the rest of the night and all the wine she had. She took a deep breath, closed her eyes and consoled herself with the fact that she was safely home alone in the apartment.

She made her way to the bathroom by stepping over her pile of clothes in the kitchen and looked in the mirror over the sink.

Mascara ran down her face and her eyes were puffy and bloodshot. Her stomach was beginning to hurt, too.

What a miserable day it's going to be, she thought as she swallowed Ibuprofen with a handful of cool tap water.

She showered, put on clean clothes and drove to the Coop to buy Coke and find something tolerable to eat. She decided on a loaf of crusty bread and a box of pasta – *penne rigate*. Either would be good with a little olive oil or butter. It was all her stomach could tolerate.

The easy grocery trip drained all her energy, so it became clear that she'd spend the rest of the day at the farmhouse even though she wanted to sightsee. She berated herself for wasting a day in Tuscany with a hangover.

Her anger with Garrett had subsided, but she didn't want to think about him. She wished she could talk to Stella, but the international calling rates were too high. A quiet day was her best option.

In the late afternoon, she went to the pool, hoping no one else would be there, but the Fishers were by the pool again. She started to say hello, wanting to speak English to someone, but they were arguing.

"I don't care if you hate it here," the mother said. "We're staying for the week."

"But I'm missing my baseball games."

"Get over it, Alex. Do you know how many people would like to visit Italy? You're a lucky kid."

"How come dad doesn't ever come?"

"He can't take time off work. You know that. How often do I have to tell you?"

He huffed and put on his headphones, escaping into his own world.

Mary didn't talk to them and sat down in a lounge chair at the opposite end of the pool. But she wasn't able to stay long, because she had to go back to her apartment for more Ibuprofen and Coke. Miserable, she was second-guessing her decision to stay on in Italy alone.

Before sunset, she moved to the rooftop and found her sketches from the prior night. She read her journal, too, and realized how much she'd been bottling her frustrations with Garrett for the past several months.

With the Atlantic Ocean between them now, it was more apparent to Mary that she and Garrett had been drifting apart for a while. And maybe the issue was less about drifting apart and more about an inability to grow closer, she thought.

Mary took solace in her sketchbook. She liked the big drawings from the previous night because they were passionate, loose and full of expression. She'd produced an abundant amount of art in a short period of time, too. In spite of the unpleasant events that inspired her latest works, she was pleased with them, thinking some were even worthy of framing.

As the sun dropped toward the horizon, she felt like having a glass of wine, even though earlier that day she declared she'd never drink again.

She was on her second glass when she heard the distant growl of a motorcycle, reminding her of Luca. The rumbling drew closer until she heard it outside the farmhouse.

She was sure it was him, and she wanted to talk to someone, anyone. He was a stranger, but she knew he would understand and maybe help her feel better. She went downstairs to the apartment and splashed cold water on her face so she would look a little fresher then she headed outside.

Chapter 40

IN THE GRAVEL COURTYARD, Luca and Giovanni stood next to the large olive-oil cask. They were talking, and it sounded like business. It was animated and serious.

Luca happened to look her way. He went silent and his mouth dropped open.

His strong reaction startled her, and she looked over her shoulder to see what was behind her, but there was nothing. She had elicited his reaction, and it made her blush.

Giovanni turned to see what had captured Luca's attention. He looked at Mary and Luca and shook his head. He began to rant in Italian, and it sounded like he was giving Luca a brotherly reprimand.

Mary imagined he was saying something like, "Don't go near her, she's a walking disaster. An emotional, self-centered American bitch who already has a boyfriend. You're inviting trouble."

Luca ignored his brother and approached Mary.

"Good evening, *bella*," he said as he kissed each of her cheeks.

Her recent pain numbed.

"Hello."

"Are you okay?" he asked.

He must have sensed her stress.

"Better now. Red wine can numb an aching heart."

She surprised herself with her immediate candor, but she hadn't been able to talk to anyone about the tumultuous two days.

"What?"

"Garrett had to leave, and I'm here alone now."

"What?"

"I know it sounds crazy. But he had to return to the U.S. for work, and I couldn't bear to go with him. I've waited so long to see Italy, and it would've broken my heart to leave now."

He smiled.

"So you love Italy more than Garrett?"

"Huh?"

Mary hadn't considered this thought, but she realized she did love how inspired and enthusiastic she felt when she woke up every morning, today excepted. She loved the buried emotions it stirred.

"How long will you stay now?"

She blurted out all the details.

"I'm keeping to my original plans. I'm going to stay here until Saturday, and I have friends to visit in Greve in Chianti on Sunday. Then I have to be in Rome on Tuesday morning for my flight."

"Let's work on this one day at a time."

He smiled and it made her feel calm again.

"How about tomorrow?" he asked.

"Tomorrow? Thursday?"

"Yes, what are you doing tomorrow?"

"Umm, I'm not sure. I've lost time for sightseeing, but I can't miss Florence, so I'm thinking about driving there."

"*Perfetto!* I will be there, too. You could spend your morning with Michelangelo, your afternoon with Botticelli and your lunch with me."

His invitation surprised her, and she didn't reply immediately.

"I'll take you to a favorite place for lunch," he said. "It is a simple family trattoria. Forget the fancy tourist traps."

Mary was definitely interested, but she felt hesitant to agree. Her mental banter started up again, and she thought about Garrett leaving, almost sleeping with her pizza server, and planning lunch with Luca. She thought she might be crazy for thinking Luca was her long-lost lover from another life, but she also thought lunch was innocent enough.

"Um, yes, that sounds like a lot of fun."

"Let me write down the location for you."

He returned to the office and came out with a piece of paper.

"This is the address of my family's store. Please meet me there, and we will walk to lunch near Mercato Centrale. Is one o'clock good for you?"

"Sure, thanks."

"It is not too difficult to find."

"I should be fine. I have maps, and I'm usually good with directions."

"*Perfetto*. I will see you tomorrow. Ciao!"

"Ciao!"

She went upstairs, excited and a little uncertain about the following day. She still didn't know what she was going to do about Garrett, but at this point, he seemed destined for her list of ex-boyfriends.

Chapter 41

MARY ROSE EARLY and changed into running clothes for an easy morning jog. She enjoyed the fresh air and the sounds of birds, dogs, roosters and church bells. It felt so comfortable and familiar, but the crunch of each step on the gravel road toward Terzano made her remember this wasn't home. It wasn't the city. It was a new experience, and thankfully this morning was off to a better start than the previous two.

Back in the apartment, she showered and slipped on a fitted white cotton sundress with narrow shoulder straps scantily covering her pale pink bra. She let her hair hang long and put on her silver hoops and father's watch. Then she tucked her maps and camera in her tote bag and headed out.

Patrick Sullivan was sitting outside again, but the dogs weren't by his side this time.

"Hi, Mary."

"Hi."

She wondered if he did anything other than watch people come and go.

"Sightseeing today?"

"Yeah."

"Where to? Siena?"

"Nope, Florence."

"Florence? That's where Giovanni's brother Luca works. You should go to his leather shop. Maybe he'll give you a hefty discount. He likes American women."

"What?"

She wondered if somehow he knew she was going to meet Luca.

"Luca's quite the ladies' man," he added.

"Is that so?"

She played it cool.

"Yup. Take the discount on the jacket, but don't fall for anything else."

He laughed at his own comment.

"Got it."

She got into the car and pulled away to end the conversation. It was none of his business and chances were he was only stirring trouble.

Mary arrived in Florence and followed the guidebook recommendation to park on Florence's south side in an area called the Otroarno - the other side of the River Arno.

She headed to the opulent Pitti Palace and Boboli Gardens, once home of the Medici. It was only the beginning of her sightseeing in the birthplace of the Renaissance.

After touring the palatial estate, she walked north and entered a shopper's heaven. There were art galleries, mosaic tile works, textile stores, paper-goods boutiques, souvenir shops, bakeries, pizzerias, *gelaterie*, antique jewelry stores and t-shirt shops. She noticed a leather store called Le Pelle and made a mental note to visit it on her way back to look at a stylish brown leather jacket displayed in the window.

When she reached the Arno River she crossed the Ponte Vecchio - the old bridge. Open to pedestrians only, it was lined on both sides with small but elegant jewelry stores. Many tourists were admiring the dazzling stones and shiny metals in the shop windows, and she planned to do the same when she returned at the end of the day.

The beautiful city was smaller than she expected, and more overrun with tourists than she ever could have imagined. The Piazza del Duomo, home of Florence's famous Santa Maria della Fiore Duomo and its Baptistery, was so full of tourist groups it was hard to navigate. She was impressed with the massive red tile dome of the Duomo and snapped photos as she surveyed its perimeter, but didn't have time to wait in the long line to enter the church. She tried to get close to the bronze doors of the Baptistery, but it was impossible, so she mapped out her next destination - The Accademia, home of Michelangelo's David.

After a 20-minute wait, she entered the hall where David was grandly perched at the far end under a cupola of natural light. A fabric drape filtered the sunlight, creating a soft ambience around the famous sculpture. At first, he appeared smaller than she expected, but perspective was playing tricks on her. He was at the end of a deep hallway and elevated on a pedestal. As she approached and stood beneath him, he became larger than life. She couldn't believe she was there, and she strolled around the full circumference of the statue, misty-eyed, amazed by the beauty and impressed by the talent of Michelangelo. He had captured David's physical strength and warrior calmness simultaneously.

She moved to a bench in the entrance hall and quietly admired the carved marble, striving to memorize the sight and her emotion. As she looked around the gallery, she realized how fascinating it was to watch people's expressions when they entered and saw David for the first time. She watched sightseers enter the room, and like her, their jaws dropped as amazement filled their eyes.

Mary stayed about an hour, not only admiring David, but Michelangelo's unfinished "prisoner" statues. She meticulously studied every little chisel of his painstaking work, in awe of his talent and vision.

Afterward, she followed her map and came to the address of Luca's family store, Pelle di Rusconi SRL, or Rusconi Leather.

Chapter 42

SHE ENTERED THE SMALL SHOP and a clerk turned to greet her. The woman, about forty, had pursed lips and shiny dark hair pulled tightly into a ponytail. She scrutinized Mary's clothes, shoes, hair, jewelry, makeup and nails, and decided Mary wasn't Italian, because she greeted her in English.

"May I help you?"

"Thanks, I'm here to see Luca."

On cue, Luca descended the circular metal staircase near the rear of the store, and she gasped when she saw him. He wore a dark, lean-cut navy blue suit – a huge contrast from the clothes she had previously seen him wear.

"Ciao, Mary."

He approached and lightly embraced her, and as she started to back away he pulled her closely to him for a brief moment that sparked an instant flame.

"Thank you for coming. You look beautiful today."

"Thank you."

She tried to use humor to tone down the intensity.

"And you have clothes without paint on them."

"No paint, only a tie for color."

It was light blue silk, patterned and styled like those she'd seen in the Florentine shop windows. The pale color brought out his blue eyes, and she thought about how unusual it was that he had such blue eyes since all his other features were so dark.

"I picked one I knew you would like."

He winked and Mary blushed.

"You did well," she said. "I like it."

The clerk made a "tsk" sound.

"Forgive my manners. This is Laura, she has worked for our family for many years and is one of our best employees."

He was plainly trying to sweet talk this opinionated friend.

"Hi, I'm Mary."

Laura's scowl didn't go away. She remained quiet and acknowledged the introduction with a minimal nod.

"Are you ready for lunch?" Luca asked.

"Yes, of course."

"Let's go."

They hurried out to get away from Laura's scrutiny.

"Is she always like that?" Mary asked.

"I'm afraid she is always like that when it comes to personal matters. Sorry. But she is good with customers."

He offered an apologetic look and continued.

"We don't have far to go."

He touched the small of her back, but only for a moment to guide her gently around the sidewalk's corner. The simple touch added fuel to the already burning fire between them.

Mercato Centrale was a short walk away, and they entered the heart of it. She was surprised they were going to an area filled with tourists because she thought he wanted to take her somewhere the tourists didn't go. They traveled through a section of the market before darting behind a booth filled with leather purses, belts and wallets.

"Those are not made in Italy, but most tourists don't know or care because the prices are so low."

He was clearly irritated.

"But here is a place where you will not find tourists."

They had arrived at a trattoria in the middle of Mercato Centrale, marked by a small sign above the door, out of sight of anyone walking by.

She doubted she would have ever noticed it.

Chapter 43

L‌UCA OPENED THE DOOR to a modest, family-owned eatery, open only for lunch, and he told her they created a fresh menu each day.

"Look at the chalkboard for today's menu, but if you trust me, I will order for you."

"I trust you."

Only with my food order, she thought.

Luca spoke to the man behind the counter, but Mary understood little. Then he led them to a wooden table with a bench seat along the wall. He gestured for her to sit before he slid in beside her. Sitting on the bench, they had a full view of the trattoria's activity, and since the seat was narrow, their legs and arms brushed against each other every so often. Each time it happened, tremors of excitement darted through her body.

The server delivered sparkling water and a half liter of *vino rosso della casa*. Luca must have ordered it when they first entered.

"Do you like pork?" Luca asked.

"Yes."

"I will order roasted pork for us. It is always tender and delicious."

He kissed his fingertips in the same way Mr. Moretti did, making Mary smile.

The server returned with a basket of crusty white bread and Luca ordered for them.

"I like this place," Mary said.

"The tourists haven't found it yet. Most people walk by and never notice it."

"I can understand why. Their signs are hard to see."

"It is a family trattoria, and most of the diners live in the neighborhood. Do you see the white-haired man?"

He nodded toward the opposite wall where an elderly gentleman was eating Bistecca Fiorentina, drinking wine and talking in an animated manner to a gray-haired man next to him.

"He is the owner, and he is too old to work, but he comes here every day to supervise and count the money. Now look near the cash register. It is his son and his grandson. They work here, too. They have no choice."

"I hope they like it."

The grandson, who appeared to be about 17, reached into the cash register. The father slapped his hand and reprimanded him.

Luca laughed and leaned into her as he did so.

"I bet he needs money for cigarettes," Luca said.

Mary flashed back again to Mr. Moretti and his complaints about his son. She couldn't believe the similarity.

"I have never tried *Bistecca Fiorentina*," she said. "But an Italian friend at home encouraged me to have it while I'm here."

"The beef is so tender and juicy," he said. "There is a trattoria near the farmhouse, where you should have it. It's a large cut and best shared. Maybe I can take you one evening?"

"Um, sure. But I'm only here a few more days."

"Where is home?" he asked.

"Philadelphia."

"I know Philadelphia. I spent most of my childhood and teenage summers in the U.S. with my cousins near Philly, as you call it. They live in New Jersey."

"Did you spend those summers at the Shore?"

"Yes, in Point Pleasant. Do you know it?"

"Yes, my uncle has a beach house near there, and our family took many summer vacations in the area."

"It's a fun place," he said.

"It is. I imagine that's the reason your English is so strong?"

"Yes, but my mother also began teaching me when I was a child, so I learned to speak English and Italian at the same time. She knew it well and was determined I would, too. Then I studied it in high school and college. It was necessary to work for my father. I needed strong English-speaking skills for our retail business and our small export business to the U.S."

"Do you go back often?"

"Once or twice a year on quick trips to see customers. I should go more often, but it's hard to leave here. My father counts on me to manage daily business, so that leaves me little time to travel."

"What about Giovanni? Does he work with you too?"

"No. It is a long story."

He said this with a bit of tension in his voice, so Mary didn't probe.

"Where do you go in the U.S. now?"

"Mostly New York City."

"Do you take your family?"

She needed to find out if he was married.

"My family?"

"A wife? I thought I saw a lady on your motorcycle?"

"No, no. I am not married. You saw my nephew's girlfriend. I took her home on Sunday."

"Oh, okay."

She was happy to hear this news. Even though she had a ring from her boyfriend back at the apartment, she didn't want him to be married.

"But when I'm in New York, I visit my uncles, aunts and cousins," he said.

"I love New York. It's so close to Philly, but I don't go as often as I'd like. It's too bad, because there's so much to do there."

She and Garrett rarely made the trip. She liked the athletic things they did, but also liked visiting museums and going to the theater.

"Yes, it's amazing," he stated. "Like you."

He raised his wine glass.

"*Salute.*"

He casually put his free hand on her knee.

It was warm and felt wonderful, but she was a bit surprised by his boldness. She didn't push it away, though.

They ate slow-roasted pork covered with light gravy, white beans drizzled with extra virgin olive oil and a mixed green salad with olive oil and balsamic vinegar. They polished off the bread and red wine, and Luca was right, it was all simple and wonderful.

During the entire lunch, he never asked about Garrett and she didn't bring him up either.

Afterward they each had espresso, and Luca suggested they walk back to his store.

"We were in a hurry when we left, but I want you to see our products."

He grabbed her hand as they walked. He was confidently moving in, and she didn't resist. She couldn't. Her head tried to convince her otherwise, but she was unable listen. There was a force at work stronger than reason.

Chapter 44

It was shortly before three when they arrived, and the store would be closed for lunch for another half hour. So Laura was gone, and Luca was able to take a few minutes to show Mary their well-made jackets and fine leather accessories like wallets, belts and key fobs. He explained a buyer could appreciate the quality of their products, especially the jackets, by the large pieces of leather they used in their designs, rather than several small pieces sewn together. And it smelled wonderful.

"I want you to try on this jacket," he said.

It was dark brown suede, hip length and double-breasted with buttons. A belt wrapped around the waist, and it was exceptionally soft. It was styled much like the one she'd seen in the store window in the Otroarno area.

"Let's take it upstairs to my office."

A devilish look crossed his face.

She followed him up the circular stairs to the spartanly furnished work area. The loft occupied half the area of the retail space, with a freestanding white melamine desk and a simple red plastic chair. Filing cabinets lined one wall. Stacked boxes lined another. The boxes had handwritten descriptions in black marker, and she didn't recognize the Italian words. Overall, it didn't look like he, or anyone, spent much time here.

"This is my office. Sometimes I am here, but usually to collect paperwork. I spend most of my time in an office at the factory in Santa Croce sull'Arno."

"Where?"

"A town about 50 kilometers west. We cannot have factories in Florence, only retail shops."

He took off his suit jacket and tie as he spoke.

"Really, why not?"

She watched him unbutton the top of his white shirt. He was incredibly sexy.

"The factory smell is offensive, and it is noisy. No one would want to live near it. So, all the factories are outside the city."

Mary nodded.

"My father inherited this business from his father and he loves it, but frankly, I do not. I will sell it someday and do something else."

He looked like he wanted to say more, but stopped.

"Like what?"

"I'm not sure I know you well enough to tell you."

They were standing close together now, and he toyed with her, leaning in like he wanted to kiss her, but stopping and locking his gaze onto hers. There was nothing but longing in his eyes, and her lips tingled in anticipation of a kiss. Slowly and gently, his lips found hers and at their first touch, a chill ran through her body, and she had the same feeling as the first time they saw each other. His mouth was warm and his were lips soft, perfectly fitting hers.

"I couldn't wait to do that," he whispered, remaining close to her face. "If you let me get to know you better, I will tell you everything you want to know."

He caressed the fine line of her jaw before seeking out her dress's low neckline. He coyly traced the soft inside edge of the fabric from one side to the other.

"I couldn't wait to do that, either."

Everything was moving fast but it was impossible to stop him.

"Do you like Firenze?" he asked.

His fingers slithered along the neckline, each time going a little lower.

"It's beautiful and so rich in history, but it's smaller than I expected, and I like that."

Her voice was quiet. Intimate.

"It makes it easy to see everything, but it would be better without the loads of tourists."

"It is a city filled with the world's best art. Yet the most stunning work of art is standing in front of me now."

He pulled her body to his for a deeper kiss that cast a dizzying spell.

"We are alone until 3:30," he whispered while unzipping her dress.

She gasped, surprised by his move, but she still couldn't stop him. After he pulled off her dress, he looked at her body in the dainty pale pink undergarments. She was glowing from the sultry afternoon light seeping through the window blinds.

He pulled his shirttails from his pants and unbuttoned his shirt. His skin was smooth and dark, and he pressed his body against hers, inching her backwards against his desk so her body weight rested on the furniture's edge. They kissed hungrily, fiercely.

He stepped back from her and picked up the suede jacket.

"Put this on."

As if intoxicated, she slowly took the jacket.

"I want you," he said.

He softly glided his hands over her stomach and hips.

She started to slide her arm in one sleeve of the jacket.

"Wait," he said. "Don't put it on yet. First you need to take that off."

He looked at her bra.

Under his spell, she unhooked the bra and delicately removed it, dropping it on the desk behind her.

"Here," he said, "Now you can try this on."

Her face flushed as she slipped both arms along the slippery satin lining while he held the jacket open for her.

"Yes, you are beautiful in this, as I knew you would be."

He stood back and looked at her nearly naked body now adorned with the leather jacket.

"Turn around."

She did.

"Yes, you are gorgeous."

He didn't move - he only looked, hypnotically. He motioned her to come forward. She slightly opened the front of the jacket and took a few steps toward him.

In the manner of a tailor, he slowly ran his hands over her shoulders, chest, and waist, checking the jacket's measurements. He steadily ran his hand down her back and over the swell of her tush to check the overall length but let his hand linger at the hem. His fingers slipped into the open space where her legs met her buttocks, where her nerves were tingling. She sensed his teasing hand's radiating warmth, but he didn't touch her.

He whispered, close to her ear.

"I will need to take it to the workshop for a couple of adjustments so it will fit you like a second layer of skin."

She could feel the warmth of his breath.

"So, you will need to give the jacket back to me."

She turned so that her back was to him. Slowly she slipped it off, teasing him. She placed it on the desk, and he pressed his body rigidly into hers, his smooth chest against her back, then lifted her hair to kiss the back of her neck.

"Mary..."

His voice trembled. They were both melting. He was about to say something when they heard keys in the door downstairs. He looked at his watch.

"Shit, Laura is early."

He cupped her breasts and ran his hands down her torso and deftly slid one over the silky material covering the sensitive, throbbing area between her legs.

"I want more of you," he whispered, close to her ear.

Every nerve in her body tingled.

He leaned away from her ear so he wouldn't shout directly into it.

"*Buona sera,*" he yelled down the steps to Laura.

He kissed and caressed her a few seconds longer.

She turned and looked at him, struggling to figure out what had happened, and she reluctantly stepped away to pick up her clothes. But before she could reclaim her bra, he grabbed it and then looked at her panties.

He whispered, "We need to take those off, too."

"What?"

He slid his finger under the lace, and bent over to glide them down her legs. He kissed her abdomen, and her body shuddered.

"You'll walk around Florence this afternoon, naked under your dress, and you'll never be able to stop thinking of me."

He stepped back and gazed at her.

"I'm keeping these," he said, with the bra and panties in his hand.

He ran his hands over her torso.

"I'll give them back to you later, because I will see you again."

After she stepped into her dress, he slowly zipped it so Laura wouldn't hear it downstairs. She grinned bashfully while he buttoned his shirt and put on his tie, never taking his eyes off her. He grabbed the suede jacket, and once downstairs, they had a brief conversation with Laura before hurrying outside for privacy and to escape Laura's never-ending judgment.

"I wish we had more time, but I'll call you," he said.

He kissed her lightly on her forehead and squeezed her ass in a flirty way, before his lips met hers for a final kiss.

They strode in opposite directions and when Mary turned back to catch a last glimpse, he was doing the same.

Chapter 45

MARY HEADED TOWARD the Uffizi Gallery, thinking about him and making an all-out effort to squelch her burning physical desire. Passing a lingerie store, she quickly considered buying a replacement bra and panties, but she didn't. She loved being naked under the dress and how aroused and feminine he had made her feel.

She traversed Piazza della Signoria to reach the Uffizi Gallery, observing the piazza's sites – the Fountain of Neptune; the marble execution marker of Savonarola, the leader of the Bonfire of the Vanities; the reproduction of the David statue; the Palazzo Vecchio and the many Loggia dei Lanzi statues. Only steps away, she reached the Uffizi with a pre-printed ticket Luca had given her before they left his office. He told her the best door to enter to avoid the long queue.

Once inside, she proceeded to the second floor and looked at the early pre-Renaissance art, with no depth or perspective, continuing through the galleries until she found one of the Renaissance's most famous paintings – Botticelli's Birth of Venus. She admired it for a long time, much as she did with Michelangelo's David. Then she sat down, pulled out her sketchbook and began to write.

> *Sandro Botticelli's work is before me with the paint he mixed and* the strokes he made. I understand his Venus, naked and exposed, with the winds of change blowing on her. Like Venus, I am ready to let the forces of nature carry me as they want.

Mary finally walked away from the painting to look at another Botticelli masterpiece – The Allegory of Spring. She was equally moved by this painting and was compelled to write more.

The power of love. The celebration of innocence. I can feel myself on
the canvas dancing naked under the night stars, thinly veiled –
not much different than I am right now. I keep picturing Luca
in my painting...I can't stop thinking of him.

She had more homage to pay, to another artist and another man
in her life. She found Flora, Titian's painting of a goddess of spring
and flowers – the painting that inspired the song Ian wrote for her.

She remembered that perfect summer night like it had happened
only yesterday. She and Stella were on the open-air patio of their
favorite cantina. Bright lights of yellow, red and green festively
illuminated the area and pitchers of margaritas and buckets of
bottled beer decked most tables.

Ian was bartending, and as he mixed classic margaritas for
Mary and Stella of tequila, triple sec and fresh lime juice, he told
Mary he was glad she showed up.

She laughed, thinking he said this to all the ladies, but within
minutes she learned he really meant it.

He said her eyes had captivated him the first night they met a
couple of weeks earlier, and he wrote a song about her.

Her body turned to liquid as he handed over the margaritas and
grabbed his acoustic guitar from behind the bar. He stopped a
Johnny Cash CD in the middle of "Walk the Line" and headed to
the vacant stage. He summoned the attention of everyone on the
patio with a whistle and told the crowd he wanted to play a song for
Mary, "the pretty lady at the bar with long dark hair and soulful
eyes." He told the crowd she reminded him of a famous Titian
painting he had seen as he backpacked through Europe. It was in
Florence, Italy, at the Uffizi Gallery, and the painting was called
Flora. He said Mary had the same eyes as the woman in the painting.

All Stella could say to Mary was, "Oh, shit, here you go, again."

And Stella was right.

"One look from you and I was never gonna be the same..." Ian
crooned about his longing for the girl with the Titian eyes.

In fact, that was the name of song – "Titian Eyes."

Now, Mary stood before Flora as Ian had done. She stared at Flora's deep brown eyes, and while she didn't look like Flora, she understood why the painting inspired his romantic soul. She missed the tenderness of their relationship.

When she left the gallery, she sauntered along the Arno and watched a group of shirtless young men play soccer on a small field next to the river. She took a close-up of the handsome Romeos before crossing the Ponte Vecchio. This time, she window shopped along the string of jewelry stores, wanting to take most everything home with her. The sparkling diamonds reminded her of the ring hidden in her apartment, the one she would have to return soon. She had to breakup with Garrett. Regardless of how she analyzed it, her actions were speaking louder than anything.

She wandered the city streets, found the quiet Piazza of Santo Spirito and sat on a park bench watching the neighborhood's activity. Older men sat outside the tobacco shop while the occasional tourist strolled by. She decided to head back to her car, but before leaving the city, she found a *gelateria* with more flavors than she'd seen yet. She tried a new flavor – pistachio. It was excellent, but she liked *limone* better.

She returned home in the early evening and planned to eat dinner on the rooftop. While cooking pasta, someone knocked at the door. It was Rossana with a cordless phone. Mary smiled, but Rossana scowled.

With some confusion, Mary took the phone. She assumed it was Garrett, and she wondered what he'd said to upset Rossana.

"Hello."

"Good evening, *bella!*"

"Luca! Hello! How are you?"

She was truly surprised.

At the same time, Rossana made the exact "tsk" sound Laura did earlier in the shop.

"Better now that I hear your voice," Luca said. "I want to see you again."

Mary giggled, which made Rossana frown more.

"What are you doing tomorrow?" he asked.

"I'm thinking about going to Siena and Monteriggioni."

"You will like those cities, everyone does. But let me suggest something else."

He moved in on another opportunity to be with her.

"Giovanni just reminded me we have a meeting with our accountant in the morning. After the meeting I don't need to return to Firenze, so I could show you the Chianti region, if you don't mind seeing it from a motorcycle."

She couldn't say no. She didn't want to say no. She wouldn't say no.

"Um, sure, I –."

"Okay, *bene*," he said, not giving her time to finish, "Can you be ready at ten o'clock?"

"Yes, thank you."

"*Ciao, bella!*"

She handed the phone to Rossana who waited impatiently and now shook her head, as though completely disgusted with Mary. She knew Mary arrived with a boyfriend and was now spending time with Luca. Rossana clearly didn't approve.

Mary spent the rest of the evening in the apartment reading and sketching. She fell asleep early with the windows open and rested peacefully until awakened by the morning sunlight, a crowing rooster and barking dogs.

Chapter 46

MARY DRANK COFFEE and ate a roll at the rooftop table. A jet soared overhead, locusts chirped and distant church bells chimed. These were now familiar sounds that comforted her.

After a warm shower, she put on olive cotton pants and a pale pink shirt that made her dark skin glow. The shirt had an elastic scooped neck, front and back, so she could push it off her shoulders for a more feminine look, but she decided to keep her shoulders covered. Instead of sandals, she wore the more practical choice - running shoes. It seemed wiser, since she'd be riding on a motorcycle.

Dressed and ready to go, she grabbed her camera and went back to the rooftop to take shots of the distant vineyards. She wanted to capture the scenery at different times of day and hadn't taken any morning shots yet.

At 10 a.m., she grabbed the backpack Garrett left for her to use. She filled it with her wallet, sunglasses, camera, extra film and batteries, a sweater and a scarf. Before she left the apartment, she checked her appearance in the bathroom mirror. She put on lip gloss and made sure her earrings were clasped. This was a compulsive habit because she never wanted to lose them.

After a final appraisal, she spoke aloud.

"Mary, I hope you know what you're doing."

She hurried downstairs.

Giovanni was the first to see her, but he barely acknowledged her. Like his wife, he didn't seem to approve of her spending time with Luca.

Luca's reaction was completely different. He smiled adoringly.

"*Buongiorno*, Mary. The day is beautiful, like you."

She instantly pictured Mr. Moretti's smiling face, which comforted her.

"Thank you, Luca. Good to see you, too."

He wore lean-cut chocolate brown jeans, laced dark brown leather boots and a fitted white tee. He looked handsome in white, and the shirt fit like his work shirts, just tight enough to show off his muscles.

Her heart beat rapidly and she hoped it wasn't obvious to Luca.

"I must speak to Giovanni in the office, but I'll be right back."

Mary hoped this would give her a chance to catch her breath.

The two dogs wandered up, wagging their tails and Luca patted their heads before he walked into the office.

"What are their names?"

"The black one is Gigio and the yellow one is Brontolo. I'll be back in a few minutes."

While Mary scratched the dogs, Patrick Sullivan appeared. She wanted to ignore him but it was impossible.

"Touring today?" he asked.

"Yes."

"On that?"

He pointed to the motorcycle.

"Yes."

"With Luca?"

"Yes."

"I see."

He nodded his head as though he predicted it. Then he quietly took a seat near the office to watch everything. She wondered how much Patrick knew or if he was simply an instigator.

It wasn't long before Luca returned with a second helmet and the altered leather jacket, oblivious to Patrick's watchful eyes.

"Here is your jacket," he said. "Let's take it inside so you can try it on."

She nervously agreed, thinking of the encounter with the jacket the day before.

In the apartment's kitchen, he put the helmets on the table and helped her slide on the jacket. He checked the fit and approved.

"*Perfetto*," he said.

"I love it, thank you!"

She hugged him.

"You are the perfect model for it."

"I never asked you how much it is."

He put his finger to her lips.

"Say nothing of money. It is my gift."

"Luca—"

"Shh, please accept it."

"Thank you," she said with a blush and took it off.

Without hesitation, he put his arms around her and kissed her.

"You make me crazy," he said, pushing her shirt off her shoulder.

"I've been dying to do this again."

He kissed her neck and shoulders making her desire for him heat from simmering to a fast boil.

"Are you ready to go for a ride?" he asked.

"Um..."

She wasn't sure if he meant on the motorcycle or on him.

"To tour Chianti."

He grabbed the helmets.

"Of course," she said.

She was surprised by his sudden halt, but she loved him toying with her.

"Let's go," he said.

Outside, Patrick was now talking to the Fishers.

"Oh, there are the other Americans," Mary said.

Luca glanced in their direction but showed no interest.

"Have you ridden a motorcycle before?" he asked.

"Yes, but only a couple times."

"You'll be safe. As long as you hold on tight."

He flashed a flirtatious look making her heart race more.

He mounted the bike while Patrick and the Fishers watched the whole scene.

"We'll head to the Chianti highway, and I'll take you to my favorite place for a picnic."

"Sounds good."

She buckled the backpack around her waist to make sure it would stay on and climbed on the bike behind him.

"Put your arms around me as tight as you want," he said.

She placed her hands on his waist, beneath his rib cage and slipped them along the soft tee until she locked them together. His muscles were firm, and his shirt was soft against her skin. She loved his body's scent and she kept inhaling, committing it to memory.

"Pinch me if you want to stop any place," he said and away they went.

Chapter 47

THEY EXITED THE LITTLE hamlet and rode through densely wooded areas with occasional sights of vineyards, centuries-old villas and olive groves. They passed quaint restaurants tucked along the roadside, and she often saw little signs for Vendita Diretta, or direct wine sales, at farms. Most signs were like the simple black painted weathered wooden signs for the Ribelli and Cielo.

Sprawling farmhouses, cypress trees, chestnut trees, lavender and oleander dotted the roadside.

They finally reached Castellina in Chianti, a walled hilltop town, and Luca parked on its south side.

"Let's grab a drink," he said.

They entered the picturesque town along a narrow street and followed its winding pedestrian paths lined with small shops and wine-tasting establishments called *enoteche*. Many German and English tourists were strolling through the town enjoying its quiet allure. No one was in a hurry and Mary felt the same relaxed mood.

"This is the Via della Volte," he said.

Then he guided her through a passageway to a covered gravel road along the easternmost wall of town.

"Part of the old castle, this was once an open road where soldiers patrolled on horseback, but now it's an interesting place to wander and feel history. It is reported to be one of the oldest roads in Tuscany. Through these open-air windows are fantastic views of the Chianti hills."

She stopped at an opening to photograph the view, and he stepped up closely behind her. She felt his warm breath on her neck seconds before he lightly kissed the exposed skin. He slipped a hand around her torso and dazzled her again with his sensual touches.

"Thirsty?" he asked.

"Sure."

They walked a short distance and entered a small bar.

"Do you like Campari soda?" he asked as they approached the counter.

"I haven't tried it but I'd like to."

He bought two bottles and they went to an outdoor table.

"In case you don't know, the price to drink at a table is higher than to drink while standing at the bar. Tourists are confused by it. Hell, the Italians are confused, too!"

They sat down, made a toast and drank the Campari soda. The drink's bright red-orange color didn't prepare Mary for its biting flavor, but it grew on her with each swallow.

"Do you like it?" he asked.

"I've never had anything like it. What is it, again?"

"Campari, a liquor made of orange peel and herbs."

"It must be the herb flavor that's new to me."

"But you like to try new things?" he asked.

"Yes, it makes life exciting."

"That's good. So often, visitors look for the familiar and are afraid of new things, like food and drinks. We will enjoy each other."

She definitely read between the lines.

As they downed their drinks, Luca told her some of the area's history and about the recent influx of tourists and foreigners who were buying property. He said the locals welcomed the investors since it was beneficial for their economy. And with more tourism, there was more opportunity for the farmers to sell their products like wine and olive oil, and the *agriturismo* program was booming. The restaurants and *trattorie* were thriving, too.

When they finished, they walked back to his motorcycle. As they put on their helmets, Luca asked Mary if she was comfortable on the bike.

"Yes, this is a great way to sightsee," she replied.

And a great way to be close to you, she thought.

"All right, let's go," he said. "*Andiamo!*"

The farther north they drove, the more traffic they encountered. The road was hilly, curvy and narrow, and tour buses and public transit buses passed them often. Luca handled the bike carefully each time, but it took a few encounters before she stopped tensing up at their size and speed.

The popularity of Tuscan tourism was obvious. Frequent road signs advertised an *agriturismo*, a free wine tasting, *vendita diretta* – direct wine sales, a *ristorante* or a trattoria. The choices for travelers were abundant, but it was still rural, charming and quaint.

When they reached the small hilltop town of Panzano in Chianti, Luca stopped and parked his bike along a small triangular-shaped piazza.

"You might need to stretch your legs. Do you want to walk a little?"

"Sure," Mary said, glad they would be able to talk.

She took off her helmet and observed a typical day on the piazza. There was a large water fountain with old trees shading most of it. Two older men sat on a bench, talking. On another bench, a middle-aged lady with thinning, over-dyed orange hair sat alone. A little boy was curled under a tree to read a book, and a calico cat was crossing the middle of the piazza.

They walked uphill toward a large Catholic Church situated at the town's apex. The narrow pedestrian passageway was lined with houses, shops and apartments, but there was little activity. Windows and shutters on all the homes were closed to keep them cool. They passed an older man and woman slowly climbing the hill. He walked with the help of a cane, and she walked with the help of his arm. Mary guessed they had made the same stroll every day for countless years and would continue to do so until they couldn't any longer.

Luca asked her if she worked, and she told him about her job at the advertising agency.

"So, you are an artist not only as a hobby?"

"That's correct."

"I remember you carrying a sketchbook and camera at the *castello*. What do you like to do when you are not working?"

She told him she especially liked travel photography and art.

Then she surprised herself by saying, "You can look at my sketchbook when we're back at the farmhouse."

"I would like to see it," he said. "What else can you tell me about yourself?

"I feel like I've died and gone to heaven being here. It's going to be difficult to go home."

He grinned and said, "You're definitely in love."

They reached the red brick church, Santa Maria Assunta. There were about twenty steps leading to its entrance, terracotta pots filled with pink geraniums were on each step from top to bottom. She took pictures of the artful scene.

They didn't go in the church but strolled a short distance away from it and sat on a park bench under a large oak tree. They overlooked a broad countryside view. The landscape was a patch-work of farms, vineyards, orchards and forests. Luca told Mary he always enjoyed coming to the country.

"The city is noisy and crowded," he said. "This is so quiet and peaceful, and I like it. Someday I will only live in the country. It is my heaven on earth."

A chill went through her body, hearing an echo of Mr. Moretti's sentiments.

"At the farmhouse?" she asked.

"At il castello."

He looked off, like there was more to say about this, too, but he stopped.

She sensed he was pacing himself, yet she knew he'd tell her more throughout the day.

She took a photo of the view and managed to capture the older couple who had made it to the top. They were arm-in-arm, holding each other upright. She dreamed of a lifelong partner like that and suddenly thought of Garrett. She couldn't imagine growing old with him.

"Ready to head back to the bike or do you want something else to drink?" Luca asked.

"I'm ready to ride," she said.

"Okay, the next town will be Greve in Chianti, but we won't get off the bike. It's a wonderful town and one of the biggest in Chianti. This is where you will return on the weekend to see your friends. It has plenty of restaurants and shops and is popular with tourists. A great time to visit is in September during their wine festival. For three days, there are wine tastings, music and local food like *lampredotto*. You should come back in September."

He said this last sentence almost as if it was an invitation.

"I would enjoy that, but it took me a long time to have my first visit, so I can't imagine when I'll be back."

"I wouldn't be surprised to see you again since Italy is your new love interest."

He flashed a sexy smile and didn't dodge the big issue.

"What happened with your boyfriend?"

She didn't mind his candor and she wasn't surprised by it.

"He asked me to marry him before he went home."

Luca's immediate and polite reaction was to say congratulations and as he did, he instinctively glanced at her left hand, where there was no engagement ring. So his congratulations turned into a questioning look.

"I didn't give him an answer. I told him I needed to think about it. I'm so confused."

"Ahh. This must be a challenging time. I am sorry."

Without saying it, she could tell he knew he was complicating the situation.

"It is a challenging time," she said, "but I'm not letting it ruin the rest of my trip. I have important decisions to make, and I'm hoping the time alone will help."

He nodded and changed the subject.

"Are you hungry?" he asked.

She knew from Mr. Moretti that food could correct any Italian's problem, and it was a good way to lighten the conversation. She smiled.

"Yes, a little."

"In another twenty minutes we will be at our picnic place."

"Sounds good. Will we have the *lampra* –, whatever you just said?"

"*Lampredotto?* Um, no. It is stewed cow intestines. We won't be doing any stewing today."

"Well, I'm glad to hear that. I don't know if I'm in the mood for cow intestines."

They both laughed.

"Someday you will try it," he said.

Chapter 48

THEY HOPPED ON THE BIKE and continued north. She paid attention to the landmarks, knowing she would return to this area to visit Mr. Moretti's family.

Greve in Chianti was a bustling town compared to the small towns and villages she'd seen earlier. And it was located along a river.

Luca turned left in the middle of town to show her the main piazza. It was large and lined with restaurants, shops and hotels.

"This is where you can enjoy the wine festival when you return and where you will eat *lampredotto*," he said with a big grin.

North of town Luca slowed down and made a right turn onto a dirt road and stopped. A neatly painted black-on-white sign read "Castello di Vincenzo, CHIANTI CLASSICO D.O.C.G." A regal line of cypress trees bordered the long gravel driveway.

"Sorry about the dusty road. This is the only way. You might want to cover your mouth with your shirt."

After a slow, bumpy climb, they arrived at an ornate wrought-iron gate where Luca had to introduce himself by intercom. The gates opened and they entered the courtyard of the *castello*.

Mary thought it looked like another fortified villa, somewhat like Luca's place. But it was bigger.

Luca parked in the villa's courtyard, and they left their helmets with the bike.

"This is Castello di Vincenzo," Luca said. "It is owned by my father's Florentine friend, Gianmario Sabatini. When I was a child, we would leave the city and visit often. It was always a favorite place because I could hang out with Gianmario's son, Andrea. We are still close friends and today he is here in the wine tasting room waiting for us."

"What a place!"

Mary tried to imagine growing up in a home like this.

"Are you ready to drink our famous Chianti?"

"Of course," she said.

She was ready for the relaxation that would accompany a glass of wine.

In the wine tasting room, a lanky, curly-haired Italian man in a light blue fitted shirt and slim khaki pants was serving samples to two visitors.

"This is our Classico," the man said with a heavy accent. "It has been aged a minimum of two years in wood barrels only, no metal barrels."

Andrea looked up and saw Luca. His expression changed from all-business to friendly. His almond-shaped black eyes twinkled and he momentarily excused himself from the customers to hurry around the counter and embrace Luca.

"*Ciao, Luca!*"

"*Ciao, come va?*"

"*Bene, bene!*"

"This is Mary," Luca said.

"*Buongiorno,*" Mary said.

Andrea kissed each of Mary's cheek, then promptly went behind the counter again and set out two glasses for Luca and Mary.

"Riserva?" he asked.

"No, Classico," Luca said.

He turned to Mary and said, "Excuse us for a moment. It's easier for us to speak in Italian."

"No problem," Mary said.

She didn't understand them, but she didn't mind. She loved listening to the melodic language.

The two men chatted until the visitors decided to purchase three bottles of wine.

Andrea packaged them neatly in a rope-handled wooden box. It was burnished with an imprint of the vineyard's logo.

While Andrea was busy, Luca told her more about his friend. Only a few years separated them, and Andrea had gone to college but never finished. He had returned to run the family winery and establish rooms for rent, a business Luca said he would enjoy, too. Andrea didn't have formal plans to rent rooms until the fall – in time for the annual wine festival – but he sometimes made them available to customers he liked. He didn't advertise, but if an agreeable customer asked for a lodging recommendation, he would offer rooms for a reasonable price, cash only. It was an easy way to pocket some money.

The threesome sat down again, and Luca and Andrea continued to catch up on family and business affairs, with Luca sometimes translating for Mary.

Mary listened and drank. The first glass went down easily and Andrea promptly refilled it, never letting it empty. She pulled out her camera and took pictures of the tasting room, eventually getting the two handsome men to look her way for a shot. Mary walked over to a stairway that looked like it led to a cellar, and Andrea told her she could go down.

The cellar had a stone floor with dim lights, a cool resting place for the vino. There were rows of barrels resting on their sides, filled with aging wine. Fascinated by the barrels' nearly six-foot width, Mary took several photos of the orderly rows, spigots and labels. Some labels were handwritten in chalk on slate.

She could hear the two talking and laughing upstairs, and when she returned, she caught sight of Andrea handing a large wicker basket to Luca.

"Ready for lunch?" Luca asked.

"Sure."

"Follow me."

"Ciao, see you later," Andrea said.

Andrea winked at them as they walked away.

Yet another charming Romeo, Mary thought.

Chapter 49

THEY MEANDERED through the manicured garden and patio behind the main building. Then they walked down a long cypress-lined path ending at a huge flower-filled urn on a pedestal.

Before they reached the path's end, Luca said, "Come this way."

He cut through a gap in the trees to a picnic area under a canopy of old oak trees.

"Here is *la mia trattoria*."

His eyes twinkled, then he lightly kissed her on the lips.

She was excited about this quiet place to eat, drink and talk.

The contents of the basket Andrea had packed were covered with a folded cotton tablecloth that had a design of large orange poppies. Luca spread it on a cement table and one by one brought out everything in the basket in order of importance. Two bottles of Castello di Vincenzo Chianti Classico, a corkscrew, two glasses, prosciutto, *salumi*, mixed cheeses, grapes, marinated sun-dried tomatoes and water.

He held up the water bottle.

"I don't think we need this," he said.

He put it back in the basket.

"We have expressions in Tuscany about water. It makes rust, ruins bridges and the fish pee in it."

Mary laughed and thought of Mr. Moretti's expressions about wine while Luca uncorked the bottle.

As they sat across from each other on turquoise-cushioned benches, Luca offered a toast.

"To my new friend, Mary. Welcome to Chianti."

"*Salute*," she said and smiled.

Chapter 50

"So TELL ME MORE about your life in Philadelphia."

Mary talked about her job and her apartment. She told him about how close she had been to her father and how stressful it was after his death because she'd lost a best friend, too. She caught herself playing with her father's watch as she told Luca about him. Then she described her sister and their differences.

"She's the type of tourist who would never try anything new."

He nodded.

She also told him about Stella and how long they had known each other, much like his friendship with Andrea.

"It's too bad she's not here in Italy with you," he said.

"No doubt."

Stella would be perfect company.

The wine made it easier for them to open up, and they finished the first bottle quickly.

Luca opened the second bottle as effortlessly as Mary opened cans of Diet Coke, and she couldn't help but watch the muscles in his arms flex as he did it. He poured the wine and raised his glass.

"I'd like to make another toast. To Mary, the lady with storybook eyes."

He leaned forward as he took a closer look at her dark brown eyes.

"My mother's eyes were the same."

He had said nothing but warm things about his mother, and she liked this about him.

"Everyone has a story, Mary. Tell me yours. I want to know more about you and how you found yourself alone in Italy. This is a personal journey – it is not just about the travel. Am I correct?"

She found comfort in the wine and sipped more but didn't speak right away. She was moved by his intimate question, but she knew she was feeling the wine's effect, too, and she didn't want to be sloppy with her tongue or her emotions.

She inhaled deeply, and when she exhaled, she felt the muscles tighten in her stomach. She wanted to unleash her hopes and fears, and she hoped he wanted a sincere answer to his question. She believed he did. His body language said so. He sat quietly. He was patient, confident and comfortable, seeming simply pleased to be in her company, waiting to hear her story.

She looked up at the trees' dark foliage and caught glimpses of the sky. It was bluer than blue - a perfect azure blue, *azzurro*. This romantic setting, unlike any place she'd ever been, coupled with the independence she had created by staying alone, eclipsed the life she'd brought to Italy. She realized she could take a chance with Luca and be open and honest. There was nothing to lose.

"I believed my life was complicated until this very moment. As I was just thinking of how to respond to your question it became clear to me."

He listened attentively, his blue eyes big and soft.

She took another comforting drink and faced him.

Nothing to lose, she thought. Nothing.

She silenced any consideration of emotional infidelity toward Garrett.

"I'm so happy to be here," she said. "It's a dream come true, and it's more beautiful than I could have imagined. I feel like I belong here. This country - and you - have awakened my soul, forcing me to be honest with myself. During this short visit, this very short visit, I've been forced to listen to my heart, which I have been trying to ignore for at least the last year."

She stopped and took another drink before continuing.

"I was telling it to be quiet while I listened to everyone around me."

He nodded.

After deep breath, she made another confession out loud.

"I fell in love with Garrett, but I don't think it's the kind of love that will last a lifetime. More importantly, it's not the kind of love I want or the kind of love that brings me joy."

She sighed and stopped talking for several minutes, reflecting on the previous days. Luca didn't interrupt.

"I've been creating a life with Garrett that meets what other people expect of me – to find a responsible husband and eventually have a family. But I now realize that I can sum up my life in a sentence – I let their fears become my fears."

Luca nodded as if he knew exactly what she meant.

"My mother and sister can't understand why I'm thirty-two and unmarried. They keep saying, 'You need to grow up and be more responsible.' I think they're afraid I won't follow their dreams and do what makes them comfortable. As a matter of fact, they would be furious if they knew I was here alone with you."

She looked around at the peaceful setting and almost laughed at its "danger." She took a swallow of Chianti and let out another cleansing sigh.

"There's more to my story, though. I married my college sweetheart the summer after I graduated. Danny and I met our freshman year and we dated all four years of college. We married the summer after we graduated. When I look back, I think I married him because I thought I was supposed to. My mother urged both my sister and me to marry after college, and I wasn't strong enough to defy her."

Luca kept listening, showing no judgment, and she didn't hold back.

"I got pregnant about a year after we were married, but we lost the baby. It was horribly painful, and we weren't mature enough to handle it. It ended in divorce not long after the miscarriage."

She took another drink.

"Nothing has been the same since. I promised myself I wouldn't marry again unless I had found true love. It's this promise that's making me question my feelings for Garrett."

Tears welled up and she didn't fight them. She let them stream down her face, trickle under her chin and roll down her neck. She didn't wipe them away, because she needed to feel them.

She felt like she'd dropped an entire adult lifetime of hurt and frustration on Luca. What she was feeling now wasn't just about the last year but about the last ten years. She didn't know what to say or do next.

Luca made it easy for her, sensing it was best to be quiet. All he did was pour more Chianti in her glass.

Mary looked up at the pure blue sky peeking through the green foliage and the beauty soothed her. She felt like she had some clarity now, but she knew confrontations were right around the corner. Until then, she wanted to savor this moment in time and this place on earth. She liked that she and Luca were comfortable with silence, in the same way two people who've known each other for a long time can be. They simply let the wine flow and the rhythm of the day pulse.

"I understand," he said. "You have been searching to find yourself. I am not much different, and it's fair now that I tell you about me."

Chapter 51

Mary was relieved she'd sensed correctly that he wanted her honesty and openness. Now she realized he needed someone to talk to as well.

"I almost married this year," he said. "But my fiancée and I were not right for each other, same as you. She was only worried about her looks, fashion and money."

Mary kept her eyes on Luca as he continued.

"One weekend in the spring, we went to Venice to meet with a famous seamstress who was going to make her wedding dress. The price was outrageous, and I was startled by Lia's expectation. It seemed like a waste, and it started a fierce argument. She stormed from our hotel, calling me a peasant and telling me to find someone else to marry. She told me I wasn't driven enough because all I talked about was my desire to move to the country and live in the *castello*. She said it would be boring. It hurt, but I am glad she said these things, because we would have never survived happily."

He was quiet for a second before becoming somewhat defensive.

"I don't think country life is boring at all, and I always thought I would marry someone like my mother. Lia is nothing like her."

He paused and took two large gulps of wine.

"I've had one conversation with Lia since that day, and it was one too many."

He sounded angry, but she knew all too well how long it took to recover from a break-up.

"And my family, well, my family is complicated, like all families. But mine is really 'fucked up' as you say in English. I have one brother, Giovanni, and you know him. He is nine years older than I am, and I don't think he has ever liked me. You see, I was adopted. His father was a widower and married my beautiful mother, who was unable to have children. They decided to adopt a baby, and they chose me."

"Lucky for you to have a good family."

"Yes, I agree, but Giovanni always thought our parents were too easy on me. He thought I was favored, although we both always had the same opportunities. He and I grew up knowing we would work for our father, who would pass on his leather factory to us, as my grandfather did to him.

"But Giovanni lost that opportunity when he and Rossana were teenagers. At 17, she became pregnant, and it nearly killed my father, who lives by the Catholic Church's rules. He disowned Giovanni and never allowed him to work at the leather factory. He said he would not be disgraced in front of his employees."

"That's harsh punishment. I'm sure he's forgiven him by now."

"No, today it is the same as it was when it happened."

"That's unbelievable."

"I was young, eight years old, yet I remember it vividly. My brother and father screamed and yelled at each other. It was frightening. When Giovanni did not concede to breaking up with Rossana and giving their baby to the church for adoption, my father stopped talking to him and hasn't since.

"Before the family blow-up, my father bought the *castello* as a summer residence for the family, but it was mostly for my mother. She lived in Chianti once and longed to return, rather than live in Florence. So the *castello* was meant to be a retreat. My mother was never happier."

He stopped again, smiling as he recalled his mother.

"She was so wonderful. I couldn't have asked for more love from a 'real' mother."

Mary adored his affection toward his mother.

"So, the farm next to the *castello* was part of the purchase, but my father never intended to keep it. He said it was too much to care for, and he wanted to sell it. But weeks after the purchase, my mother was diagnosed with cancer of the pancreas. She needed immediate and frequent treatments, and she was incapable of traveling. The cancer took her life quickly, and she died before she could see Chianti again."

He stopped for a moment and Mary wanted to say something, but she was speechless. She couldn't imagine losing a mother at such a young age, especially one who so lovingly adopted him.

"Before she died, she must have persuaded my father to keep the farm and allow Giovanni, Rossana and their baby, Marco, to live there. I can't imagine my father would have made that decision alone. But no one in our family ever lived in the *castello*. My father refused to visit since it reminded him of my mother and caused him such heartache. And he refused to sell it because it was like losing more of her. He was a stubborn man, but when he looked at her, his eyes were soft and caring. It was the only time he showed his true heart."

Mary smiled.

"But my father still disowned Giovanni. He let him live on the farm under the condition that Giovanni make his own income from the farm's produce, selling grapes and olives and making his own wine and olive oil."

Luca paused to drink more wine.

"With the popularity of tourism in Tuscany now, he and Rossana have done well by making it an *agriturismo*. Do you know how the *agriturismo* system works?"

"Not really."

"By Italian law, an *agriturismo* must sell product made on its own property in addition to the rentals. The government provides financial supplements for doing this. This helps Rossana and Giovanni. They have always needed all the money they can earn."

"I can't believe your father is still angry after 25 years or so?"

"Yes, Mary. He is a stubborn old man now, and his health is poor. He has a weak heart. So he has transferred the leather factory management to me, and upon his death I will inherit the entire business and the *castello*. Giovanni will inherit the farm."

His look became distant for a moment, but he kept to his narrative.

"We have many good workers at the factory who have been there since my father started the business. Some even worked with my grandfather. And we have a strong manager, so I don't have to be there all the time. That is why I am at the *castello* so much. I go on the weekends to get away from the factory and sometimes during the week. I've had more time since the break-up with Lia, too."

"Do your father and brother speak now?"

"No. Each tells me what he wants the other to know. I don't like being in the middle, but I have no choice."

"What a tough situation."

"Yes, but we make it work. I see Giovanni often now that I am restoring *il castello*. It has been a hobby, and I'm much like my mother. I love the region of Chianti. In fact, someday I will live here year-round. I want to grow the winemaking capacity of the entire property. I might try to buy surrounding vineyards. It's always been my dream. Always. As a teenager, I spent weekends at the empty *castello*. My friends and I would visit and have parties. Sometimes we'd bring girls, but it was typically only the guys."

He stopped and looked straight into her eyes.

"I don't know why I am telling you so much. I never tell anyone all of this."

"I'm glad you are. It's interesting to learn more about you and your family."

"All right. I'll go on. As a teenager, I felt like I belonged here, but I had no choice other than to work for my father. My destiny was chosen by him, and I appreciate the opportunity, but someday I want to make my own choice."

He paused for a moment.

"If I can give some advice, I know you're in a difficult situation with Garrett, but recognize your hands aren't tied. You have a choice, and you should listen to your heart."

He raised his glass.

"It's been my fortune to meet you, and maybe I can -"

He stopped, carefully choosing his words.

"Maybe I can spend more time with you. I like being with you and talking to you."

"Thank you. I feel the same, and you're right. I do have choices, but I have been afraid to make them."

With this, the intimate conversation ended, and an unspoken bond formed between them. Mary realized she shared more emotion with Luca in an hour than she had with Garrett in a year.

Luca lightened the conversation by talking about the food in the picnic basket – the prosciutto, cheese, olive oil and bread.

This led Mary to tell him everything about Mr. Moretti and her favorite market. She told him more about her scheduled visit for Sunday dinner with his family.

"That's a great opportunity," he said. "You will love all their food and the family, I am sure. And you will eat for hours and hours. The daylong feast overwhelms most Americans, but you will have a wonderful time. I know it."

They finished the wine and the food, and Luca suggested they explore the grounds.

Chapter 52

LUCA SHOWED HER an old thatched-roof playhouse and a hedge labyrinth where he and Andrea once played as children. It was a quiet, isolated setting where he easily stole sweet kisses from her.

The property was beautiful, but overgrown. Andrea was making progress, but still had much work to do. It was clear Andrea and Luca had similar passions for renewing beauty to old, ruined homes.

The entire afternoon was mesmerizing, and Mary could barely soak it all in.

It is like heaven on earth, she thought, exactly as Mr. Moretti said.

Everything was old but exquisite. They passed large terracotta urns with chips and cracks, eroded statues of gods and goddesses, rusty wrought-iron gates, mossy stones and crumbling staircases.

The wine, coupled with the artistic scenery and being close to Luca, softened her mood, providing a welcomed sense of euphoria. Mary discovered a pot of basil and pinched off a leaf to smell it. She closed her eyes and permanently linked the memory of its scent to the perfect day.

They returned to the wine shop with the basket emptied. Luca spoke to Andrea, and Mary saw Andrea hand something to Luca, but she couldn't see what it was until he turned toward her. Two large brass keys on silk tassels were in his hand.

"I cannot safely drive after all this wine," he said. "Andrea has given us keys for two rooms in the house so we can nap. I hope you agree."

"That's smart," Mary said. "We should always drink where there are beds!"

They both laughed at her comment, reading between the lines.

"Follow me," he said.

They entered the main building's formal foyer and climbed a well-worn flight of tile stairs with a wrought-iron railing. At the top, he gave her a key.

"I'll be across the hall."

An awkward pause followed, and he softly spoke in Italian.

"*Il tempo viene per chi sa aspettare.*"

"What?"

"Good things happen when one waits."

He ran his fingers through his hair. He was right, and it was what she honestly wanted to hear him say.

"I agree," she said.

"I'll wake you in about an hour."

He softly kissed her forehead.

"By then I will have dreamt of having another perfect day with you," he said, then smiled and turned away.

Mary melted and walked weak-kneed into her Tuscan bedroom.

It was a simple room with white linens and white curtains. There was a four-post walnut bed with a nightstand on each side of the bed with small table lamps. A large cherry wood armoire faced the bed.

"This feels like home," she said out loud as she pulled down the cotton duvet and got under the covers.

She buried her face in the pillow and shut her eyes. All she envisioned was Luca and his baby blue eyes. She replayed the day's events until she fell asleep.

About an hour later, Luca knocked on the door.

"Mary?"

He knocked again.

"Are you awake?" he asked.

She stretched and looked at her watch. Two hours had passed. She was surprised she slept so peacefully for so long.

"Almost. Come in."

He opened the door as she started to sit up.

Her long wavy locks fell over her shoulders, and the late afternoon sun cast a gentle glow.

Luca didn't hesitate a moment and came to the bed's edge.

"You are so beautiful," he said. "I can't stop saying it."

He slid his hands under her hair to cup her shoulders, and kissed her forehead delicately.

She held her breath, afraid to move and cause the tender moment to end.

He lightly pressed his lips to her cheekbone. He kissed her eyelid then the soft skin on the outside edge of her eye.

With the warmth of his breath against her, her lips parted, anticipating a kiss and yearning to feel his lips on hers. She felt adored by him and wanted time to stand still.

He tenderly stroked her chin and tilted it up, then traced her lips with his finger before he kissed them.

He looked at her while softly running his fingers through her hair, then pushed it aside and slowly slid a finger under the shirt's elastic and moved the sleeve down to expose her shoulder. He lightly touched her skin before his lips kissed the same place.

Her every nerve tingled and warmth radiated wherever he touched.

"Your skin is like silk," he whispered.

The window was open and a breeze fluttered. She felt incredibly feminine and vulnerable. Looking deeply into his eyes, still not saying a word, she poured out her longings. And he did the same. They wanted more from each other, and they shared their mutual desires without uttering a word.

"I want to hold you," he finally said. "And let this desire keep simmering until it comes to a boil. I'm crazily attracted to you."

In a gentle move, he rolled her into the middle of the bed and held her. He played with her hair and lightly kissed her several times.

"We should go soon, *bella*. The sun is beginning to set, and we need to get on the road. I'll meet you downstairs in the wine shop. I'll be waiting for you."

He started to stand up, then leaned back toward her and whispered.

"I've waited a lifetime, and I will keep waiting."

He put his finger to her lips, so she didn't have to say anything in return, and he left.

She lingered in bed thinking of him. This was more than a physical attraction.

Chapter 53

Back in the wine shop, Mary and Luca said their farewells to Andrea and promised to return soon. They hopped on Luca's motorcycle and this time Mary let her body fully mold to his, feeling both safe and scintillated. The early evening ride was beautiful as the hillsides were turning gold in the Tuscan sunset. She occasionally nudged Luca to stop and let her capture a photograph, but she was happiest riding with her arms wrapped snugly around him.

After they passed through Panzano in Chianti, Luca slowed down to make a turn into the hamlet of San Leolino. He drove up a short, steep hill on a narrow street winding through some tightly spaced homes, arriving at a shrine dedicated to the Madonna. Beyond it, he pulled into the gravel parking lot of the Pieve di San Leolino Church.

"Bring your camera, and we'll walk to the church. There is a cool, breezy spot where you can take pictures of the western sky, and see a sweeping view of Panzano in Chianti."

At the overlook, Mary snapped some shots of the evening horizon. Then she set her camera on the brick wall and peacefully enjoyed the setting.

Luca stepped behind her and gently removed her ponytail holder so her hair could blow in the breeze.

"You are so beautiful," he said. "I may never stop saying it."

He put his arms around her waist and kissed her neck and shoulder.

As he held her, he whispered, "Where have you been?"

She wanted to say, "looking for you," but she didn't.

When they arrived at the farmhouse, Luca parked the motorcycle so he could give Mary a warm hug.

"This has been the most wonderful day in a long time. I want to spend more time with you, but I have to return to Florence tonight for a meeting early tomorrow morning."

"When will you be back?"

"Tomorrow afternoon."

"I'm supposed to leave the farmhouse tomorrow. The reservation is over and –"

Luca interrupted before she could continue.

"Let me find Giovanni and talk to him."

In a few minutes, he returned and said the apartment did not have a new renter for the following week, so she could stay as long as she wanted. He also said he and Giovanni worked out the payment, too. She wouldn't be charged anything additional.

"That's great news, and it's generous. Thank you."

"There's one condition for you to stay."

"Yes?"

"You must save tomorrow evening for me. Promise?"

"Absolutely."

He kissed her passionately and took a couple steps backwards to his motorcycle, never taking his eyes off her as he put on his helmet and mounted the bike. He pulled forward, but stopped and turned around for one last look, and then she watched him ride away until he was out of sight.

Upstairs, she poured a glass of Chianti and headed to the rooftop. She was thrilled and a wreck at the same time. She felt so much joy about Luca, but knew she couldn't ignore that she was betraying Garrett. She hadn't yet refused his proposal and she was with another man. The conflict was intense. She grabbed her travel journal from the table and wrote.

> I am so conflicted between the known and the unknown. What is better? Safety or passion? And why can't I have both?

She went to bed later and fell asleep thinking of the situation, her subconscious mind seizing the topic. She dreamt she was in a restaurant with Luca, and Garrett came in. She was engaged to

Garrett, but they were fighting and unhappy. When Garrett saw Luca, he seethed and told Mary she had to make a decision.

"Is it going to be me, or him?" Garrett said in the dream.

Mary decided it was time to take a chance with Luca.

"The engagement is over, Garrett," she said.

Garrett clenched his jaw and his brow furrowed.

"You're going to regret this decision," he said. "And this is final. If let me walk away right now, you will never have another chance."

Mary let Garrett go and turned her attention to Luca, thinking he would be happy with her decision, but he was busy talking to the couple at the next table.

She watched him talk. He was pleasant, happy, handsome - and emotionally available. But she knew little else. She didn't know his father or his friends. She had never seen his home. And they'd never made love.

Suddenly, she felt scared. But in her dream, there was no turning back.

Chapter 54

THE DREAM WAS FRESH on Mary's mind when she woke up, and it created an empty feeling. But she realized she didn't have to make a decision about anything or anyone yet. She could simply enjoy Italy.

She made coffee and reviewed the maps for directions to Siena and Monteriggioni. She put on the same white dress she wore to Florence, leaving her undergarments in her suitcase, just the way Luca preferred. She liked it now, too. It was liberating.

When she arrived in Siena, she carefully followed the signs to the old Medici fort on the west side of town where she was able to park free. She hiked uphill toward the town's center with several other tourists, recognizable by their maps, cameras, visors and water bottles.

Even though she was a tourist, too, she didn't want to act like one. So she slowed her pace and stopped at a bar for Campari soda. She stood at the counter and took her time drinking the pungent aperitif, watching the patrons come and go. Some customers stopped in for *caffè* and others for quick shots - *gotini*. Many read the local newspapers, and she liked to listen to their banter about the latest news, though she didn't understand it.

The Campari soda lightened her step as she proceeded toward Siena's city center. The first major site on her path was the Church of Santa Caterina, where she stopped to take a few photos of the large brick exterior accented by colossal cypress trees. Then she went in to see the preserved remains of St. Catherine.

After seeing the 600-year-old saint's head and tiny thumb, she ventured up the hill to find Siena's famous Campo, a shell-shaped, sloped piazza. She read that it served as the site of the Palio, a famous, centuries-old bareback horse race that decided the rivalry between Siena's neighborhoods twice each summer.

To find it, Mary followed large tour groups whose guides carried colorful umbrellas and flags.

When she got there, the piazza's size and shape impressed her. Restaurants lined the upper level and she took pictures from every angle, including the Torre Mangia, or bell tower, and the majestic Palazzo Pubblico, or City Hall, which was under restoration. Then she sat down on the warm brick plaza, as were many others. She people-watched, enjoying the beauty of the medieval town.

From there, she headed to the base of the Campo and went behind the Palazzo Pubblico to find the Mercato Centrale, an open-air market. Locals were selling fresh produce, wine, olive oil and other local specialties. She bought bars of soap made of olive oil. They were small, packed easily and would make excellent gifts.

Next to the market, she found Trattoria Papei, recommended for the local pasta, *pici*, a thick spaghetti. But it was too early for lunch, so she decided to come back after more sightseeing.

She visited Siena's Duomo and saw the famed Gothic cathedral's façade and zebra-striped interior brick. She thought the church's best feature was the mosaic floors depicting biblical and mythological subjects. Her guidebook mentioned the famous artists who had contributed to the church's construction, like Pisano, Donatello and allegedly, Raphael. There were statues by Michelangelo and sculptures by Bernini adorning the church, too.

From the Duomo, she strolled slowly along the streets, looking in the shop windows at the handcrafted leather goods, stationery, books, antique art and toys. She found a wonderful ceramic shop where the artist, Francesca, was painting newly fired pieces. Mary bought more gifts for her friends and family, including ceramic-topped wine stoppers painted in decorative Sienese patterns. For herself, she bought a plate to hang in her kitchen.

She took pictures along the narrow brick streets and later found her way back to the trattoria. She sat at a yellow cloth-covered table for two. Lunch was a good opportunity to read more in her guidebook and decide on her next destination.

The guidebook provided a lengthy description of the Palio race, and she tried to imagine a horse race in the Campo. She read the entire chapter in the guidebook about the custom, immersing herself in the story of the race:

~ Of the seventeen neighborhoods, or *contrade*, in Siena, only ten compete due to space limitations in the Campo.

~ A lottery system is used to assign horses to each *contrada*.

~ The huge level of pride in claiming victory drives bitter rivalries, and anything is done to assure a victory, including kidnapping rival jockeys and outright bribery. Both are considered acceptable behavior.

~ The horses are cherished and virtually worshipped, while jockeys are only tolerated as a way to get the horse across the finish line.

Mary also learned from the book that each *contrada* has a name – the Snail, the Owl, the Caterpillar, and more – and distinctive colors and flags. Banners for different neighborhoods were hung in the shops, but Mary hadn't realized each represented a *contrada*, so she decided to look at them more closely after lunch.

She read that people in the town also celebrated the race with neighborhood parties, a flag-throwing competition, music, costumes, parades and feasting. Mary found it hard to understand this level of competition in a city as small as Siena.

Her server, Paolo, was an older man with a head full of gray hair, and he spoke English well.

No worries about a proposition like the one she'd gotten from Roberto, she thought.

She ordered *vino rosso della casa*, the red house wine, and *pici cardinal* – thick, spaghetti-like noodles in a savory red sauce.

Paolo said this was his favorite dish and he recommended it.

She loved every bite of the firm pasta and wished she could make it at home. She decided to ask Mr. Moretti for help when she got back to Philadelphia.

Paolo was disappointed she ordered only pasta, but she realized the decision was smart because it was so filling, especially alongside the bread he served. He tried to convince her to have dessert, but she opted for only a cup of espresso. He looked disappointed that she didn't eat more.

She promised him she would have gelato on the Campo and she did. This time she tried strawberry and thought it was delicious, but *limone* was still her favorite.

She stopped in a tourist gift shop to look at the colorful *contrada* flags of the Palio. She wanted to buy one for her niece's bedroom and she couldn't decide between the flag of the neighborhood of the Goose, *oca*, because it looked somewhat like Mother Goose, or the Caterpillar, *bruco*, because of its charming little green mascot.

The storeowner saw her trying to choose.

"I am *oca*," he said, meaning he lived in the Goose *contrada*. "We win always."

Mary didn't like his pompous attitude so she defiantly bought the Caterpillar flag.

Chapter 55

Back in her car, she carefully navigated the maze of one-way streets to leave Siena. Then she drove north to the small walled town of Monteriggioni. Historically, it was a Sienese outlook post and over seven hundred years old. Its fortified walls and 14 towers were intact, with a small village enclosed. It was very small – under a half mile in diameter – and well preserved.

She parked in a large lot and strolled up a small hill along a path of lavender to the gated entrance. The fragrant plant made her think of Luca and their meeting at *il castello*. She'd thought of him all day, and she couldn't wait to see him for dinner.

In the town's small piazza, she watched young children kick a ball. She navigated the streets while admiring the ancient medieval architecture. Small homes lined up next to each other, made of brick and stone with solid wood doors. House numbers were hand-painted on tiles and potted flowers were as bountiful here as everywhere else she'd been in Italy. She found a wine-tasting shop, thinking she would buy something new to try. She decided on a bottle of bold Brunello.

She drove back to the apartment, and when she got there, she drank the legendary Brunello and nibbled on some prosciutto and Parmagiano-Reggiano.

"I love Italy," she said out loud.

The wine and food warmed her soul, and she daydreamed about the night ahead.

After showering and changing into a white skirt and patterned blue blouse, she was ready. It was early, so she opened her journal to write.

> *This is a rich slice of life, feeding my heart and soul. I feel so alive!*

But Garrett was at home working and probably worrying about her, she thought. And she was with another man. She was in the heart of Tuscany wanting to jump in with both feet with Luca, but she couldn't ignore her commitment to Garrett. But she didn't want to break up with him by phone. She knew she was being selfish, but she decided she would wait to talk to Garrett.

When Luca arrived, she invited him to the rooftop to enjoy the Brunello, prosciutto and cheese. As they snacked, Mary showed him the sketches she'd done of the scenery.

"Your art captures the soul of this country. I like them and think others would, too."

"Thanks. I've felt so much passion while I've been here. Hopefully it came through in the work."

"I haven't known you long, but I wish you were able to extend your time here. We could get to know each other better."

She smiled at the thought of it.

"I'd like that, too, but I have to take care of things at home first."

She was primarily talking about Garrett, and Mary knew Luca understood that.

"I'll count the days until you can come back," he said, moving in for a kiss.

As they stood on the roof under a warm sunset, his tender lips slowly met hers. Their kissing intensified and desire burned, but they controlled themselves.

After the first glass of wine he asked, "Are you ready for dinner? We can go to a local trattoria."

She wondered if it would be the same restaurant where Roberto worked, but thankfully it wasn't.

Dinner in the little rustic restaurant was *delizioso*. She ate *ribollita*, thick stewed vegetables over day-old bread, a local specialty, and they shared tender Bistecca Fiorentina. But Luca was more memorable than the food.

Some older customers in the trattoria recognized him and looked at Mary questioningly.

"*Mary è la mia amica nuova dagli Stati Uniti.*" - "Mary is my new friend from the United States," Luca said.

When the older women tried to ask him more questions, he tormented them with silence and they gruffly turned away. "They live for gossip," he said and laughed.

"Tell them you found me lost in the country. My breadcrumbs were eaten and I couldn't find my home, like Hansel and Gretel."

"Hansel and Gretel?" he asked.

"Yes, the fairytale kids who go into the woods, get lost and end up in a witch's cabin. Do you know the story?"

"Ah, we have a similar story, *Nennillo and Nennella.* But there are no breadcrumbs, it is bran."

They both laughed.

"How was your day?" he asked.

Mary described her fascination with Siena and Monteriggioni, and he shared insight about the Palio and the fierce level of competition within the city.

"The event is like turning back the calendar to medieval times, and you have to see it to believe it."

He tried to help her understand that as a Florentine he would always be shunned by the Sienese who characterized Florentines as arrogant and pompous. The rivalry between Siena and Florence had existed for hundreds of years, but Luca was worldly enough to appreciate the differences between the cities. He also said he sometimes thought about who his real parents might be, and it was entirely possible he was Sienese, he told her. He didn't know how he ended up in Florence when he was a baby, so he did not speak negatively of Siena like many Florentines did, including Luca's father.

Mary said, "No matter the history, I love Tuscany - both Florence and Siena - but especially the area between them."

"You mean Chianti, then. Tell me what you love."

"The geography is a perfect palette. Everywhere I look, I feel like I'm seeing a painting or I'm in one. It's so natural and there's harmony between the architecture and the land. The houses ramble and flow in sync with the geography."

"Yes," he said. "You are right. And think about this, most homes were built hundreds of years ago when people didn't travel, have televisions and magazines or exposure to outside influences. They created these houses based on their instinct and sensibility. It is natural art."

"I never thought of that."

She was fascinated by this concept.

"Homes were functional, yet they managed to be beautiful, too," he said.

"And it's obvious they were built with time and care, not hastily," she added.

Luca smiled.

"What else do you love?" he asked.

"I love this," Mary said, lifting her glass of wine and taking a sip as she continued. "I love the orderly rows of vineyards, and I love strolling along them and thinking about how long grapes have been a part of man's life."

Luca beamed at her as she kept talking.

"When I watch the farmers prune the vines, I understand how much work it takes to produce a bottle of wine, and I realize it's a passion, a labor of love. People's lives are attached to the land, and they work so hard."

"Very hard. My brother and his wife can tell you about it."

"I feel like I've stepped back in time in the vineyards. When I close my eyes, I hear ancient music and laughter. It's magical."

"It is, I agree. Dare I ask if there's anything else you love?"

"Yes, the food. It's so fresh and tasty and such an important part of life. At the supermarket, I've seen couples selecting ingredients and having animated conversations about what to prepare for dinner. I've never seen anything like that at home. I love that the meals are long and never rushed, and I like the habit of late dinners, too."

"You sound like you've found a new home," he said, winking. "Chianti suits you well."

He lifted his glass.

"*Salute!*"

"*Salute!*"

They both took a sip of wine.

"Do you mind if I continue?" Mary asked.

"Please do."

"I love that you keep things forever - that things aren't so disposable. Furniture is made to last and it's taken care of. Doors and shutters are solid wood and not hollow or synthetic. Flowers are in real terracotta pots, not plastic made to look like clay. And pots filled with gorgeous flowers, trees, spices and herbs are everywhere."

She drank some more wine.

"Everywhere I go, I feel like I'm in a romance movie," she said.

"If you are in a movie, then you are the stunning leading lady. I hope you don't mind if I ask, but would you consider me for your leading man?"

Mary blushed and even though she was sitting down, she felt her knees go weak again. He was so charming.

"I would be the envy of many women," she said.

Their connection was paradoxical. It was comfortable, but exciting. When she was with him, she felt an intense enthusiasm to experience life and new adventures. She also wanted to experience him.

After the delicious dinner they returned to the farmhouse.

"Give me thirty minutes, and I'll be back," Luca told her.

"Okay," she said, a bit confused.

He walked toward the *castello*, looked back at her and winked.

"I'll be back very soon," he said. "I have a surprise."

She couldn't imagine what he was doing, but it was exciting to know he was doing something to surprise her.

She poured the last glass of the Brunello and took a sip. Then she freshened up in the bathroom. Her cheeks were rosy, so she decided not to put on any more makeup other than lip gloss. She brushed her long hair and changed into a thin, light-blue cotton sweater, no bra. She slipped off the lacy thong she wore beneath the skirt, too. Then she went to the dark bedroom and lay down. She smelled the lavender fragrance from her pillow while she looked out the window at the night sky and mentally replayed the evening with Luca at the trattoria.

The doorbell rang and she hurried downstairs to meet Luca, who was waiting with a small lantern.

"Let's go!" he said as he grabbed her hand.

"Where?"

"It's a surprise."

"I love surprises," she said.

"Who doesn't?"

Garrett, she thought, but didn't say so out loud.

The lantern illuminated their way as they walked along the shortcut to *il castello*. They were on the same path Mary discovered days before. Every few steps he stopped to kiss her.

They entered the *castello* through the same door as she did on her first visit. From the foyer, they turned left to enter a corridor that led to the inner courtyard.

In the middle of the courtyard was a thick pile of blankets, a dozen lit candles and a basket with a bottle of wine.

"Welcome, Cinderella."

"Now I truly feel like a leading lady."

But this is much better than a movie, she thought.

Luca's face glowed in the soft lighting.

"Come," he said.

They sat down on the soft blankets, and he poured Chianti into two glasses.

"*Salute!* To Cinderella!"

"Cheers, Prince Charming!"

She closed her eyes, drank the Chianti and felt time meld. Past, present and future became one.

Luca kissed her lovingly.

Then they talked and giggled, occasionally stopping to kiss or fondle.

Mary kept looking around the courtyard, soaking it in and loving every minute of his magical, mystical home.

The wine bottle was empty, the candles burned low and their moods were soft and mellow.

Chapter 56

"LIE DOWN NEXT TO ME," Luca said after he blew out the flames.

They were on their backs, side by side.

"Look at the brilliant stars," he said.

This is heaven on earth, Mary thought again.

"I told you I stayed here often when I was a teenager. I'd come with my friends and we would party through the night, laughing and drinking. Zipping up my sleeping bag and falling asleep under the stars was my favorite part of the night. I'd lie here looking up at them, knowing they'd witnessed every event here on earth. I'd also dream of my mother and wonder if she could see me. When I was little, she would put me to bed and say, 'You are my moon, my stars, and my sun.' I always thought she meant that I was her son, like s-o-n. Then one night, lying here, it dawned on me that she was calling me her sun, s-u-n, all those years!"

He laughed at himself and continued.

"Another expression she always said to me was, 'I love you from the top of my head to the toes of my Uffizi's.' It was a fun play on the pronunciation of the gallery's name – oo-feet-zee."

Mary looked at Luca intently as he went on.

"She studied English, music and art, and was so smart and loving. I miss her, and the one place I've always felt connected to her is right here, under the stars. If she can see me, I am sure it is here, and I hope she is proud."

He paused for moment, still looking skyward.

"I used to dream of having a beautiful girlfriend and bringing her here. I wanted her to gaze up at the stars with me and love being here as much as I do."

He was silent for a few moments before continuing and Mary didn't say anything, either.

"I think I dreamed of you, exactly like this."

He squeezed her hand.

Mary was awestruck by this romantic moment. She pulled their locked hands to her face and kissed the backside of his hand. He smelled like the earth, like the summer's night air and the spice of Chianti.

"I didn't have a magical place like this to stargaze," she said. "But when I was a kid, we loved to swim at night, when the water felt so warm. Then we'd get out of the pool and lie on our concrete driveway, feeling the warmth it held from a full day of sun. I can remember it so vividly. The pavement was hot, and it was rough like sandpaper. I would lie and wait to see a shooting star. I'd try to find constellations, too, but it was more about the elusive shooting star. One summer night we saw hundreds during a meteor shower. I think it was in August."

"*La festa di San Lorenzo*," he said.

"What?"

"The Perseus meteor showers. We saw the same stars."

He swiftly rolled above her.

"*Sei mia bella stella*," he said. "You are my beautiful star."

He couldn't hold back any longer. His lips found hers and kissed hungrily, devouring her.

She did the same, pressing and biting his ravenous lips with hers.

Desire raged through their veins, but Luca made a swift tempo change. He slowed and softened to gentle, lingering kisses.

Mary pulled his body closer to hers, and slid her hands along his back, around his neck and through his hair.

Their bodies entwined as they kissed and rolled on the soft blankets.

Mary never wanted it to stop.

Nearly out of breath, Luca backed away for a moment.

"The first time I saw you at the farm, it was -"

He stopped and took a deep breath.

"It was -. Well, let me try to explain how my life changed in a moment."

With the arched columns of the *castello* and the starry sky as his backdrop, she watched Luca take a deep breath. Mary knew the words he was about to say. She was sure of it.

"On that summer day, I heard your voice, but my back was to you," Luca said. "I simply turned around, and there you were. The wind stopped blowing, the birds stopped chirping and the clocks stopped ticking. Time stood still. I didn't know where I was, and I felt like maybe I was someone else. It's hard to describe, but I felt like I had stood there all my life waiting for you, to see you, to be together again. Until that moment, I didn't know I had spent my life looking for you. Nothing that happened before mattered, because you were back."

He paused, looking at Mary's face to see if she understood.

"Do I make sense or do I sound like I've had too much wine?"

He laughed at himself, but Mary knew he needed to hear her answer.

It was difficult to speak, but her words finally trickled out.

"I felt the same, and I never experienced as much peace as I did in that moment. It seemed like I had found something I was missing, too. It was like I found someone I didn't know I was looking for."

"Yes, exactly."

He kissed her tenderly before he spoke again.

"But I have to be sincere. I didn't want to believe it. I resisted it, but when you showed up here by accident, I had the same feelings again, equally as strong. When we stood at the tower lookout, it seemed like you and I were where we were supposed to be. Right there, with each other. And as the days went on, I told myself I was imagining it. I rationalized it as an overreaction to my recent break-up. I tried to ignore the feelings and 'be tough.' By the time you came to Florence for lunch, I convinced myself you were visiting for a brief time and we could have fun for the week – you know, uncommitted fun – because I'm wildly attracted to you."

He kissed her again before continuing.

"I heard a voice telling me there was more to this feeling and more to us. I couldn't silence the noise. Little by little, I acknowledged those first feelings were real. The strength of the yearning I have for you is something I've never felt before. It's like there is something bigger than us pulling us together."

"I know," she said. "I feel the same, and I went through similar emotions. I admit it's confused me, too. But right now, here with you, I know it's real."

He pressed his lips to hers and kissed her as though he never wanted to let her go.

"I'm so happy we found each other," he said.

He shut his eyes and traced her face, neck and ears with the tip of his finger. Then he whispered.

"Our souls already know each other, don't they? It's our bodies that haven't met."

His lips found her eyelids, the tip of her nose and her neck.

"I want to know everything about you," he said.

Her chest filled with warmth. She felt a fiery ball of energy and light inside her, radiating love and growing brighter in his presence.

With his eyes still closed, he kissed her while his hands explored. Their desire intensified.

"I have an idea. Please trust me."

He sat up and pulled off his long-sleeved black tee. His smooth skin glowed in the moonlight as he rolled the cotton shirt into a long strip. Then he slowly wrapped it around his face to cover his eyes, tying it behind his head to make a blindfold. He whispered again.

"If I can't see you, it will make every other sense stronger, and I want to memorize you, every delicious morsel of you. Will you let me?"

She didn't say anything, but eased her sweater over her head and handed it to him. She lay topless on the blanket as he felt to find the sleeves and make another long sash. He carefully tied it around her head.

"I like this," he said as he traced her lips with his fingers. "I like you."

With their senses of touch and smell heightened, he brought her hand to his chest and placed it over his heart, where he held it for a few minutes before he moved it away and pressed his torso to hers. They kissed and explored. Slowly. Blindly. Full of desire. Their hands and mouths sought flesh to kiss, fondle and caress.

"I want you every way imaginable," he whispered.

He tenderly traced her shoulders, arms and elbows to her fingertips. His mouth followed his fingers' trail, kissing and nibbling. When his lips reached her hand, he sucked the length of each of her fingers. His mouth was warm, soft and hungry for her. He retraced his path up her arm and went down the other. Slowly. Carefully.

She listened to his breaths, kisses and occasional moans. She pictured what their bodies looked like pressed together in the old castle. Her every nerve was alive as his mouth traveled back to her neck and lips, his hands following. With every warm breath against her damp flesh, she felt the power of his love.

His lips worked their way down her torso to her belly button, then around her waist, up her chest and back to her neck. His hand occasionally grazed her breast and sent shivers through her body.

Wanting more, he slowly removed her skirt and moaned when he realized she wasn't wearing anything under it. He kissed the back of her knees. He wrapped her feet in his strong hands. He nibbled on her hips.

"Sit up," he said.

He moved behind her, wrapping his legs around her and lifting her hair to kiss the back of her neck, driving her mad with desire. He kept kissing her neck while his hands traced the side of her body and ran through her hair.

He took his hands away, and she couldn't sense where they were until she felt their warmth at the base of her spine. His hand hovered above her skin, then touched the tingling flesh.

She could barely control herself. Not being able to see him was powerfully erotic.

"I want this to last all night," he whispered in her ear.

She imagined still being in his arms with the rising sun.

"It's a perfect night," she said, hearing her own voice quiver. "You're so perfect."

Luca explored and found Mary's every bone, tendon, muscle and nerve, but withheld his attention to her most erogenous areas. He wanted to make her wait to have her desires fulfilled.

Lying down again, he returned to her lips.

"You are so delicious," he said. "I want to make love to you."

"I want you, too."

She helped him take off his remaining clothes, and their limbs tangled. She moved her hands across his smooth back and arms, grabbed his hard shoulders and squeezed his buttocks. Her legs swaddled his.

Their bodies writhed.

"I have to see your face and the desire in your eyes," Luca said, breathless and aroused.

He pulled off their blindfolds and looked into her eyes as his hand slid to her breasts. Then his mouth followed. He had waited to savor these delicate mounds of flesh and his tongue rolled over her taut nipples, making her insane with desire. He devoured her breasts and she was going crazy.

He slithered one hand down the middle of her torso and between her legs. He delicately touched her and moved to watch his own fingers trace her sensitive, slippery folds of skin.

Her back arched. She was so ready for him.

It was time. They couldn't wait any longer.

He kneeled above her while his hands slipped under her. He grabbed her buttocks, and then slowly, very slowly, entered her. Mary closed her eyes and swirls of color and light flashed stunning auras. When she opened them, she saw Luca looking at her, and they both moaned in pleasure, frozen for a moment.

Their bodies glowed in the moonlight and they couldn't press their bodies close enough together. He slowly pulsated in and out, careful to notice her every reaction to his moves.

Their mouths searched for each other, wanting more.

Their bodies rocked, and they couldn't let go. They didn't let go.

As they climaxed, Mary felt the rhythm of life speed to a fiery tempo, one that made her reconsider everything she'd known about life and love up to this time.

Then they were still. Naked and silent. They needed no words.

They kissed, they touched, they fondled.

They giggled, they gasped.

They fell asleep with their bodies fully tangled, like old grapevines clinging to their posts.

Chapter 57

MARY AND LUCA AWOKE under a blanket on Sunday as the sun was rising. A rooster crowed, a dog barked and church bells rang.

"Good morning, *bella*."

Mary beamed, thrilled to see him. She kissed the tip of his nose.

"Good morning to you."

They wrapped their naked bodies around each other.

"I will never forget last night," he said.

"I won't either."

She felt her body flush with warmth.

"We fit together so perfectly," she said. "And I don't know about you, but I'm ready for more."

"You're reading my mind."

They made love under the morning sun and afterward she nuzzled in and put her head on his chest while he played with her hair. She loved his body's scent.

"Today is your visit with the Morettis, isn't it?" he asked.

"Yes."

"I've been thinking of a plan. How about if I take you?"

"That would be nice, if you're available."

"Yes, I am. And will you go to Venezia on Monday?"

"Yes, I'd like to, unless you have another suggestion."

"Venezia is magical and romantic. It is a place where the past lives in the present, and it is stirring. You, an artist, would love it."

"Based on how you just described it, how could I not go?"

"If you choose Venezia, we can have more time together, too. Here is what I'm thinking. I'll drop you off in Greve in Chianti this morning and I'll pick you up in the afternoon. We can go to my apartment in Firenze where you can stay tonight. Then you can take the morning train to Venezia. Bring a backpack with everything you need for overnight and tomorrow."

"That sounds like a great idea."

"Well, I am selfish. It gives me more time with you."

She kissed him and snuggled in more tightly.

"I like how you think," she said.

Eventually they made their way back to her apartment. She made coffee and they drank it while she looked through her notes for the Morettis' address.

Throughout the morning, they watched each other's every move, completely obsessed. And when they caught each other looking, all they did was giggle. There was no modesty. They openly admitted their fascination, and they were giddy.

Moments before they were ready to leave, there was a knock at the door. It was Rossana with the cordless phone and a frown directed at both Mary and Luca.

Mary knew who it was before she answered.

"Mary?"

"Hi, Garrett."

"How are you? Are you doing well?"

"Yes, it's been wonderful. I've done some sightseeing and relaxed."

"You're okay? No problems?"

"I'm perfectly fine. I'm leaving to meet the Morettis in a few minutes."

"All right," he said. "I just needed to hear your voice."

"I'm fine."

Tension was still present, and Mary thought it was best to keep the conversation brief. Evidently Garrett did, too.

"Okay, I'll let you go," he said.

"See you on Tuesday."

"I miss you."

She heard the line click. He didn't wait for her to reply.

As she handed the phone to Rossana, she felt her eyes get misty, so she went to the bathroom to wipe them with a tissue. Living such a fantasy with Luca she had begun to ignore the pain that would come with breaking up with Garrett. She took a deep breath and decided to mentally put him in a little box, like the ring, and tuck him away in the deep recesses of her mind. She owed him an explanation and the truth, but it wouldn't happen for a few days.

Luca didn't ask questions when she returned to the kitchen. He wrapped his arms around her.

This comforted her and she chose not to talk to him about Garrett. But she did ask about Rossana.

"Why was she so irritated?"

"She is bitter, like Giovanni."

Chapter 58

THEY MADE THE SCENIC DRIVE to Greve in Chianti on the Chianti highway in Luca's small black Fiat, or at least she thought it was black. It was hard to tell with the thick layer of dust covering it. And the inside was just as messy - clothes, a gym bag and a soccer ball were strewn across the back seat.

"You'll find some of your clothes in that bag," he said.

His face blushed a bit.

She unzipped it and found her bra and panties from the day in Florence. As she stuffed them in her backpack, they both laughed.

"Did you think I was crazy that day?" he asked.

"Crazy, yes. Hot, yes."

He smiled.

"So you play soccer?" she asked.

"No, but I play football." He laughed. "We don't call it soccer."

"Oh, that's right."

"I'm in a league that plays on Friday nights, but I skipped our game last Friday so I could see you."

"I'd like to see you play."

"You will when you come back," he said and winked.

He easily followed the directions to the home of Mr. Moretti's sister on the east side of town. A curvy road led them up a steep hill, past some apartments and a cemetery, then through vineyards and olive groves. Within a kilometer, they arrived at the entrance to the farm.

They turned off the paved road and drove downhill along a dirt road between two vineyards. The end of each row was accented with a rose bush.

"The roses are pretty," Mary said.

"Yes, but they're not for decoration. Insects and mold attack the roses before the grapes. It helps the people working the vines to know the plants' health."

"Interesting."

As they approached the house, the vineyards changed to olive groves. It was beautiful, and Mary understood why Mr. Moretti missed Tuscany, but she realized she had never asked him why he left. She made a mental note to do so when she got home. Just past the olive groves they arrived at a small gravel driveway lined with lavender. It led to the stucco-covered farmhouse.

Two women hurried outside to greet them.

Mary guessed the two women were Mr. Moretti's sister, Stefania Costa, and her daughter.

"*Buongiorno! Mary?*"

"*Sì,*" Mary said.

The older woman hugged her and kissed both of her cheeks.

"*Sono Stefania. Piacere.*" - "I am Stefania. Pleased to meet you."

"*Piacere,*" Mary said.

"Garrett?" Stefania asked as she looked at Luca.

"*No, non sono Garrett. Sono un amico di Mary e abito in Toscana.*" - "No, I am not Garrett. I am a friend of Mary's, and I live in Tuscany."

"*Un italiano! Piacere!*" Stefania exclaimed.

Luca explained he was simply giving Mary a ride, but Stefania insisted he stay, too. They went back and forth with Luca saying he appreciated her offer but he couldn't stay because he had work to do. But Stefania insisted he must stay. Ultimately he accepted the invitation.

Mary later learned from Luca that he knew he was going to stay from the moment of Stefania's first invitation.

"The back-and-forth dialogue is a typical Italian manner of accepting invitations," he told her on the car ride home. "It usually takes two requests and two denials before a commitment is made, and it happens very quickly, with everyone knowing all along the final answer will be 'yes.'"

To Mary, the interaction was funny, and she was glad he accepted Stefania's offer, because the day was truly special.

After their greetings, they went straight to the kitchen where there were steaming pots, countless plates of food in various stages of preparation and a huge, open fireplace along one end of the room.

Stefania poured Prosecco to welcome Mary and Luca and everyone drank the sweet, sparking wine. It was the beginning of a four-hour feast at the Costa house.

They moved outside to picnic tables set on dry, rocky soil and thin grass. Their yard was surrounded by the serene Chianti hills, and Mary couldn't believe this was their view every day.

Luca helped translate and make introductions to Stefania's two daughters, Chiara and Claudia, her sons-in-law and six grandchildren.

Stefania complained, saying they didn't have traditional Sunday dinners like this as often as they did in years past because her family was too busy. But Mary's visit was an event their mother had ordered the family to attend.

The meal started with large platters of antipasti, and Mary feasted on more varieties of meats and cheeses than she'd ever seen, accompanied by thick, fire-toasted bread drizzled with bright green homemade olive oil.

For their *primi piatti*, or first course, they ate long and short homemade pasta. The long pasta was *pici*, with two different sauces including a Bolognese-type sauce and a wild boar ragu Stefania had started making at six that morning. Mary had two short pasta dishes – penne, tossed with grilled broccoli, tomatoes and a white sauce and *ditalini* with artichokes, ham and olive oil.

Stefania made Mary try them all, and Luca laughed at the expressions Mary made as she tried to eat everything and keep Stefania from fussing at her for eating too little.

Feeling ready to burst, Mary was surprised to see the *secondi piatti*, a second course of grilled meats. Stefania served fresh-grilled pork ribs and sausage roasted outside over the open fire. Mary took small pieces and played with her food. It was delicious, but she had no room in her stomach, and Luca occasionally took some bites to save her. Just when she thought she'd survived the feast, Stefania served grilled zucchini and green salad, and Mary ate as much as she could.

Throughout the meal, the homemade Chianti complemented everything. Luca stayed near her side the entire day and translated for everyone. Mary told them all about Mr. Moretti's market and how often she visited him.

Stefania asked if Giovanni was a good son, and Mary said that he was, but he needed to work more hours in the market. Stefania replied that she needed time with Giovanni to straighten him out. It was clear Stefania ruled her own family with an iron fist.

She looked at her offspring and said, "No lazy kids here."

The Costa family talked about the lack of rain and how dry everything was. Now that Mary had explored the vineyards and rural areas, she understood how intensely the weather influenced their livelihood.

More than anything, though, the lunch discussions revolved around the food they were eating, its origins and how it was prepared. Stefania reminded her daughters never to change the family recipes and always to cook with the freshest ingredients.

When Chiara told her mama that she sometimes bought frozen vegetables when she had no time to cook after working all day, Mary thought Stefania was going to have a heart attack and die at the table. With Stefania's dramatic reaction, Mary dared not mention all the Lean Cuisine meals she'd eaten in her life.

They finished the feast with fresh fruit and firm cakes dipped in *vin santo*, a sweet wine. Finally, they all drank a shot of grappa to help their digestion.

Mary loved their passion and hearty enjoyment of the meal and the company, and she loved being by Luca's side. He flirted with Stefania, making her act like a young schoolgirl, and he played with the kids, too.

Mary took plenty of pictures for Mr. Moretti, and when it was time to say goodbye, Stefania gave her bottles of their homemade olive oil and Chianti as gifts for Mr. Moretti. Stefania told Mary she was worried she would never see her brother again, crying as she handed Mary the bottles.

After the long goodbye was over and they had promised to return, Mary and Luca hopped back in the car. In the heavy city traffic with lots of horn blowing, it took over an hour to get to his apartment. The congested Florentine streets made Mary nervous, but Luca navigated them well.

Chapter 59

LUCA'S THIRD-FLOOR STUDIO apartment was sparsely furnished, like his Florentine office. Its best feature was a small balcony with sliding glass doors and long sheer curtains framing it. The southwestern view faced distant mountains where the sun hung low.

Luca opened the sliding doors to let in fresh air and the city street noises came with it. Mary changed into a pale blue cotton sundress in his tiny bathroom. She already felt herself becoming aroused just knowing she'd be alone with Luca for the night. Their chemistry was intense.

She went from the bathroom to the balcony where Luca was standing with a glass of wine.

The sun's glow highlighted his fit body, and when he turned to look at her, his expression melted. He put down the glass, embraced her and kissed her madly. They stumbled backward into the room and fell onto his bed, their bodies shaking with desire.

"I can't wait another minute," he said.

"I can't either."

They ripped off each other's clothes and made love with the windows open, the light from the setting sun streaming in the room.

"This was the most memorable sunset of my life," he said after he caught his breath.

She looked at Luca's sculpted body with hers next to it. They were a perfect match, physically and emotionally.

Mary thought she could fall in love with him. Then she thought she might have fallen in love with him already.

They talked and laughed in bed before redressing, then went to a local trattoria for wine and antipasti.

Mary couldn't believe she was eating again, but she loved the homemade meats and cheeses served at the eatery.

As they ate and drank, they never stopped looking at each other. They were in their own world, like the passionate couple Mary had seen in the Philadelphia airport before her flight to Rome.

Luca offered suggestions for her day in Venice, and Mary took notes in her journal.

On the way to his apartment, he insisted they stop for gelato. He ordered a small cup of chocolate and she decided not to try anything new. She ordered her favorite - limone - the perfect ending to a perfect day.

They returned to his small apartment where they made slow, sweet love. They fell asleep in each other's arms with the door open and a fresh breeze blowing in, both oblivious to the rest of the world.

Chapter 60

T HE ALARM CLOCK BUZZED at 5 a.m. so Mary could catch the morning train to Venice. While neither of them wanted to be awake so early, they were pleased to wake up lying next to each other. They began the morning quietly, looking into each other's eyes and kissing gently.

"It's already a good day," Luca said.

"I agree."

"Who will be the first to get up?"

"I don't know if I can."

They teased each other a little more before Luca stood up and headed toward his tiny bathroom.

As he walked away, Mary admired his naked body and a chill ran the length of her torso. She absolutely adored him.

He stopped and turned around to catch her looking at him.

"I'm not sure I'm ready to leave you," he said, and he climbed back under the sheet and caressed her body. They kissed and played for several minutes until they were out of time.

"Shower and *il caffè, va bene?*" he asked.

"Definitely."

In thirty minutes, they were dressed and fueled with espresso. He took her to the Santa Maria Novella train station on his motorcycle where she boarded her first train in Europe.

As the Italian countryside flew by, Mary read, wrote and dreamed. It was nice to enjoy the sights without having to drive.

She arrived at the Santa Lucia train station promptly and was ready to see as much as possible in the one-day visit. Her loose plan was to take a taxi along the Grand Canal to St. Mark's and walked the narrow sidewalks back to the station exploring as much as possible. Her short day in Venice turned out to be wonderful and she couldn't wait to tell Luca everything that happened.

At 8:20 p.m. her train arrived in Florence. Luca was waiting for her to go back to the *castello* for her last night in Italy.

"Tell me about Venice," he said once they were settled in his Fiat.

"It was fantastic. I can hardly wait to go there again when I have more time."

"I hope I'm with you next time."

She melted but continued.

"When I got to Venice, I did as you suggested and rode the 'Linea 1' water taxi the length of the Grand Canal to St. Mark's Square. I was lucky to find an open seat in the front of the taxi."

"Was Venice crazy with tourists?"

"Packed, but I can understand why everyone wants to see it. There's no place like it, and it was grander than I imagined. I loved the palaces and grand homes, so I took lots of photos. I would love to see them inside. I picture them filled with heavy silk drapes, big oil paintings, thick tapestries and crystal chandeliers."

He smiled as she described her image of the palaces.

"I love the gothic arches, leaded windows, orderly columns, boat docks and mooring posts. It looks like most need repair, but they were still gorgeous. I read a comment in a book before coming to Italy and someone called it 'elegant decay.' I couldn't describe it better."

"True. An excellent description."

"It was interesting to travel on the water. I never thought about it being the only way to deliver things. I saw one boat full of plumbing supplies and another carrying huge bags of flour and sugar."

"It is an unusual way to live. Locals have to use the water taxis, same as the tourists."

"Those old Chris Craft private taxis look like they should be carrying glamorous movie stars. Oh, and I finally saw the gondolas near St. Mark's Square. Some tourists were riding them on the

Grand Canal, but it looked like a choppy ride. Riding them on the small, quiet side rivers looked better to me."

"Believe it or not, I've never been on a gondola," Luca said. "Someday, I'll have to. And what did you think of San Marco?"

"There were tons of tourists, but I tuned out the people and just admired the architecture. It made me think of my father – he was an architect. If he had been there with me, he could have explained all the different styles – Gothic, Renaissance, Baroque."

Mary looked at Luca in the driver's seat. He was smiling and taking in everything she said.

"When I got to St. Mark's Cathedral, the bells were ringing, but it was only 10:50 a.m., so they were chiming out of time. I decided it was Venice was saying 'hello' to me. But the line to tour the cathedral was so long, I didn't go in."

"Next time," he said, winking.

"I went to Caffé Florian on the Square and drank a glass of Prosecco, as you recommended."

"It was very expensive, I'm sure. But it's a time-honored place to sit and enjoy the atmosphere. Were the bands playing?"

"No, but something else interesting happened. A lady was sitting at the table next to me, alone. She started sobbing while I was there."

"What?"

"I was worried, so I asked her if everything was okay. She was an American, and she was clearly relieved to hear me speak English. I asked if she needed help, but she said she doubted I could fix a broken heart."

"Poor lady."

"Her name was Miranda, and she told me she'd recently broken up with her Italian boyfriend. She said she couldn't help but remember dancing on St. Mark's Square with him at midnight less than six months ago. That night, she said, she thought they'd be together forever."

"She is lucky you sat next to her."

"Yes."

Mary decided not to tell Luca the rest of the story because Miranda had strongly advised Mary to stay away from Italian men.

She told Mary she'd lived in Bologna for the past two years with her Italian boyfriend, a professor at the University. Then two weeks ago, she came home to find him in bed with another woman, a young American exchange student. After he betrayed her, everyone told Miranda he was a ladies' man. She immediately moved out of the apartment they had together and shipped her things to California. She was staying her last two nights in Venice before flying to Los Angeles.

Miranda accused all Italian men of being untrustworthy mama's boys and bad news.

Mary continued.

"We talked a little, and then she said she was going to Harry's Bar for a Bellini and invited me to come with her. So I did."

"It sounds like you drank your way through Venice!"

"Almost, but for lunch I only drank water," she said, laughing. "I didn't have time to sit down and eat, so I bought a panini from a bar and ate while sightseeing."

"You ate like an Italian."

Mary smiled, then continued telling Luca about her day in Venice.

"After Harry's Bar, I said goodbye to Miranda."

Mary thought about Miranda's parting words. They were another strong reminder to stay away from Italian men.

"From there, I headed to the Rialto Bridge. It was so crowded, but I bought some millefiori pendants for gifts in a little shop. Then I went over the bridge to the Rialto market as you suggested, but I was too late for the open-air fish display. The produce and flower stands were still open, and now I know why Mr. Moretti always hand picks my produce. Everyone here does it the same way."

"I'm glad you went. It's fascinating to be there in the early morning when the fishermen are bringing in the fresh catch of the day. Maybe I can take you someday."

"After the market I put away my map and explored the narrow streets behind the market, away from the tourists. I loved seeing everyday life in Venice. I took photos of laundry hanging from windows and the colorful flower boxes. I could have taken rolls and rolls of photos. It was so romantic and inspiring. I want to paint some of the things I saw today."

Luca couldn't help but smile at Mary's enthusiasm for Venice.

"Then I went back over the Rialto Bridge and wandered until I found the train station. I didn't have much time, but I saw enough to know that I want to go back. Oh, and I bought a cool vintage necklace, too. Just before I got to the train station, I saw it in the window of a small jewelry shop. I wanted to buy something unique to wear that would remind me of this magical place."

"Good idea," Luca said. "And you must come back and spend more time in Venice. There are so many other fantastic places I want you to see - the Cinque Terre, Fiesole, Talamone and Bellagio, to name a few. You must see them all with me. I promise I will make them very special."

The thought of traveling to romantic Italian cities with Luca caused a familiar wave of heat to rush through Mary's body.

Chapter 61

W HEN THEY GOT BACK TO THE FARMHOUSE, Mary changed clothes for dinner and put on the white dress she wore in Florence and the long silver necklace she bought in Venice. They decided to eat at the same rustic trattoria where they had dined before.

She left the bedroom and climbed the steps the rooftop where Luca was waiting at the table, drinking Chianti with the table lantern lit. She sat next to him as he poured wine for her.

"*Salute!*" he said.

He smiled and gazed deeply into her eyes, then his eyes traveled down her body. As soon as he saw the necklace, his expression froze. He inched forward.

"May I?"

"Sure," Mary said.

He took the pendant in his hand.

"This is the necklace I bought in Venice," she said. "It's a pocket watch, but it doesn't work. I like it because it's stuck at 7:11 – my birthday is July 11."

"*Dio mio*," Luca said, shaking his head as he examined it. "This is unbelievable."

"What?"

"How do I explain this?"

He stood up, went to the balcony's edge and looked toward the castle tower.

Mary wasn't sure if he was upset, angry or confused. It was hard to tell.

He turned back to her and ran his fingers through his hair.

"I'm stunned," he said.

She remained silent, waiting for him to speak. He finally did.

"Last summer, I started working on the *castello*. The sky was so clear one day I went to the tower lookout to enjoy the view. San Gimignano was visible, which is rare. While I was standing there, I took off my watch to wind it."

He pointed to the Timex watch on his wrist he wore every day.

"It slipped from my hand and fell through the cracks in the floor, landing at the bottom of the tower. The watch is old - a gift my mother left for me."

Mary listened attentively.

"I went to the lower steps and dismantled some of the staircase to get to the dirt floor. It was pitch black, so I used a flashlight to look for it."

He paused, running his hands through his hair again. He took a big gulp of wine.

"I found the watch and lying next to it -"

He took a deep breath and raised his eyebrows.

"I found the same pocket watch you are wearing."

Mary gasped.

"What?"

"I know it is the same. It was broken and stopped at 7:11."

"What?"

"It seems like it wants to return to the *castello*," he said. "This is quite spooky."

"No kidding! But how did it end up in Venice?"

"I can't say for certain, but I suspect Lia sold it. When we were in Venice in April, the same weekend we broke up, I gave it to her. I told her about finding it in the castle tower, thinking it must have been there for years. I thought it was romantic and probably had an interesting story. I thought she might like to make a necklace of it to remind her of me when we were apart. She laughed when I gave it to her, and said it would clash with her Gucci. I should have known she wouldn't like it, because she only wore status items."

"This is definitely a sentimental piece, not something of significant value," Mary said. "That's what appealed to me."

"Where was the jewelry store again?" he asked.

"Near the train station."

"I bet she sold it on her way out of town. She was furious with me. I'm sure that is what happened."

"What are the chances I would buy it?"

He took the pendant in his hands and studied it again.

"Yes, it is the same, except the chain is new. I gave it to the wrong person," he said. "It was meant for you."

He sat down again.

Mary felt like it was a sign - an otherworldly force at work. It had to be. While she pondered its meaning, Luca kept shaking his head.

They sat quietly, and every now and then he would shake his head or run his fingers through his hair. He finally suggested they head to the trattoria.

Mary ate *pici* again for dinner, but this time it was with a cheese and pepper sauce, *cacio e pepe*. She enjoyed the thick hand-rolled noodles, but they were in a daze throughout the meal. Whether it was fate or coincidence, the pocket watch cast a new dimension on their bond. After they talked some more about the watch, Mary told Luca that she had originally planned to stay at Cielo and was only staying at Ribelli because of some broken plumbing.

He laughed in disbelief.

"See, my dear, we were meant to be together," he said. "And now I want to take you back to the castle so we can sleep under the night sky."

"Of course," she said.

Chapter 62

THEY LAID OUT THE BLANKETS and quickly undressed, except Mary kept the special necklace on. The locusts chirped, the air was warm and the night sky was filled with stars. They didn't want to fall asleep because they wanted to spend as many waking minutes as possible together. Their lovemaking was free and passionate and just before they fell asleep, Luca held Mary and looked at her intensely.

"Promise you'll come back here, like the pocket watch came back. You're meant to be here."

"I want to," she said.

"Wherever I have a home, you have a home. Come back and be with me."

Mary was comforted to hear him say this. It validated he wanted to be with her. She had wondered if the whole experience was a fleeting dream or her vivid imagination at work. Now it was clear to her it wasn't.

"Let me take care of my situation at home, and then we'll talk."

"I understand," he said. "When you are ready, do you want me to come to Philadelphia? I could only stay about a week, but I would like to see your home and know everything about your life there."

"I would like that," she said and nestled into his body, easily relaxing.

Soon, they were both asleep under the stars.

Chapter 63

As the sun was rising, Mary and Luca woke up and held each other, not speaking a word, as if silence would delay having to say goodbye.

Finally Luca spoke first.

"I know you are leaving today, but you will still be with me. You always have been."

He held her closely, but time marched on, and their busy days needed to start. Luca couldn't stay until she was ready to leave for Rome because he had an early meeting at the factory.

They went back to Mary's apartment, cleaning up, holding each other, kissing and holding each other some more. When it was time to say goodbye, they promised to stay in touch.

"We will always be together," he said holding her hand to his chest as they stood outside by his car. "Time and distance will not separate us."

Then he climbed into his Fiat and drove off.

She blinked away tears and went back into the apartment. She looked around, not wanting to leave. But it was time. She finished packing, making sure not to forget the engagement ring hidden in the armoire. She reached in the corner where she hid it, and as her fingers searched for the box, she found something else next to it. It felt like a book.

She pulled it out along with the ring box and gently flipped through the delicate yellowed pages of the small leather book. Some entries were dated 1963, and she knew a few of the Italian words used - *papa, Americano, amore, gallerie di Uffizi*. It looked like it was a diary. She looked inside the front and back covers for a name but couldn't find one. She couldn't read most of the handwritten Italian, but a feeling came over her that she was destined to find the diary. She flipped through the diary again, landing on a page with a detailed freehand drawing of the pocket watch she purchased in Venice. She compared the drawing to the necklace she was wearing, and it was undeniably the same. The drawing was finely detailed, and her mind raced to determine how the pocket watch and diary could be related. She remembered Luca saying that some of the furniture in the farmhouse used to be in the *castello*.

The diary hadn't been touched in nearly forty years. But she realized reading it might help reveal the mystery behind the pocket watch. She decided to take it home and have Mr. Moretti translate it, knowing she would return it to Luca. She wouldn't have the opportunity to tell him about the diary until after she was home, but she was sure he wouldn't mind if she took it for a little while. Mary couldn't wait to know the secrets the diary might reveal.

She reluctantly opened the ring box to see the diamond again. She ran her finger over the stone and began to think about how nervous she was about her upcoming encounter with Garrett. She closed the box and put it in the backpack.

After she zipped her suitcase, she inspected the apartment to make sure she hadn't forgotten to pack anything. Then she made a final stop at the bedroom window for one last look at the view outside. It was going to be another gorgeous day, but it was time to say goodbye to the familiar vineyards, olive groves and forest. She gazed at the castle tower and remembered the first magical day with Luca. She had fallen in love with Tuscany and with him, too. She couldn't stop her feelings even if she wanted to.

Reluctantly, she carried her bags downstairs.

Chapter 64

As she stepped outside, she heard a familiar voice.

"Hello, Mary. How are you today?" Patrick asked.

He was sitting at the table, drinking coffee from a large mug and smoking a cigarette. Gigio and Brontolo were with him, and the dogs got up and pranced around her.

"You must have brought your mug from home," she said, making small talk.

"Yes. Damn Italians only drink it one fucking shot at a time, but I need to drink a few mugs like this to wake up every day. Believe it or not, I pack my own coffeemaker every time I visit."

"I drink big mugs at home, too, but I've really enjoyed the Italian's *caffè*. I bought a stovetop coffee maker while I was here so I can make espresso at home, but I'll probably only do it on the weekends."

He raised his eyebrows as if to say, "Whatever makes you happy."

"You missed the Fishers," he said. "They're heading back to the U.S. today, too. Said they're flying to Philadelphia and this is their last trip, but I'm sure someday that wacky lady will tell her son the truth, and he'll want to come back to have it out with his father."

"What?" Mary asked, half-listening.

She knew Patrick was a busybody, and she didn't have the time for him today. Mary put her suitcase in the back of her rental car. She was ready to leave.

"The Fishers. Angela and Alex. You met them, didn't you?"

"Briefly."

"Luca didn't tell you about them? You've spent so much time with him. I was sure he'd tell you about their relationship."

His snooping annoyed Mary, but her antennae went up.

"Tell me what?"

"Unbelievable! You'd think he'd learn from his mistakes. These Italian men are so fucking arrogant sometimes. So handsome Luca took advantage of another American lady?"

He let out a hearty chuckle with a "tsk-tsk" then a sigh.

"It figures," he said.

"Take advantage of me?"

"He has a reputation. If you find out you're pregnant, don't expect him to marry you."

"Excuse me," she said abruptly.

Her personal life was none of his business.

"Didn't you notice how much the Fisher boy looks like him? Mary, he is Luca's son. You didn't see the resemblance? Maybe the blond hair confused you. Luca never married the boy's mom. Got her pregnant one summer and now the only time Luca sees his son is when they come here. I've watched that lad grow up summer after summer. He hates coming. He thinks it's boring, and the only thing he likes here is the spaghetti," Patrick laughed. "He would rather be back in Jersey at the Shore with his friends."

Mary's face turned red, fueled by anger and embarrassment.

"You're sure of this?" she asked.

She hadn't considered it until now, but there were physical similarities between Luca and Alex.

"Yes. Luca sends them money, but he doesn't want a relationship. He's pompous, if you ask me. I can't imagine he'd be good for anyone, but he sure has a penchant for American women. You know, you're not the only woman who received one of those brown suede jackets from him."

"Well, it's time for me to hit the road," she said, not admitting anything.

She shook his hand to be polite and maintain her composure.

"Goodbye, Patrick. Enjoy the rest of your trip."

Chapter 65

SHE STUFFED THE BACKPACK into the passenger seat while Patrick watched, then took off. When she was a safe distance from the apartment, the stream of tears she'd been holding back rushed down her face. She was in shock. Her mind reeled.

She wrapped her hand around the necklace and held the pocket watch.

Mary had thought she and Luca were soul mates, brought together by fate. But now she was doubting that, thinking she might have been swayed by romance into overlooking the obvious.

She got to the point in the road where the castle tower was visible, and she stopped to look back at it. She wanted to talk to Luca, but she couldn't reach him. Her cell phone didn't work in Italy, and she didn't what she would say to him anyway.

Mary didn't know how she could tell if Patrick was telling the truth. She wondered if he was just a troublemaking busybody or if he was right about Luca.

She drove on.

Mary thought about how she had shared the skeletons in her closet with Luca and how he had the same opportunity to share his past with her, too. She thought they had been honest with each other. Mary began to wonder if her ability to make character judgments was seriously flawed.

She remembered the unsolicited advice from Rae Lynn on the plane and Miranda in Venice. Mary realized they had warned her, but she had chosen not to listen.

She tried to sort through every moment with Luca in an attempt to arrive at the truth.

She thought about Luca showing up often at the *agriturismo*. Maybe he was trying to find visitors for quick dates. Or maybe he still had a relationship with Angela.

She wondered how often these trysts happened. He could provide leather jackets for them all. He could have a new woman with every weekly rental cycle.

But Mary thought their connection was something special. He said he'd been waiting for her. He admitted he tried to deny the feeling that they were lost soul mates, but ultimately he said he recognized they were real. And he asked her to come back to Italy.

She looked at the pocket watch again. It was hard to believe there wasn't some type of unseen energy at work.

If Alex is 15, then Luca was only 17 when he became a father. He said he spent the summers in New Jersey. It must have happened there.

She played out all the possible scenarios, wanting to give Luca the benefit of the doubt, but that was difficult. Their relationship lasted less than a week.

Mary knew she loved the excitement of meeting someone new, and she was having a hard time breaking her habit of falling hard for men like this. Her romantic notions always overrode any logical thoughts.

But Luca seemed different. Their experience was so real, so intimate. Then she realized she had thought the same exact thing about other men.

In the three-hour drive to the airport, she denied Luca's play-boy nature, then rationalized it. Eventually she got angry, but her anger wasn't directed at Luca. It was directed at herself.

Mary debated if there might be something wrong with her. She wondered why she couldn't be happy with the handsome, successful man who had brought her to Italy. She questioned why she needed more than that – why she needed a soul mate and romance and sex in a castle. Why she needed international adventure and passion. And why she hadn't just gone to the movies or read a romance novel instead.

Mary's drive from Siena to Rome was miserable, just like the last one, but it was miserable for different reasons.

By the time she arrived in Rome after a final stop at an Auto-Grill for gas, coffee, a brioche and some Perugina candy, she'd convinced herself the time with Luca might be a secret she would have to keep forever, except from Stella. With the newly discovered but unconfirmed knowledge of his Casanova style, it was unlikely she would ever see or hear from him again. And if she did, she would have to be the smart one and let it go. A long-distance relationship with a guy in Italy was an absurd idea.

Mary decided Luca and Garrett had to go. It was time for a clean slate. Maybe a new city and new job.

Back at the Ribelli, Patrick found Giovanni and asked when Luca was coming back. Giovanni told him he'd be back in the evening to help with some building repairs. Patrick knew it was a fact that Alex was Luca's son, but he exaggerated about the suede jackets. The only other lady he'd seen wearing a similar jacket was Luca's ex-fiancée, and everyone who met Lia agreed she was a money-seeking bitch. Patrick was happy when Luca kicked her to the curb, too.

Patrick could hardly wait to see Luca's reaction when he shared the news of his departing conversation with Mary.

Sometime during Mary's eight-hour flight home, the phone in her apartment rang until the answering machine picked up the call.

"Mary, my sweet Mary, how I miss you already. Please call me when you arrive at home. I want to be together again. Soon. *Ciao, bella.*"

PHILADELPHIA

IN THE PHILADELPHIA AIRPORT, the Fishers were at baggage claim. They had been on Mary's flight, but it was the first time she'd seen them. She spied on Alex from across the baggage carousel. He looked identical to his father, with the same physique, skin color and blue eyes. The only difference was that his hair was dark blond, unlike either of his biological parents.

She shook her head in disgust with herself and her blindness.

Mary hopped in a taxi, relieved to be off the plane and out of the airport. The flight felt longer than eight hours, because it was uncomfortable and crowded. Every seat was occupied, and she restlessly waited in her confined space to be home. She needed to fix her mess and it was impossible from an airplane, leaving her feeling more like a prisoner than a passenger.

Her first call was to Garrett's cell phone. There was no response, so she called his office number. The receptionist answered and said he was traveling and would be back the following day.

Mary wondered why he would be traveling when he knew she was coming home today.

She wanted to throw her phone out the car window, but it rang almost immediately after she hung up.

"Sorry I missed you," Garrett said. "I'm in L.A. I rushed out here yesterday morning."

Mary didn't say a word.

"But I'm so glad you're home safely, and I want to see you."

She swallowed hard.

"When will that be?" she asked.

She needed to know how much time she would have to prepare to break up with him.

"Tomorrow night."

He muted his voice into a whisper.

"You'll never believe what's happening here. I can't talk now, but there's a huge scandal. I'll tell you everything tomorrow night."

She was surprised by his comment.

"A scandal? What's –"

He interrupted, still whispering.

"I'll tell you tomorrow. We have so much more to talk about, too. I've missed you."

His voice loudened.

"See you tomorrow around seven."

With that announcement, he hung up abruptly.

She made her second call to Stella, inviting her to come over later that night.

When Mary got to her apartment, the first thing she did was unpack her bags to find Stefania's gifts of olive oil and Chianti for Mr. Moretti. She hurried to visit him.

"*Buongiorno, signore!*"

"You are kissed by the Italian sun, and you make-a my day brighter."

Mr. Moretti hugged her.

"Italy was wonderful. It's so beautiful. And this is from your lovely sister."

He was thrilled to have the family olive oil and wine, but she told him she didn't have much time to stay and tell him about her trip. She promised to come back the following afternoon with stories and photos.

"Are you okay?" Mr. Moretti asked. "You have sadness in your eyes."

"I'm not, but I'll tell you more tomorrow afternoon when I come back with the photos. I promise."

"I worry about you. Here, take this. *Il vino allontana la malinconia.* Wine makes the melancholy go away."

He handed her a bottle of Villa Antinori Chianti.

Chapter 67

"WHAT HAPPENED?" asked Stella as soon as she walked into Mary's apartment.

She came bearing a bottle of tequila, a bag of tortilla chips and a jar of hot salsa, precisely as Mary requested.

"Pour a couple shots, and I'll start at the beginning."

Mary's eyes were puffy from crying.

Stella followed orders and poured out the tequila while they were still in the kitchen. They held up their shot glasses to toast.

Mary didn't smile as she toasted, "To Stella and to tequila – thank God for these two loyal friends."

They tossed back the shots then moved to the sofa in the living room, the tequila and shot glasses only an arm's reach away on the coffee table.

"You're never going to believe this," Mary said. "And I know you'll never tell anyone, so here goes."

"Wait a minute, let me see that."

Stella pointed at the pocket watch around Mary's neck.

"This is part of the craziness, but here, take a look."

Stella quickly analyzed it.

"It looks like it's from the early 1920s. I like it, but it feels too light, like all the mechanics have been removed."

"It's definitely broken, and the time is stuck on the numbers of my birthday."

She opened the case to show Stella.

"I bought it in Venice the day before I flew home, but let me start at the beginning. I'll get to the watch, and you won't believe where it's been."

Intrigued, Stella listened as Mary started her tale with Garrett's frenzy to keep working in Italy.

"That's crazy," Stella said. "What a waste."

"No kidding. And when he decided to come home early, I told him I was staying."

"He left?"

"Yes, but not without giving me this."

She pulled the ring box from her purse and opened the box.

"That's stunning! It looks like a really expensive diamond."

Mary explained the scene at the airport, and Stella shook her head.

"What a good situation gone bad."

"It crazier than that," Mary said. "I think I need another shot before I go on."

Stella refilled the shot glass.

"This is better than a movie. I can't wait to hear what happens next."

Mary laughed for the first time that evening, then raised her shot glass.

"To keeping secrets," Mary said.

She poured it down her throat and told Stella about her near miss with Roberto.

"Holy shit, Mary! Now I think I need another shot. To hot Italian men!" Stella said as she guzzled her own shot.

Mary couldn't help giggling.

"Roberto was a cutie, but thank goodness I didn't sleep with him. And now the real story begins."

Stella raised her eyebrows.

Mary took a deep breath and began confessing the events with Luca, starting with their first meeting at the farmhouse. Then she told Stella about the second time they saw each other when he passed her on his motorcycle and the castle tour he took her on.

"Listen to this," Mary said.

Mary replayed Luca's message on her answering machine.

"Wait a minute," Stella said. "Are you making this up? He sounds like a dream. Why didn't you tell him you have a single friend at home?"

"It would have made my life simpler if I had. And what I've told you is just the beginning."

About thirty minutes later, Mary had told Stella the rest of the story.

"So now you know it all, and you're the only person who will ever know it all."

Stella didn't say a word. She grabbed the tequila and poured out another shot for each of them.

"To Luca! What a guy!" Stella said.

They downed the shots.

"I know. He was incredible, but now what?" Mary asked.

"Now you need to let me see the tailored leather jacket. That's what."

Stella had intentionally downplayed the drama to make her clearly overwhelmed friend laugh, and it worked. Mary went to her bedroom and came out wearing the custom-fitted jacket.

"It's perfect! What great styling, and it fits you like a glove."

"Smell it."

Stella inhaled.

"Mmmmmm."

"I love it, too. But seriously, what am I supposed to do about Luca?"

"It doesn't matter, Mary. You got a great leather jacket, a great pocket watch story, and it was the experience of a lifetime. I'm just sorry to hear you peaked so young!"

They both chuckled again.

"You took photos, didn't you?"

"Yes, I dropped off the rolls tonight, and I'll pick them up after work tomorrow."

"Damn, I want to see this guy."

Mary pulled her knees into her chest.

"He's hot, and he's so passionate, but I'm sure I made a mistake getting involved with him."

"Because he has an illegitimate child?"

"No, that's not the main issue, but that's definitely upsetting. I have no idea what the real story is there. I just can't believe I fell so hard for someone I hardly know and right on the heels of Garrett leaving. I'm such a pathetic romantic, and I keep making the same mistakes over and over."

Mary rocked her body on the sofa with her arms tightly wrapped around her knees.

"Mary, you're being hard on yourself, but I would probably do the same. Remember you're deep in the middle of this, not to mention full of tequila. It's hard to have clarity at a time like this."

"The emotions with Luca were so intense, and because I've felt them, I don't ever want to feel anything less than that again. Ever. I loved it. I really thought I'd found my soul mate."

"Maybe you did," Stella said. "The best advice I can give is that you don't have to make any decisions yet because you don't have enough information to do so."

"But I've hurt Garrett and caught Luca in my reckless behavior."

Mary buried her head between her knees.

"I have to break up with Garrett. I've lied to him, I've cheated on him, and I don't deserve him."

"What is that Shakespeare line? 'One that loved not wisely but too well?' That's you. Well, you and me."

Mary nodded, and her best friend continued offering advice.

"It was a great experience, the stuff movies are made of, and you learned some valuable lessons about yourself. Now you're going to have to let it play out. You can't solve it from this sofa right now. You're going to have to see Garrett and hear his story about why he made such a dramatic decision to go home. There may be more to it than you realized. And at a minimum, you can be thankful for Luca. He gave you an unbelievable life experience. It may not feel like it right now, but you'll move on. You will live through this with or without Luca and with or without Garrett."

"I'm sure you're right, but it's so hard. I'm analyzing everything and pressuring myself to decide. I guess if Garrett is 'the one,' he'll give me time to decide. If Luca is 'the one' and not a phony

Prince-Charming-on-a-motorcycle, he'll do the same. But I have to make a decision at some point. That's what I'm dreading."

Stella smiled, obviously hurting for Mary and wanting her best friend to have all the happiness in the world. So she did the only fitting thing, she poured out two more shots of tequila.

"Mary, I know you're struggling, but let's look at the bright side. You had more sex in Italy than I've had in the last year!"

Chapter 68

MARY PICKED UP THE PHOTOS, sat down on a park bench and slowly went through them separating the duplicates for Mr. Moretti. She studied the images of Luca and still felt the same about him. The attraction was bigger than life, and she was more confused than ever.

When she arrived at the market, there weren't any customers in the store. Mr. Moretti motioned her toward the bar stools behind the cash register.

"Sit down here beside me," he said. "I want to know everything about Italia."

"Mr. Moretti, it was incredible, better than I could have imagined. Your family treated me like I was family, too."

He beamed.

"Of course they did. That's how we are."

"Here."

She handed him a stack of photos.

"*Dio mio!* Look at Stefania! She looks so much like our mother now. Her grandchildren are so big."

"The kids were so sweet. I took peppermint sticks to them, and they loved them."

He kept flipping through the photos, smiling while his eyes welled up with tears.

"I miss them so much-a. I wish I could go home. If Giovanni would take care of this market, I could go somewhere."

She flashed back to the Florentine trattoria and the three generations of workers in the restaurant, better understanding Mr. Moretti's expectation of his son. Luca's father was no different with him either.

"They would love to see you. They asked non-stop questions, and the grandchildren want to come to the United States."

"Mary, who is this man?"

He pointed at Luca.

"A friend I met."

She blushed as she said it.

"Mary, he never looks at the camera. He looks at you always. And he has love in his eyes. I can see it. Who is he?

"His name is Luca, and he is the brother of the *agriturismo* owner. We met by accident. After Garrett came home early, I spent a lot of time with Luca."

"What? Garrett came home early?"

"Oh, I haven't told you yet. Garrett came back to Philadelphia after three days in Italy because of a problem at work. I was so angry when he left, but apparently the problem at work is more serious than I understood."

She stopped for a moment, wondering what Garrett would tell her later that night.

"Regardless, I was furious and refused to come home because I loved Italy so much. It felt like home."

"I understand and I would want to stay, too. Tell me more about Luca."

Mary shared how she met Luca and where he lived.

"I like-a this guy already."

She told him about the day in Florence at his leather store, but not every detail.

"His store? He owns the store?"

"Yes, it's his father's business. He will inherit the factory and the store someday."

"Luca is a worker," Mr. Moretti said, nodding his head approvingly.

"Yes, he is. He's wonderful, but I was angry with Garrett, and I probably behaved selfishly. I don't want to tell Garrett about all the time I spent with Luca. I've made a mess of my life."

"Mary, it is okay. You will figure this out, like I did."

His eyes twinkled as he said this.

"What do you mean?"

"You do not-a know the story about my wife, Regina, but I think I should tell you now. I met my Regina about four weeks before she was supposed to marry another man. Her family liked him, but she was not in love.

"In a new job, I was deliverin' groceries. A store in her hometown was on my route and she worked there in the afternoons. When we met, I couldn't stop lookin' at her. She was so beautiful and made my heart beat so fast. I fell in love the first time our eyes met, and so did she. We were meant for each other."

Mary remembered the first encounter with Luca. It felt like Mr. Moretti described.

"I arranged to make every delivery to her store. Three days before the wedding I begged her not to marry the other man, and she finally cancelled her wedding plans. Her family was-a furious with us, but we married anyway and loved each other every minute. I still feel the same love for her today."

"I didn't know that story. You were so lucky to find each other and to have such a happy life."

"It eez-a happy story now, but at the time it was difficult for everyone. She cried. Her family cried. Everyone cried. But it worked out."

He showed great pride in his decision.

"So why did you come to the U.S.?"

"She is the reason. She wanted to be near her sister who moved here after she married an American soldier. I would do anything for Regina, and I left my *famiglia* for her. I don't regret it."

His expression became serious, and he spoke next like a father.

"Listen, Mary. I know I introduced you to Garrett, and I think he is a decent man, but I rarely see you together. I tell you, I worry about you. Listen to me, he needs to put you on a pedestal and treat you like the angel you are. Do not make decisions too quickly."

"You're right. I keep trying to figure out what to do."

She paused for a few minutes, then told him about Garrett's proposal.

"Well, usually I would say congratulations, but I don't know what to say. You are not-a wearing the ring."

"No, I haven't answered him yet. The proposal was so awkward. We were at the airport when he was leaving. He was angry, and it wasn't as romantic as he planned and -"

She stopped talking, drifting off in thought.

"At the airport?" Mr. Moretti asked, frowning.

"Yeah, at the airport."

"Mary, you were in a special place, in Toscana. It is where I proposed to my Regina. Why didn't he do it there?"

"Well, there were the work problems, and -"

She drifted off again, this time remembering Luca - at the picnic, at the *castello*, sleeping in the courtyard.

"I am worried. It seems Garrett always has work problems. It is important to work hard, but not to sacrifice time with loved ones."

Mr. Moretti pulled a bottle of Grappa from beneath the counter and poured some into two small glasses.

"Here, my dear. We need a drink. *Salute.*"

He said more in Italian that she couldn't understand, and they emptied their glasses.

"You are thinkin' too much," he said. "Listen to your heart to find the answer."

They sat in silence before he went back to the photos and asked more questions about his sister. Looking at every photo carefully, he noticed changes to the house and landscape.

He said repeatedly, "My Italia is so beautiful."

"Yes, it is, and all these photos are yours to keep."

"Thank you, Mary. You are like my own daughter."

He kissed her on the forehead.

"You're welcome."

She felt like she needed to be alone. She grabbed a box of pasta, a jar of tomato sauce, two bottles of Chianti and a loaf of bread.

Mr. Moretti told her she didn't have to pay anything since she gave him all the photos of his family.

"Thank you."

"Here is a new basil plant, too," he said. "I am sure you need some. Take it with you."

With one foot out the door, she remembered the diary. She couldn't believe she'd nearly forgotten to mention it.

"Mr. Moretti, there's one more thing."

She put her bag of groceries on the counter and reached in her purse.

"This is something I found in Italy. It looks like a diary."

He scanned the first page.

"Yes, you're right."

"I'm really curious to know what it says. Do you have time to read and translate it?"

"For you, of course."

"Thank you. I'll be back soon. Do you need me to bring anything to you?"

Mr. Moretti and his wife didn't drive, and she knew Giovanni was unreliable for help.

"No, *grazie*. You have done enough."

Chapter 69

MARY PUT THE GROCERIES in the kitchen and saw her answering machine flashing again. The message was from Italy.

"Mary, my sweet Mary, I need to talk to you. I'm so sorry you heard about Alex from Mr. Sullivan. That bastard took great pleasure in telling me how surprised and upset you were, and I believe he liked watching your pain. I know you are confused. You should be. Please call me, and I will tell you the story. I have nothing to hide from you. I never found the right time to bring it up. I told you I want to share everything with you. Please call me when you arrive home. Please. It hurts me to know you are hurting. *Ciao, bella.*"

Hearing his voice, Mary started to cry, but she couldn't bring herself to return his call. She didn't know what to say yet.

She put away the groceries and watered the basil. She paused to smell it before she put it on the kitchen table. The aroma was so alluring, and it transported her back to the day with Luca at Castello di Vincenzo.

She opened a Chianti bottle and poured some into a glass. As she drank it, she listened to Luca's message again. She grabbed the journal she had carried in Italy and sat at the kitchen table with the basil. She broke off a small leaf and put it to her nose. The scent awakened her sensual emotions, and she closed her eyes to fully take in the aroma, trying to find words to describe it.

Sun-worshipper, plush and green, tantalizing aroma asking for attention. Earthy, ancient and perfected by time, shared by generations, by kings and peasants. Scathe me and I become richer. Squeeze me, crush me, tear me, boil me, simmer me and I become more to you. I lure you in, then I become you.

She closed her eyes again and imagined a rustic forest, smelling the scent of basil and the earth.

Smells like making love on a thick blanket under a moonlit sky, the smell of the earth and damp air while ancient music plays, warming my soul...

She finished her first glass of wine. The taste of it made her yearn to return to Chianti. She looked at all her photos again and then decided to look at her large sketchbook.

After several minutes of looking around her apartment, she realized where it might be. The last place she'd seen it was on the rooftop table at the Ribelli, so it was now most likely in a trash can. Rossana wouldn't save it.

She fantasized about going to the airport, taking the next flight to Rome, driving to Tuscany, getting her sketchbook and seeing Luca. But she wouldn't or couldn't. It was gone and so was he. Probably. Already the memories of him were becoming cloudy.

While in Chianti, she had decided to end her relationship with Garrett and continue to get to know Luca, but now that Mary was home, she was filled with uncertainty. She met Luca when she was highly emotional, and she thought she probably imagined that their relationship was more meaningful than it really was.

Now it was time to be honest with herself, and she still thought she needed to take a break from dating.

Her phone rang and she answered, in spite of the caller ID showing it was her sister.

"Hey, Mary!"

"Hi, Catherine."

Like always, Mary wasn't in the mood to talk to her sister. But she especially wasn't in the mood now.

"You're home! When am I going to see you?"

"Will you be at mom's house this weekend?"

"Yes, you know we never miss Sunday brunch with her. It's you who's rarely there."

Thanks for the dig, Mary thought.

"I'll be there," Mary said. "Mom wants to hear about Italy and see the photos I took."

"Me, too," Catherine said. "And Peter and your adorable niece will be there. She wants to see her favorite aunt."

"I'm her only aunt."

"But she may not be your only niece. Guess what? I'm pregnant again! Twelve weeks."

"Catherine, that's wonderful! Why didn't you tell me sooner?"

"I was nervous, like it might upset you, because, well –"

Another dig.

"How silly of you, Cat. You know I'm happy for you. Are you going to find out if it's a boy or a girl?"

"Nope, we want to be surprised. So do you have big news for me?"

Mary knew this was coming.

"No news. I'm not engaged."

"Oh, Mary. You must be so upset."

"No, I'm fine. There's more to the story, but I'm not in the mood to talk about it right now."

"Mary, I'm your sister. You can always talk to me."

Yeah, right, Mary thought.

"Let's wait until Sunday."

She knew this would drive Catherine crazy, and she selfishly took pleasure in dragging it out.

"Are you sure? Liv is taking a nap, and I have plenty of time to talk."

"Thanks, but I gotta run."

"You're going to make me wait?"

"Yeah. See you Sunday. Tell Liv I love her and I have presents. Maybe I can see her sooner and take her to the park."

"This week is busy, but I appreciate the offer. Let's plan on Sunday. Okay? Bye."

"Ciao," Mary said and hung up.

Then she started sobbing. Catherine was right – Mary wanted to have children. But first she needed a husband.

Chapter 70

WITH CLAMMY HANDS, Mary set the black velvet box on her coffee table minutes before Garrett arrived. He knocked and let himself in, looking as handsome as ever in a tailored suit and starched white shirt with the top two buttons unbuttoned. He kissed her quickly but couldn't hug her because his hands were full.

"Welcome home! I figured you might want a break from the red wine."

He held up a bottle of Ketel One vodka.

"I think a couple drinks might help us get through everything we have to talk about," he said.

He pulled tonic water and limes out of his duffle bag along with the alabaster grapes.

"You owe me for carrying these all the way home from Rome."

He teased her as he set them on the kitchen counter.

"Thank you," she said.

With his arms free, he hugged her tightly.

She felt uncomfortable knowing she would deliver bad news to him soon, and she dreaded the lies she might have to tell. Her face flushed, her heart raced and her stomach churned.

"I've missed you so much and before you say a word, let me tell you how sorry I am about my work conflict," he said tenderly, still holding her.

She backed away. It was hard to look him in the eye, but she did.

"Garrett, what's –"

"Shh. Don't worry, I'll tell you everything. Let's mix some drinks first."

While he mixed the vodka and tonic, she sliced a lime.

With drinks in hand, they moved to her leather sofa and turned to face each other. The ring box was in sight, but neither mentioned it.

"You look so refreshed," he said. "You got some sun, didn't you?"

"Yes. I was outdoors a lot."

"I want to hear all about Italy, but I have to explain and apologize for what happened at work."

"I'm so curious. What's the scandal?"

"Good news first. The Palmer deal closed."

He lifted his glass to toast.

"Cheers."

She clinked his glass.

"You earned the commission, that's great."

"Yes, we made the sale, but that's not the major news."

"What is?"

"Max is gone."

"What?"

"He was fired by the Board of Directors."

"No!"

"He was. There was inappropriate activity with the Palmer deal. I knew there was something wrong with the numbers, and that's why I incessantly scrutinized them."

"You're kidding! What was going on?"

She was surprised he was telling her so much since Garrett usually kept every piece of information about work confidential.

"Max has been receiving kickbacks from some of our customers. And Jake Palmer, the CEO, is suspected of giving him personal money."

"How did you know?"

"The financials weren't right, so when the deal didn't close, I let Tom know my suspicions. He looked at the figures and agreed there was a serious problem. By the time I called him from that payphone in Tuscany, he told me I needed to come back to the office because the news was going to break. It would have been bad to be out of the country and unavailable."

"I'm still in shock. How's Susanne, have you heard?"

"No, I'm keeping a low profile and not asking questions. The good news is Tom's the acting president right now. It might mean a faster opportunity for a vice president position for me, if I continue to report to him."

"That's the bright side. You work so hard. You deserve it."

Now she felt horrible. She had no idea of the scope and seriousness of what was happening at work when he was in Italy. She felt spoiled and selfish. At a time when he truly needed her, she turned her back on him, and she didn't like her behavior at all. She felt like she'd failed a real-world test on morality and ethics.

"Mary, I couldn't talk about it. I'm so sorry to have withheld information from you, but it was sensitive and privileged to the people involved. The attorneys made it explicit that we couldn't say anything, and I held most of the information as the primary liaison for the account."

"What happened to Max?"

She tried to focus on the facts while still berating herself.

"He left the country the day I got back to Philadelphia, telling everyone he and Susanne were going scuba diving in the Cayman Islands."

"That's salt on the wound. You paid more of a price than Max did by giving up your vacation while he drank rum cocktails and worked on his tan."

"I have a feeling we won't see him or his money for a long time, if ever. The Caymans are a haven."

"Who would've guessed?"

"I think it's been going on for years, but he got too greedy with the Palmer deal, and Jake Palmer was smart enough to catch it, or at least that's what he's saying now. I think Palmer knew he was being watched and tried to bail before he was caught, too."

"They know you weren't a part of it, right?"

He got up to refresh his drink.

"Yes, thank God. I'm clean, so there's nothing to find."

When he returned, he sat next to her and put his hand on her leg.

"But none of that is what matters. We need to talk about us."

"You're right, Garrett."

She felt a pain in her stomach.

"You've made a decision?"

"I think I need more time," she said.

She misjudged Garrett. He was committed to her more than she had given him credit for, and he was creating a plan for their future. She needed time to think, and more importantly, she needed to grow up and stop her immature behavior.

"Why do you need more time?"

"Garrett, marriage is an important decision, and I know that too well, having failed once at marriage already. I want to be fair to you, and I want to be fully committed if I say 'yes.' My track record isn't good, and I really want to get this right. I've been in Italy vacationing, and I want to make this decision at home in my everyday world. I want to be practical and realistic about what we have."

She picked up the box from the table and handed it to him.

"Hold onto this, and I'll let you know."

"Mary, I didn't propose the way I wanted to. I was angry and frustrated about work, but I meant every word I said at the airport. When I think of my future, you're always in the picture. Everything I do now, I do for us, and the family we will have. I love you, and I want to marry you."

"Garrett."

She began to cry.

"Just let me have some more time, please."

"I'll wait. I know you're worth it."

She put her head in his lap and he stroked her hair. She couldn't stop crying as she thought about the mess she created.

Chapter 71

THE FOLLOWING DAY Mary returned to work and her normal routine. She had two important phone calls to make.

The first one was to Luca.

She practiced what she would say and decided not to tell him Garrett was still in the picture. She would tell him a long-distance relationship wouldn't be easy.

After dialing, he didn't answer, so she left a quick voicemail. She thanked him for the time together and told him he didn't owe her any explanations about Alex. She assured him he held a special place in her heart. Then she asked him to stop calling.

Saying goodbye to a possible future with Luca was hard, but she couldn't imagine dating someone she barely knew who lived across the Atlantic Ocean.

At lunch, she made her second call. This one was to Garrett.

She invited him to her mom's Sunday brunch, and he accepted, saying he would cancel his plans to run a 10K road race because he preferred to be with her. The compromise surprised and pleased Mary, since he'd never done anything like it before.

At brunch, Mary gave out her gifts, and everyone loved them. She brought photos, too, leaving the ones of Luca at home in a shoebox in her closet. She spoke so passionately of Italy that everyone agreed they wanted to visit, too.

Liv and Mr. Dolittle the beagle stayed by her side every minute, and she dodged her sister's questions about the lack of an engagement by talking about the pregnancy.

She was relieved to leave the brunch unscathed by Catherine, and she was eager to spend some time with Garrett. They went downtown and took a long walk.

As they strolled, Garrett opened up.

"Mary, I love you. What can I do to make our relationship better?"

Taken aback, she seized the opportunity to express her concerns.

"Okay," she said. "I'll give it to you straight."

There was nothing to lose. The marriage decision was pressing, and it was time to get to the heart of the matter.

"I want to feel more important in your life, but it seems like your work and training schedules are your priority."

"You have every right to feel this way."

She was floored. His reply derailed her thought of suggesting things might be over.

"The shake-up at work made me realize how much I've been putting my job before everything else. I need to focus on things that matter most, especially the time we can share."

She didn't comment. She wanted to hear more.

"Will you please give me a chance to show you how much I love you? I want to spend the rest of my life with you."

His sensitivity was refreshing and reality confronted her.

This was home.

Garrett was her boyfriend.

And she was ready for a family.

Suddenly, the visit to Italy seemed so remote. It was as if it happened years ago and was millions of miles away. It felt more like a dream.

"It might take time," she said. "I'm going to quote you now, 'Actions speak louder than words.'"

"You're right. I'll show you."

In the upcoming weeks, a new sensitive and caring Garrett emerged. He worked fewer hours and gave up some training time, too. He planned dates he knew she would enjoy.

A couple times, they took the train to New York City where they visited art museums and went to the theater. He found some local bands and took her to small venues to hear them, and he found trendy restaurants for them to try. Impressed by his effort, she was having a ball with him, and they were spending more time in bed, too.

The doubts she felt steadily waned, and she could imagine a lifetime together. She knew she was confident in her feelings about Garrett when a letter arrived from Luca in August and another in September, and she wouldn't let herself open them. She knew the letters would confuse her, and she needed to give everything to her relationship with Garrett. But she was unable throw them away. So she kept them in her closet, in the shoebox with the photos she had taken of Luca.

Chapter 72

IN MID-OCTOBER, Garrett invited Mary to his parents' house in
Rye, New York. He didn't go often, and this was the first time
he'd asked her to join him. She looked forward to the opportunity
to get to know his family better.

En route, they stopped at her sister's to see Liv and check on
Catherine. She was having another healthy pregnancy, and all the
talk was about the baby on the way. Mary found herself admiring
her sister's pregnancy and all the adorable baby clothes she was
receiving as gifts. It made her feel a strong urge to have a baby,
too, but she didn't express this to anyone, especially Catherine.

When they arrived at the two-story brick house in Rye, it was
dark and didn't look like anyone was home.

"I hope I told them the right weekend," Garrett said.

The front door was locked, so he used his key to unlock it.
When they got inside, he turned off the security system. The
house was cold, as if shut down for the winter.

"This is odd," Mary said.

"It sure is. Let's look around and see if they left us a note."

They found nothing in the foyer, and she looked in the
kitchen, while he headed to the garage.

The refrigerator contained condiments with no fresh food.

"This makes no sense."

"Let's look out back," he said, after he returned to the kitchen.

Mary wasn't sure why he wanted to do this, thinking they
wouldn't find any new information outside, but she followed him
anyway.

When they stepped outside Garrett said, "Come this way. I
want to show you something."

She took his hand, and he walked toward an old oak tree and pointed up.

"Let's go up there," he said.

"What?" Mary asked, laughing. "You think we'll find your parents in that tree house?"

"No, they're in Boca Raton until Christmas. We have the place to ourselves."

Garrett winked.

"What?"

"Yes, I thought I'd surprise you. Follow me."

Up they went into the tree house. Garrett pulled a small flashlight from his pocket and shined it around. The tree house was big enough for about six adults to stand comfortably.

"This is great, Garrett. You never told me about this place."

"You don't know everything about me."

He wrapped his arms around her.

"This is where I was happiest when I was kid. I spent hours here. So I knew it would be the best place to ask you to marry me."

Mary gasped, not expecting this.

On one knee, he took her hands in his.

"Will you marry me? Will you make this the happiest day of my life and say 'yes'?"

Mary's eyes filled with tears.

"Yes, Garrett. Yes, I'll marry you."

He stood up, hugged and kissed her, then pulled the familiar black velvet box from his pocket and opened it. But the ring inside was different. It was a large emerald cut solitaire with sapphire baguettes.

"It's a new ring, for new happy memories," he said.

She loved his thoughtfulness and hugged him tightly after he slipped the ring on her finger. They kissed and held each other before Garrett spoke again.

"Take a look at this," he said.

He opened a hinged door on the tree house roof.

"Look, we can see the sky. This is where I used to study constellations."

"You?" she asked, almost as startled as when he told her he liked Italian films.

"Yeah, I wanted to be an astronaut so I memorized all the constellations."

"I can't believe I didn't know this about you."

Stargazing reminded her of Luca, and she forced herself to dismiss his memory.

"How about some champagne?" he asked.

He climbed down and quickly came back with a bottle, glasses and a few candles. They drank by candlelight then went inside where they spent the night snuggling and making love under thick blankets in a chilly guest room.

During the drive home the next morning, after she called her mom and Catherine to share the news, she and Garrett decided spring would be a great time for a wedding. It was only six months away. He suggested they go back to Italy for their honeymoon, promising this time he'd leave work behind.

"Maybe we should try a new place," she said. "Let's really have a fresh start."

It needs to be somewhere Luca isn't, she thought.

"Don't worry. I'll plan something we'll love."

Chapter 73

MARY STOPPED IN THE MARKET to tell Mr. Moretti her news and buy wine.

"I've never seen you so happy! Congratulations!"

"Thank you. We're not going to wait too long. We'll have the wedding in the spring, and we'll keep it small with our closest friends and family."

"Yes, I agree."

"We're going to have it at Garrett's parents' house, and I want you to be there. Will you be able to come to Rye, New York?"

"Where is Rye?"

"Near the Connecticut border."

"Maybe Giovanni will drive us. Can he come?"

"Of course."

"Okay, we will be there."

She bought two bottles of Chianti and remembered to ask him about the diary. She felt obligated to send it back to Luca. She took it without permission and it belonged to his family.

"Mary, I am sorry. I asked my nephew to translate because you know my English is not so good-a, but he is slow. I know it has been many weeks, but he said his job is busy. I give to you later, okay?"

"Sure. It will be interesting to know what it says about my necklace, but it's not a big deal."

Especially now, she thought.

Mary promised to come back soon and left.

Mr. Moretti looked under the register where he kept his grappa. Next to it was a large white envelope with the diary translation.

Since the store was empty, he talked to himself.

"If she reads the diary, she may want to contact Luca. She seemed so happy and needs to enjoy her wedding plans. The diary will-a confuse her."

He opened the grappa and poured a shot.

"*Dio mio*," he said. "I make a big decision about her destiny by not giving her the translation. My hearts tells me to give it to her, but my head says do not. I hoped I am right."

He drank the grappa and shook his head.

In the upcoming busy weeks, Mary forgot to ask about the diary. Mr. Moretti didn't mention it either.

Chapter 74

ONCE THE ENGAGEMENT was announced and the wedding plans started, time flew. The spring wedding was set for the first Saturday in June, so they had to plan quickly. It wasn't too difficult, especially since they were limiting the guest list to fifty people. Mary wanted to keep it simple and intimate. After all, it was her second wedding.

The ceremony and reception would be under a white tent in the Hansens' backyard, and Stella helped Mary find an exquisite, vintage Versace silk dress. She would wear her mother's pearls, just like her mom and sister had done at their weddings.

She wanted Mr. Moretti to walk her down the aisle, but her mom insisted Mary's uncle do it again, stating it would be a family insult not to ask him. Mary conceded but planned a special dance with Mr. Moretti.

Catherine gave her a handkerchief with blue embroidery – the one Catherine carried with her own bouquet.

Wedding bands were purchased from the same jeweler who kindly exchanged the first ring.

Mary selected a bouquet of loosely gathered pale pink and white roses, accented with long strands of ivy. She ordered the bouquet, corsages and centerpieces from her friend Terri Rue who owned a floral shop.

All the details were coming together, but a few weeks before the wedding it started to get tense. After dinner one night in Garrett's condo, Mary pulled out the La Panetière menus for the rehearsal dinner. She wanted to review the selections with him, since his parents were paying for it.

"Mary, I don't have time to think about it. You make the decision and call my parents. They're not worried about the expense, so choose what you want."

She flashed back to their Italian vacation planning and felt the same irritation with him. She stared at the menus while drinking Ruffino Chianti Classico purchased earlier in the day from Mr. Moretti. In that moment, she realized she and Garrett had fallen back into their old roles.

With major changes at Garrett's company, new responsibilities increased his time at the office. And the more he worked, the more he coped by working out. He even registered for a May triathlon, telling Mary he wanted to be fit for the wedding. So they spent increasingly less time together.

She now realized their dynamics hadn't really changed, but she didn't react as emotionally as she did before. She convinced herself it was wedding stress and not a relationship issue, but she needed to talk about it with Stella. So she went to Garrett's bedroom and called her.

"It's been weeks since we've met for margaritas," Mary said.

"No kidding," Stella said.

"Tomorrow at six? I need to talk."

Chapter 75

THE FOLLOWING EVENING, Mary went straight to the cantina after work. She got there before six, knowing she'd have to wait for Stella to arrive. She ordered a classic margarita and pictured Ian making it for her. She took a couple of sips thinking about how much her life was about to morph from the time when she dated him. She said a silent toast to him.

"Mary?"

It sounded like Ian's voice.

"Ian?"

She peered over her shoulder. It was him. She spun around, almost falling off her barstool.

"You're back?" she asked as he hugged her.

"Only tonight. I'm here with my new band."

Her palms got clammy and her heart raced.

"I hoped I'd see you," Ian said.

"Where do you live now?"

There were so many questions she wanted to ask him.

"No place really. The band formed in Austin, but now we live in our van and in cheap hotels while we tour. Last night, we played in Baltimore, and we're heading to New York City tomorrow. We stopped in for a few drinks after I told the guys I used to work here and that the place has great margaritas."

"What fun," she said.

She wondered why he didn't try to call her, but at the same time, she wasn't surprised.

"How've you been?" he asked.

"Busy, getting ready for my wedding in a few weeks."

"Who's the lucky guy?"

She blushed and told him. The whole time she described Garrett, she realized how surprised she was to be telling Ian she was marrying a pragmatic, conservative investment manager. She was doing everything she'd told Ian she never wanted. She was settling and getting comfortable. But Ian was polite and didn't challenge her decisions at all.

Stella was later than expected, so Ian bought her a second margarita and they kept talking. She made sure to tell him about visiting the Uffizi Gallery.

"I still love your Titian eyes," he said.

His comment warmed her heart the same way it had the first time.

"That song is always the girls' favorite ballad at our shows. When we're famous, you can tell everyone it's about you."

She smiled, but crying would have felt better.

They chatted a little longer before he left with his band buddies. He didn't offer to stay in contact, which was a wise idea, and she couldn't stop thinking about this smack in the face. Seein him reminded her of the intimate, soulful connection she'd always dreamed of having with a man. The kind of connection that wasn't likely with her future spouse.

"The timing is crazy," Stella said when she heard about who Mary had just seen.

"I know. I can't believe it. Do you think it's a sign?"

"I don't know, Mary. Are you looking for a sign?"

"I don't think so, but I can't believe the timing either. It's so weird."

Mary faded off.

"It's like I'm being challenged about my decision to marry Garrett."

Stella started to ask questions, but now Mary didn't feel like talking, so she shrugged them off. She was too emotional and knew she'd get more confused. She needed to leave things alone and let the wedding happen.

Chapter 76

LESS THAN 24 HOURS AFTER drinking margaritas with Stella they were talking again. Stella called from a hospital's emergency room and could barely talk because she was crying so much. She'd broken her right ankle after falling off a ladder while creating a display at work. An orthopedic surgeon reviewed the x-rays and told her she had to have surgery when the swelling decreased. And her right ankle had to be non-weight bearing for six weeks after the operation.

"It's going to be impossible to be your maid of honor," Stella said.

She sobbed, apologizing repeatedly.

Mary was upset and cried, too, but knew the situation couldn't be changed. Now her only substitute was her sister. It was the right thing to do, so she invited Catherine to be her matron of honor, and she was all too eager to accept.

"This is the choice you should have made in the beginning," Catherine said. "It's funny how things work out the way they're supposed to."

Mary cringed as she listened to Catherine's response, and fortunately they were on the telephone so Catherine couldn't see Mary roll her eyes.

Two weeks before the wedding, Mary confirmed orders and reservations. When she reached the tent supplier, they couldn't find her order. The customer service agent remembered talking to Mary, but said a new computer system might have accidentally deleted it. Now the tent wasn't available. The agent offered a larger one for the same price. Mary didn't answer right away, so he reduced the price and offered to provide greenery and a fountain to fill up the extra space. He assured her it would be elegant.

"It's an upgrade," the agent said.

Mary wanted to scream and say, 'forget about the wedding!' but she knew she was overreacting. The agent had worked out a reasonable solution, so she politely accepted the offer.

The week before the wedding, Garrett took a three-day business trip to California. Mary was okay with him leaving because she had the plans under control, or at least she thought she did until she realized she'd almost forgotten her mother's birthday in the midst of all the activity. She decided to kill two birds with one stone and stopped in Terri's floral shop to make a last-minute check of the wedding order and buy flowers for her mom.

"I can't believe my wedding is this weekend," Mary said as she selected an arrangement for her mom.

"It comes so fast," Terri said. "And the day itself goes faster."

"True."

Mary remembered her first wedding.

"Your bouquet will be beautiful. Do you want to see the greenery I'm going to use?"

"I trust you. You have great taste, and I know that if you like it, I'll like it. Do whatever you think is best."

The next few days zoomed by as she tied up loose ends, but everything happened as planned. Almost.

On the Friday before the wedding, she was getting ready at her apartment. She was organizing all her clothes, shoes, accessories, jewelry and toiletries for the rehearsal dinner, wedding and honeymoon. She needed to take everything to Rye, because they would leave from New York City on Sunday for their honeymoon.

While she was loading her car, the mailman arrived and handed her a stack of envelopes and a box with a wedding gift. She took everything upstairs to the kitchen table.

She closed the blinds, watered her plants and right before she was going to leave, decided to look through her mail. She froze when she saw an airmail envelope from Luca. It was badly crumpled, like the post office sorting machines had damaged it.

The postmark was March 31. Her hands trembled. The timing startled her - only eight weeks earlier. She really wanted to open it, but she debated whether she should.

Mary wondered why she had gotten the letter today, right before her wedding. She decided she couldn't open it.

She went to her closet and pulled out the shoebox with Luca's photos and unopened letters. When she had asked Luca to stop calling, he obliged. Instead, he had written.

As difficult as it was, she hadn't read any of the letters. But she kept them all. They were a secret she kept from everyone, including Stella.

After she added the newest letter to the box, she looked at the time and knew she needed to get to Catherine's house soon. Her mother was meeting them there, too, and they were going to ride together to Rye in Catherine's minivan.

Just before she started her car, she jumped out and ran back into the apartment for Luca's latest letter. She hid in the zippered side pocket of her purse and hurried out. If she changed her mind about reading it, she'd have it with her.

The rehearsal dinner that evening was festive, like a scene in a good romance movie. Garrett turned on his charm all night, staying by her side, while his family was warm and welcoming. She enjoyed every minute of the delicious dinner and cherished the time with her friends and family.

Chapter 77

THE NEXT MORNING, her mom helped her get ready for the wedding in a guest bedroom at the Hansens' house.

In the same room, Stella sat with her right leg propped up on an ottoman, watching it all unfold. She didn't want to miss anything.

Catherine and her husband, Peter, managed the downstairs activities.

The tent was delivered and assembled in the backyard early in the morning. Later the caterers arrived at the same time as Terri did with the bouquet, corsages and centerpieces.

Catherine directed Terri to the room where Mary was restlessly waiting for the big event, now alone with Stella.

"Hi Mary, you're beautiful," Terri said. "That vintage gown is so romantic."

"Thanks, I'm more nervous than I imagined I would be."

"There's nothing for you to worry about. We're all taking care of you today. Are you ready to see your bouquet?"

Terri reached into a box and pulled out the bouquet, and Mary's chin dropped.

"I received some lavender yesterday and on a whim I decided to mix it with the roses. It's an attractive accent, and I knew it would smell wonderful. Lavender is soothing, so maybe it will help calm your nerves."

Mary found herself unable to talk or breathe. She pictured Luca at the castle. His smile. The nights under the stars. The picnic at Castello di Vincenzo. The lovemaking.

"Mary? Are you okay? Do you not like it?"

"It's gorgeous, and I love it more than you'll ever know. But it reminds me of something that's hard to talk about."

She closed her eyes and smelled the lavender.

Mary pictured herself standing in the castle foyer and Luca handing her the lavender.

"I can pull it out," Terri said. "I don't want you to be upset."

"No, no. Leave it."

Mary trembled and her eyes filled with tears. She couldn't say anything else.

She reminded herself that she was trying to do the right thing and that she had to stop thinking about Luca. But she realized that was nearly impossible.

Stella spoke up from the comfort of the armchair.

"Terri, she'll be fine. She loves lavender, but do you mind giving me a few minutes alone with her?"

"Not at all."

"What's happening?" Mary asked Stella.

"You're getting married today. That's what's happening."

"I feel like there's a force trying to stop this wedding. Ian showed up two weeks ago. The letter arrived yesterday. The lavender showed up in the bouquet today."

"What letter?"

"Look in my purse."

Her leather bag was sitting on the table next to Stella's chair.

"I got another letter from Luca. Yesterday."

"Another letter? I thought you hadn't heard from him since you told him you were back with Garrett."

"He stopped calling, but he keeps writing."

Tears rolled down Mary's face, ruining her makeup.

"You didn't tell me," Stella said.

"I didn't tell anyone. And I wouldn't let myself open them."

Stella held the crumpled and torn envelope.

"Do you want to know what this says? I'll open it and read it to you, if you really want to know."

Mary stepped up to the window and looked outside where everyone was busy preparing for the wedding. She saw Garrett talking to Peter.

She knew she had to do the right thing and stop living in a fantasy world.

"Put it back in my purse," she said.

She heard herself speak, but her voice sounded like it was a million miles away.

Stella did as Mary requested and didn't say a word, but it didn't stop Mary's tears.

Once she calmed down, she reapplied her makeup and shifted gears to being a bride. Garrett's bride.

After the elegant wedding and dinner, Mr. Moretti danced with Mary to "O Sole Mio."

"You are a beautiful bride," he said as they sashayed on the dance floor.

"Thank you."

Mary beamed in his arms because he put her on a pedestal.

At the end of the dance, he said, "*Chi non ama il vino, il bel canto, e le donne rimane un stolto per tutta la vita.* He who does not like wine, songs or women is a fool for life!"

"You are no fool!" she said and hugged him.

Then they sat down at his table.

"You are right, no fool am I, but my Giovanni is."

Mr. Moretti complained that Giovanni needed to get married soon, too, as he watched his son flirt with a young, pretty caterer.

"Maybe he needs to find a nice Italian girl," Mary said.

"Speaking of Italian girls, it has been many weeks and months since you gave me the small diary. On the table of your wedding presents, I return it to you in a white envelope."

"Thank you, Mr. Moretti. I've been so busy lately I completely forgot about it. I can't wait to read it."

"Read it when you can. After the honeymoon is best, but have tissues in your hand when you read this-a diary of a young Italian lady."

His comment roused her interest, but there was no time to read it. She'd have to wait until she returned.

Chapter 78

PETER DROVE MARY AND GARRETT to LaGuardia for their honeymoon departure. Garrett kept their destination a surprise until they arrived at the airport. He only told her to prepare for a lavish island location.

"We're going to Bermuda," he announced as they entered the terminal. "And it should be fantastic. I've rented a waterfront home from a colleague, and we'll have a sailboat, too."

Their honeymoon house looked like it belonged in "Architectural Digest" and Mary felt like royalty. The days were luxurious. They spent their time in the house and pool or on the sailboat, and a driver picked them up for dinner each evening. She had no idea how much he'd paid for it, but it was more glamorous than she expected or knew they could afford.

It was somewhat odd, and perhaps irresponsible on her part, but they'd never talked in depth about their personal finances. She knew he earned a healthy salary with big commissions and he always said Mary didn't have to worry about money and that he would take care of everything.

In spite of his comments, she planned to keep her job so she'd have her own money and savings. Garrett called it her "fun money" and maybe it was, but it was also her source of independence. She wasn't going to be another Susanne, but she did plan to learn more about their financial situation when they got home.

They sailed and swam naked and made love every day. The week alone was the most relaxed and intimate time they'd ever shared. Garrett was happier than she'd seen him.

On the last day, their driver was scheduled to arrive at 10:15 a.m. to take them to the airport, so they woke up early and sat on the patio drinking coffee and eating toast one last time.

"Mary, this has been a great week. Don't you love this weather?"

"I sure do."

"I have another surprise wedding gift for you."

"Really?"

"Yes, how would you like to live in sunny weather every day?"

"What?"

She cocked her head sideways, not sure where he was going with this comment.

"I want us to move to California."

"What?"

"I've bought a condo in Los Angeles, and I worked out a deal on the retail space on the ground floor of the same building. For your gallery."

"Garrett."

She didn't know what to say next. Her family and friends were in Philadelphia and now he was changing their lives without asking her? L.A. sounded wonderful and so did the gallery, but she wanted to be part of the decision.

"Our condo is on the top floor with spectacular views of the mountains, the ocean and the valley. You'll love it."

"I'm sure, but this is a serious decision."

"It's easy. We'll have a beautiful home and a fantastic opportunity. You'll have a gallery on a street with heavy foot traffic, and your family can visit us."

"I don't know."

She felt her life spinning out of control.

"We have to. My company is opening an office on the West Coast, and I've been asked to run it. It's the biggest career opportunity of my life."

"It's great news for you, Garrett, but I'm in shock."

"It won't take you long to see how wonderful it will be. Now, let's take one last dip in the pool."

He took off his bathrobe and jumped in naked.

"Come on in, Mary!"

It was the first time ever that she wasn't in the mood for him.

Their driver arrived promptly and on the ride to the airport she didn't say much. She didn't know what to say. As much as Garrett was happy, Mary was confused.

Chapter 79

Bᴀᴄᴋ ɪɴ Pʜɪʟᴀᴅᴇʟᴘʜɪᴀ, they went to his condo, where she planned to move in. But with two more months on her apartment lease, she didn't have to rush the move.

"I'm going to take your car to my apartment to pick up some clothes and my mail. I'll be back in an hour."

"Okay," Garrett said. "I need to make a few phone calls. Why don't you pick up some sushi on your way back?"

"Okay, see you in a bit."

She quickly kissed him.

In the parking garage, she checked her purse for her apartment key, but she didn't have it. She'd left it in his bedroom, so she headed back upstairs to grab it. When she walked into the condo, she could hear Garrett talking. He was in his office with the door open, but he was on the other side of the room, so she couldn't see him.

"No, I didn't golf in Bermuda," he said. "You know I don't golf. Fuck you, Tom. Riding around in madras plaid shorts on a golf cart chasing a little white ball is not my idea of a sport. Oh yeah, I've been meaning to ask, when are you doing your first triathlon?"

Garrett laughed at his badgering of Tom.

"Did Palmer send the last payment to you?" Garrett asked. "Good, I got mine, too. The $60,000 was wired to my Cayman account."

Garrett paused.

"That's what I thought. Did Max receive his money, too?"

He paused again.

"Okay, that's good news. Before we left for Bermuda, I struck a deal with Avalon Construction for the L.A. condo. Bill Avalon said it was cleaner to give me property than cash. In the end, though, we'll all make more from him than we did from Palmer."

Another pause.

"Sounds good, see you Monday."

Mary was speechless.

Garrett walked out of office and saw Mary standing near the condo's entrance. It would have been impossible for her not to hear the conversation.

Every muscle in her body was tense, and she spoke with her jaw clenched.

"What the hell is going on?"

"Calm down," he said.

"Calm down? I think I married a criminal, and you're asking me to calm down? What the fuck is going on?"

"Mary, it's not a big deal. Everyone does it."

He moved toward her.

"Tell me exactly what 'it' is. 'It' is not something that happens in my simple world."

"Sit down, Mary."

"No, I'm not sitting down, and I'm not going to listen to your lies. I'm grabbing my suitcase, and I'm taking a taxi to my apartment. I want nothing to do with this."

"Mary."

"There's nothing you can say to explain this away."

She grabbed her suitcase, still packed from their honeymoon, and filled a laundry basket with the few clothes and toiletries she'd left at his place over the last year.

He dogged her every step, attempting to talk.

"Listen, Mary. This is for us. We can live in California. You can have your art gallery. We can have everything we ever wanted. Hell, we can buy a villa in Tuscany, and we can spend our summers there with our kids. Maybe we can buy that castle you love so much. We're going to have a great life. Let me take care of the finances, and you won't need to worry about anything."

"You're assuming you're not going to end up in jail," she said as she stormed out of the apartment, refusing to look at him.

As she slammed the condo door shut, he shouted.

"You'll be back when you realize what you're about to lose."

She didn't hear him.

She hailed a taxi and directed the driver to her address while sitting in the backseat crying.

So much for the sure bet, she thought, the guy everyone believed in, the responsible, mature, organized, disciplined, clean-cut, successful guy. He didn't play guitar, didn't have long hair, didn't have illegitimate children and didn't work in a bar, so he was the "perfect man."

Wrong.

Chapter 80

MARY ARRIVED AT HER APARTMENT and found a pile of boxes on the ground by the mailbox. Wedding gifts. What a joke. She was so angry and felt so stupid and embarrassed.

Then she noticed an envelope taped to the mailbox with only her first name on it. The handwriting was familiar and she began to quiver. She opened the letter, shaking.

It was Luca's handwriting.

She dropped everything to the floor and sat on the stairs. She took a deep breath, wiping away tears so she could read it. She held the letter with two hands to steady it because she was trembling so much.

3 June

Dear Mary,

I hoped you received my last letter to let you know that I was coming to the United States. I arrived today, and it was bold, but I came directly here to see you. I had to see you. I waited in Philly all day, but you never showed up.

I'm going home on Sunday night. Please call my cousin Frank if you can see me. He knows how to reach me.

I'm still waiting for you and always will.

Luca
Frank Fiore – 609-555-0892

"No," she said aloud. "No."

She sobbed.

What a horrible mess. He showed up on her wedding day. The same day as the lavender. And his other letter arrived in the mail the day before her wedding. They were signs.

She flashed back to Stella holding the crumpled letter from Luca and giving her the option to read it. She couldn't help thinking what would've happened if they had opened it.

"What a mess!" she exclaimed aloud.

"I'm still waiting for you and always will."

His words kept replaying in her mind.

The other letter was still in her purse, so she took it out and carefully slipped her finger inside the tattered envelope. She removed the single, folded sheet of thin paper. Her heart raced and the paper shook as she read it.

31 March

> Dear Mary,
>
> I don't know if you are reading my letters, but if you read any letter, I hope you read this one because it will help us see each other again. I know when we see each other, you will believe we are meant to be together.
>
> I have finalized plans to visit New York in June for a business trip. I arrive on 3 June and depart on 10 June. I am making my flights in and out of Philadelphia so I can see you. I will come to your apartment on 3 June, and then I will stay with my cousin Frank in New Jersey. Will you please call him 609-555-0892 and tell him the best way for me to contact you when I arrive? I want to see you more than words can say. I am waiting for you.
>
> Luca

Mary read the letter three times as she sat in the apartment entryway. He's still waiting, she thought.

This time, she had no choice. Today was June 10, the day Luca was leaving. There was nothing to lose. Nothing.

She jumped up and hurried into the apartment to call Frank. She might still catch Luca.

"Hi, Mary," Frank said. "I'm glad to hear from you, but you're too late. His flight left at seven."

She looked at her watch. It was 7:30. He had been at the airport when she'd just arrived. They may have passed each other in the international terminal. She couldn't believe they'd been so close to each other.

"He really wants to see you, Mary. He talked about you non-stop. Let me give you his phone numbers at work and his apartment in Florence. You should call him."

"Thanks, Frank."

Mary got Luca's numbers, then hung up and called Stella. She told her about Garrett's plans to move them to Los Angeles and the incriminating phone conversation she overheard. Then she told her about Luca's visit to her apartment.

"Mary, stop crying and catch your breath. Listen to me. We will do this one step at a time. I have a client who is a divorce attorney. You need to call her tomorrow morning. Until then, don't accept any calls from Garrett tonight. Come here if you want."

"You're right, and thanks, but I think I'll stay home. Garrett hasn't tried to call me. He's such an arrogant asshole. He probably thinks I'll be back. I think I really just need to be alone. But stay on alert, I may need to call and cry."

"Of course, I'll be here. And do one more thing, Mary. Call Luca. You're in a heap of pain right now, but you shouldn't let him get away. He wants to be with you after nearly a year of waiting. I think he's truly in love with you."

When Mary hung up, she could do nothing else but bury her face in a pillow and sob. When she calmed down, she took a hot shower and opened the only bottle of wine in her apartment, Gabbiano Chianti. She filled a glass and sat down on the sofa in a thick bathrobe with the shoebox full of Luca's letters next to her. It was time to open them. To read every word.

She opened the box and gently removed all the letters, putting them in order of their postmark, oldest first. She took a deep breath and opened the first one.

16 August

Dear Mary,

   Weeks ago, you asked me not to call, and I respect your
request, so I haven't. But you didn't tell me not to write,
and I hope you read this. I have decided I'm not letting
you go. I want to get everything in the open, and although
you told me I did not need to explain my situation with
Angela and Alex, I want to tell you. I was honest with you
about everything, I really was. When you were here, I never
found the right time to tell you about Alexander. I wanted
my time with you to be special and not filled with
explaining poor decisions of my youth. I will tell you
everything. Will you please give me a chance? Will you
please call me one more time?

She almost laughed when she read about poor decisions and
thought about her own. She opened the next letter, and this one
was long.

19 September

Dear Mary,

   I haven't heard from you, and I want to tell you about
Alexander. I will tell you everything here, but before I
start, I want you to remember this - we are real. We are
meant for each other. Don't ever doubt it. Remember
how you felt at our picnic? You said you were looking for
"true love." I believe you found it with me. Didn't the
pocket watch find you, too?
   Here is the story. I have nothing to hide.
   I told you about my father's anger with my brother for
his illegitimate child, and at 17, I found myself in the same
situation. I spent the summer in New Jersey with my
cousins, and we stayed at the shore every weekend. There
were parties, lots of parties. There were girls, lots of girls. I
am sure you can imagine. In the last two weeks of my

summer trip I spent some time with a girl from New York named Angela. She was the daughter of a second-generation Italian family. We never fell in love. We partied a lot on the shore that summer. I am sure you can read between the lines.

After I returned to Florence and was back in school, I received a letter from her. She told me she was pregnant and was keeping the baby. I was shocked and scared. I asked her what she wanted from me, and she only said she wanted money for the baby's food and clothes and savings for his future. I was scared and didn't argue with her. I knew I needed to find money so I could do what she asked of me.

I couldn't go to my father. There was no way. So I had to turn to Giovanni, who I knew would understand my predicament. Giovanni understood very well, but was still angry and bitter with our father for the way he'd been treated. Since he wasn't treated fairly, and since I was the adopted son, he wanted me to pay the price, too. He agreed never to tell our dad and to give me the money I needed as long as I agreed to pay him back and split our father's estate with him, upon our father's death. The way he made me pay him back was by working on the vineyard. My hands were tied with no choice. It has worked for years, as far as the financial portion of it.

As for having a son I'd never seen and who I still don't truly know, it broke my heart. Angela didn't want our son to know me and she finally married, so Alex has a stepfather who he believes is his real father. He has no reason to think otherwise. I still argued with her about wanting to see him, and by the time Alexander was seven we agreed she would start coming to Italy every summer for a week, all expenses paid by me. She would stay at Giovanni's farm where I could see him, but I promised her I would not tell him who I was. I treated them like guests.

Every year I pay for their flights, and Giovanni allows
them to stay at the farm. It's awkward, but at least I see
him once each year. Angela and I do not talk. We never
had a relationship and still don't.

Giovanni holds this secret over my head and uses it as
control over me every day of my life, threatening to tell our
father. This is the reason he and Rossana were never very
friendly to you. They saw you as another Angela. I
apologize for their behavior.

Mary, that's the entire story. A teenage fling became a
lifetime of handcuffs from my son's mother and my
brother. But I have a beautiful son, and I hope that once
he is an adult he might eventually know who I am. I am
willing to sacrifice my contact with him now to not
confuse or anger him. Hopefully he can have a happy
childhood.

I hope you understand why I never found the right time
to tell you. I hope you can forgive me for not telling you
and also forgive me for the mistakes of my past.

Let's please talk. I miss you so much.

Time stands still without you.

She read the letter a second time. It was a simple explanation,
complicated by family dynamics. Now she wished she'd read the
letter when it arrived, but she couldn't change the past. She
sighed.

2 October

Dear Mary,

I am thinking of you. The grape harvest has kept us busy. You
should be here for the wine festivals and for nights under
the clear skies. I dream of you. I wait for you.

11 November

Dear Mary,

My father is weak now, so I am helping him while I take care of the factory and store. I am busy and cannot visit the *castello*.

I am still hopeful I will hear from you, and I am still waiting for you. I always will.

He never gave up. He really never gave up, Mary thought.

12 December

Dear Mary,

My father is better, and I have more free time. My passion for you is being fulfilled at the *castello*. I am working every weekend to make it a home for us. I know you'll be back. I waited so long for you. I wait for you to return. We are so good together.

16 January

Dear Mary,

The winter is cold, but the kitchen is finished. It is ready for us to cook, eat, talk and drink together.

28 February

Dear Mary,

The second-floor bathroom is almost finished, and now I work on the bedroom. Our bedroom. I'm waiting for you.

The next letter was only six weeks old.

23 April

Dear Mary,

The bedroom walls need more repair than I expected, but it won't be long before I'm ready for you. What are you doing? Do you think of me the way I think of you? I'm

waiting for you. I always will. I hope to see you soon when
I am in Philadelphia.

Luca

Luca's passion, sincerity and commitment were moving. Their
physical encounter was brief, but the letters confirmed it was deep
and heartfelt. She couldn't believe that she'd been keeping these
letters – and him – in a shoebox for nearly a year.

She drank the wine and read every letter a second and third
time. She ran her fingers over the paper, studying Luca's handwriting, hearing his voice as he read them. The fire between them
still burned. She thought about where he might be. It was ten
o'clock in Philadelphia, so it was four in the morning in Italy.
Luca wouldn't land for several hours.

She went to the kitchen for a glass of water. The pile of
wedding presents her mom and sister dropped off while she was
on her honeymoon was stacked on the kitchen table. These would
have to be returned in the upcoming weeks. It wasn't going to be
fun.

In the middle of the pile of boxes, she spotted the envelope
from Mr. Moretti with the diary and translation. She remembered
what he said on her wedding night.

"Read it when you can. After the honeymoon is best, but have
tissues in your hand when you read this diary of a young lady."

She was ready to read it now, but before doing so, she got the
pocket watch from her bedroom and put it on. She hadn't worn it
since she accepted Garrett's proposal. She loved it, but it confused
her by reminding her of Luca. Everything reminded her of Luca,
she now admitted to herself.

She cozied up on the sofa again and opened the big white
envelope. Her curiosity was stronger now than it was the day she
found it. The envelope contained the original diary, pages of
typed translations and a handwritten letter from Mr. Moretti. His
handwriting was large and messy, and she quickly learned he
spoke English much better than he wrote it.

Mary,
You are the daughter I want always. I want for you happiness. I
did not give to you this diary before now because I have a
fear. If you read before the wedding, you will be confused
and I fear you will want to see Luca, and now you marry
Garrett.

Mary gasped. She wondered how Luca could be related to the
diary. She quickly read on.

I give to you now because I promise to translate, but it might
make pain for you. I can read the Italian, but my English
writing is weak, so my nephew Antonio make the
translation for you.

I give this with love to the daughter I want always.

I hope I make no mistake to wait after your wedding to
give to you.

Love,
Enzo

She couldn't imagine what caused his hesitation, so she dove into
the translation.

Chapter 81

The Diary

Friday, 19 July 1963

Today was wonderful! It began normally by going to the Uffizi Gallery as I do every Friday. Art class starts after lunch because our teacher requires us to study the Masters of the Uffizi in the morning. I usually go alone, and I always see Signore Tomei, an usher. He is a kind man who told me he has been an usher since he was 19 years old. He knows all the paintings, but he really knows people. He says every time he sees a visitor he can assign their looks to an Uffizi painting or sculpture. The first time I met him, he said, "Buongiorno, Flora," like the Titian painting. He likes my big brown eyes. I told him my name is Anna, but he still calls me Flora every time he sees me.

I didn't see S. Tomei when I went in today, but he must have seen me, and he played a trick on me. I approached the Botticelli Birth of Venus and at the same time, a handsome American soldier in uniform walked up. Then, S. Tomei moved behind us and in Italian said, "Lovers should hold hands in front of Sandro Botticelli." The American turned to me and asked in English, "What did he say?" Something magical happened. It was love at first sight, and all we did was laugh. S. Tomei smiled quietly with approval and went to the next room.

The American asked me if I spoke English, and fortunately, I have studied it for many years. We introduced and his name is Luke Davis from Ohio. We continued through the Uffizi to look at paintings together and talk about them. I told him I studied art, music and English.

When we were ready to leave the Uffizi, he asked me to have coffee, abandoning his soldier friends who were drinking *vino* at Piazza della Signoria. We went to a quiet bar, and we sat outside and drank coffee and ate panini. He told me he was visiting Florence for the weekend as part of his "R" and "R" or "rest and relaxation" he called it.

He traveled the world and saw places I'd only read about. His trip started in Vietnam where he served as a medic for the United States Army. From there, he and his buddies flew to Korat Royal Thai Air Force Base. While they were waiting for availability on a flight to Bangkok, he heard there were seats open for a flight to Aviano Air Base near Venice. He decided to change his schedule to come to Italy instead of Bangkok, where he originally planned to go to drink and party. He chose Italy because he said his grandfather toured here when he was in the military and loved it. His grandfather told Luke it was his favorite country outside of the U.S., so he always encouraged Luke to go if he had the chance.

Luke told me he cared deeply for his grandfather, and he pulled a pocket watch from his uniform pants and showed it to me. He said his grandfather bought it in Venice, when he was in World War I. It was silver, and he said it hadn't worked for years, but his grandfather thought it was his lucky charm because he came home safely. Luke said he gave it to him for good luck when he left for Vietnam. The hands were stuck on the time of 7:11.

Mary gasped, again. Anna had to be describing her pocket watch. She read on.

I believe it is true, it is a lucky pocket watch, because on a whim,
Luke decided to come here instead of Bangkok, and we met.
At least it was lucky for me!

Once Luke arrived here, he visited Venice, then Bologna. He
arrived in Florence yesterday and still plans to see Pisa and
Rome. He said he will go to Naples if he has time. He loves to
travel and last year, he took "R" and "R" and went to
Australia. He said he liked how the people talked there. He
saw kangaroos and koala bears, too. I would love to go there!

My life seems so boring compared to his, since I've lived in
Florence all my life and never left Italy. The only cities I've
seen are Rome, Bologna and Venice. My father says we can't go
anywhere because his work is so important. I don't understand
why making dyes for fabric and leather prohibits us from
traveling, but I am happy when we go to our country home in
the Chianti countryside. I love to spend time in the tower of
the house. The views are beautiful, especially on clear days
when I can see San Gimignano. I like that we make our own
wine and olive oil, too. I told Luke all these things, and he said
he would like to see the view from the tower.

Mary stopped reading for a moment, piecing together the story.
The author lived in the castle on the weekends, and Luke owned
the pocket watch. Maybe he ended up visiting her at the castle
and lost his pocket watch in the tower? She couldn't wait to read
more.

After Luke and I finished coffee, it was time for me to go to class, but
I did something I've <u>never</u> done. I skipped the class to have
more time with Luke. My father would be furious if he ever
learned about this.

We walked the city streets, and I showed him the famous
buildings of Florence. We climbed the steps inside the Duomo
to its rooftop for the incredible panoramic view, and I showed
him statues and paintings in some small churches. We crossed
the Ponte Vecchio and took an early dinner at a small trattoria
in Piazza Santo Spirito, and by the end of the day, I was in
love.

The only love I've ever known until now is what I've read
about in books, and Luke is everything of that and more. He's
tall, strong and muscular, with dark blond hair and baby blue
eyes. He is polite and courteous. He looks at me as though I
am a beautiful painting in the Uffizi and holds my hand
delicately like porcelain.

Tomorrow we are meeting at the doors of the Baptistery of St.
John, and we are going to have coffee on the Piazza del Duomo
before he takes the train to Rome. I wish he could stay, but I
wouldn't be able to see him because I have to go to our
country house with my parents. My *papà* would be furious if he
knew I was seeing an American soldier. As a strong supporter
of Mussolini, he has no patience for Americans and their
principles.

I can't stop thinking and dreaming of Luke. He is so adorable,
and he's more astonishing than any man I have ever met in my
life. I will count the minutes until we meet tomorrow morning.

Saturday, 20 July 1963
Today, I snuck out of my house for an hour to meet Luke on the
Piazza. In our brief time, he told me it would be hard to leave
Florence because he had already started to fall in love with me.
He said there was something unique about me, and he felt like
we were meant to be together. He said he wanted to take care
of me. I felt the same, but it was difficult for me to say these

words back to him. I've never said anything like that to anyone. At 18, I am ready to leave my family and have a life of my own. I can imagine it with Luke. I have never felt this way about a man.

Before he left, we stood in the shadow of Giotto's Bell Tower, and he kissed me like he would never let go. And I never wanted him to let go. I wanted to be in his arms forever. All I can do is smile when I remember him.

He reluctantly headed in the direction of the train station, but he suddenly stopped and returned, saying he forgot something important. He reached into the front pocket of his khaki brown pants and pulled out his lucky broken pocket watch. He handed it to me and said, "This pocket watch brought me the greatest luck in the world because I met you." Then he kissed me. "Keep this lucky charm and know I'll come back for it so we will see each other again." He kissed me again. "Do one more thing for me, Anna. Take a sharp knife tip and lift off the back cover. In the empty space, I left a note for you. Read it to find out where we'll meet again this Friday." He kissed me and walked away toward the station.

At home, I took a small kitchen knife to my bedroom and removed the cover of the watch. I found a long strip of paper rolled up with a message. I read it and laughed because it was so cute. Then it was everything I could do to keep from screaming with delight because he was coming back! Here is what it said.

> *I love you from the top of my head to the toes of my Uffizi's. Meet me again at the doors to the Uffizi on Friday at 10 a.m. I'm coming back for you.*

I can hardly wait until Friday!

Mary's mouth dropped open, and she said aloud, "I love you from the top of my head to the toes of my Uffizi's! This is what Luca's mother said to him!"

She was more confused than ever. She was torn between reading more or prying open the pocket watch to see if the note was still inside, but she decided to keep reading, eager to solve the mystery.

Friday, 26 July 1963

I arrived at the Uffizi Gallery at ten, and Luke was waiting for me, as he promised. He was standing grand and proper in his green Army uniform. A paper bag was under his arm, and he put it on the ground to hug me.

"I missed you," he said. "Rome and Naples were beautiful, but the most glorious sight is in front of me."

He asked me if I would skip my afternoon class again because he already arranged a date for us. I said yes. (I hoped this would happen!) And I hope my *papà* never finds out!

We hopped on the bus to Fiesole, and when we got there we found a comfortable shady area for a picnic. In his bag, he had a bottle of Chianti, salami, cheese and bread. We laughed, talked and admired the beautiful view of Florence from the Fiesole hillside, where it was cooler than in the city. And we kissed. We kissed and kissed and we couldn't stop touching each other. I should be embarrassed to write this, but I wanted him to take off my clothes and touch me everywhere. I wanted to do the same to him. It almost hurt not to.

Before sunset, we went back to Florence and he asked how he could see me again. I told him I was going to my country home on Saturday with my parents, and I couldn't cancel it. He

asked for the location and said he would find a way to get
there. It made me nervous, but I told him my parents always
take *riposo* from in the afternoon, like the Spanish siesta. We
decided that if he arrived after one we could have some time
with each other. I would watch for him to drive up the hill
because I would be able to see him from the tower, and he
would have to park below our house in Terzano. I would go
down the hill to meet him and take him to the forest, so no
one would see us. I apologized that I had to be so secretive, but
my parents would never approve. He said he would do
anything to see me again.

We parted near the Ponte Vecchio, and before he left, I gave
him his pocket watch and told him I left a note for him inside,
too. I told him he could read my romantic note in private. This
is what I said: *You are my moon, my stars and my sun.*

As Mary read this, she became startled again. This confirmed the
writer was connected to Luca or to Luca's mother, because these
were the exact words of Luca's mother. The mystery heightened.

Saturday, 27 July 1963
Today was the happiest and saddest day in my life. Luke came to the
farmhouse by borrowing a motorcycle from a guy in Florence
where he stayed. I waited in the tower until I saw him driving
up the hill, and he did as I told him. He parked in the hamlet
of Terzano. I ran down the hill to meet him and took him to
the forest where I had left food, wine and a blanket earlier in
the day.

We spent two-and-a-half hours by each other's side, and they
were the most beautiful two-and-a-half hours of my life.

We made love. We couldn't stop ourselves.

He was so strong and so handsome, and I want to be with him forever. I love looking into his beautiful blue eyes.

When it was time to say goodbye, it was so difficult. We want to be united again. He said he would return in six months after he finished his last tour of duty in Vietnam. He gave me the pocket watch and told me to keep it until he came back. He told me to be sure to look for another note, and he started to give me his parents' address in Ohio, saying I could always contact them to find him.

Suddenly, we heard a noise in the trees. It was *papà*. He was walking around the property and happened upon us. He shouted, and he scared Luke, who couldn't understand a word he was saying. I told Luke to run because I was afraid *papà* would kill him!

Luke dashed toward the motorcycle, and I ran to the house past *papà* as fast as possible. Thankfully, I am much faster than him because I made it to the top of the tower in time to watch Luke ride away. It would be the last time I would see him for six months.

I stood at the lookout and waved goodbye, but I knew he couldn't see me. When I couldn't see him anymore, I reached in my skirt pocket for the pocket watch. I couldn't wait to see my new note, but I had nothing to dislodge the cover. As I put it back into my pocket, it slipped and before I could catch it, the watch fell through a crack in the floor. I heard it tumble and land at the bottom of the tower. I had no idea how to retrieve it.

At the same time, I heard *papà*. He was yelling. He was furious and ordered me to my room where I would stay the rest of the night. I think I am too old to be told what to do, but *papà* is the boss of this family. No one defies him.

I can remember every detail of the pocket watch and this is what it looks like.

Antonio had left Mary a note explaining what was on the next pages of Anna's diary. He wrote, "There is a drawing of the pocket watch here, followed by empty pages before Anna continued."

Mary still had many unanswered questions, so she read on.

Thursday, 28 May 1964
This weekend I returned to the summer home for my last visit. I spent the last seven months in Florence with the nuns in the convent, hiding my pregnancy. The baby was born on 10 May and it was a boy. I asked Sister Sofia to promise to name him Luca. I never told her he was named after his American father, Luke. So now, our baby lives in the orphanage. I pleaded with Sister Sofia to keep him from being adopted for six months, because I planned to find a way to come back for him. She couldn't promise me, but I believe she wants to help me. She believed it would be better for a baby to be with his real mother.

In two weeks, I will be married to Signore Rusconi, who is a business partner of my father. My father made the arrangements and is insisting it happen. He does not want me to disgrace him again.

S. Rusconi is an older man in his thirties, and he is a widower. His wife died in a car accident, and he already has a son, Giovanni, who is nine years old. I will be a mother to a son I've never met and mother to a baby I can't have.

I have to stop writing, because I can't stop crying. I still love Luke, and I don't know how to find him to tell him about our baby. I lost his pocket watch in the tower, and my father has sold the property. Today is our last day here to pick up our things.

I've lost everything I love, but I am making a promise to myself to get Luca back. He belongs with me. After I am married, I will convince S. Rusconi to adopt a baby. I will get my baby Luca. Someday I will find Luke again, too. All I have left from Luke now is the Timex watch he accidentally left in the forest on our last day. I found it today when I snuck away to visit the place we were last together. When I finally get my baby Luca back, I will give him his father's watch, but I am worried I will never see Luke again.

The diary stopped abruptly here, and while Luca had never told Mary his mother's name, she was sure Anna was his biological mother. Anna rescued her own baby from the orphanage, named him after his blue-eyed American father and gave him his dad's old Timex. The same one Luca wore every day when he was with Mary in Italy.

Mr. Moretti must have assumed the Luca in the diary was the same Luca in Mary's photos, which is why he must have been worried about her reading the translations.

She retrieved a steak knife from the kitchen and carefully lifted the back case of the watch. Inside she found three small paper rolls, yellowed and fragile. She gently unrolled the first. Written in the same penmanship of the diary it read,

You are my moon, my stars and my sun.

Her heart fluttered as she read it, remembering Luca telling her his mother said this to him when she put him to bed as a child. She unrolled the second piece of paper.

> *I love you from the top of my head to the toes of my Uffizi's.*
> *Meet me again at the doors to the Uffizi on Friday at 10*
> *a.m. I'm coming back for you.*

She smiled. This was Luke's note to Anna. Luca loved when his mother said this expression, too. The story of the pocket watch and diary would be unbelievable news for Luca, as it told the story of his parents.

She unrolled the third note, the one Anna never read because the pocket watch slipped through the cracks of the tower floor.

> *Don't forget, I will be the brightest star in the night watching*
> *you and waiting for you. I will be back in January 1964.*
> *Wait for me at the Uffizi Gallery on the last Friday of*
> *January at 10 a.m.*

This note made Mary sad. She wondered if Luke came back, and if he was unable to find Anna because she was at the convent. Their love story probably stopped here because it was unlikely they ever saw each other again, based on what Mary knew.

Mary couldn't fall asleep that night. Garrett never called her and at five in the morning she picked up the phone and dialed.

Chapter 82

"P<small>RONTO</small>," Luca answered.

"Luca?"

"Mary? Mary! Is it you?"

"Yes, it's me, and I found your note on my mailbox last night."
She paused, unsure of where to begin.

"I hoped I would see you. I miss you."
Tears welled.

"I've missed you, too. I didn't know how much until yesterday.
I have so much to tell you, and I'm in such a mess."

"Are you okay? What's wrong? It's very early in the morning for
you."

"It's hard to talk about this, but the day you arrived, I wasn't
home because I was at my wedding. I married Garrett."
Tears began to roll.

"No."
He didn't hide the disappointment in his voice.

"Yes, but there's a problem, and the marriage is already over."

"What? It has only been one week."

"I'll have to explain more later, but it's definitely over."

"Are you okay? Did he hurt you?"

"I'm okay, but he has some legal problems."

"What can I do for you?"

"Can you keep waiting for me?"
He laughed happily.

"Yes, of course. That's easy, because I'm lost without you."

"Maybe I can come there soon?"

"Tomorrow?"
She giggled.

"I wish, but I have to find out how to get out of this marriage, and I need to hire an attorney on Monday."

"This is serious."

"Yes, it is."

"I wish I could come back to help you," he said.

"Thank you, but I'll be okay. I have my family and friends to help."

"I want to hold you right now and make you feel better."

"Me, too."

More tears welled.

"I will call you every morning before you go to work until I can see you again," Luca said. "Okay?"

"Sure."

Her heart melted.

"What time is best?"

"Just before I leave at 7:30. That would be good."

"Okay, I will check on you every day," he said.

"I would like that."

"It's so comforting to hear your voice. I've dreamed of hearing it for months. I never gave up, Mary."

"I know you didn't."

"I am sure you are exhausted. Do you need to sleep now?"

"I probably do."

She definitely did.

"Okay, I will call you tomorrow morning at 7:30 Philadelphia time."

"Thank you."

"I'm sorry for your pain, but we are lucky. We will get through this together."

"Yes, we will."

Her heart fluttered.

"I will say goodbye but only for a day."

"Okay, I like that, but before we hang up, I have a question. What was your mother's name?"

"Anna. Why do you ask?"

Mary gasped. It was definitely true.

"I'll explain later."

"Okay, you have me intrigued. You did from the day I met you."

ITALY

Chapter 83

ON THE FOURTH OF AUGUST, the train stopped at the Siena station, and Mary thought her heart was going to stop, too. She looked out the window and he was standing there, waiting for her. Brown jeans. White tee. His hair still long.

His face showed the same expression at their first meeting, a look of adoration and joy, the look that was permanently etched in her mind.

She hurried off the train, ran down the steps through the underground tunnel and sprinted up the other side.

"Luca," she said when he was within arms' reach.

Like a dream, everything moved in slow motion except her heart that raced and her knees that shook. She dropped her duffle and tote bags to the ground, and they tightly wrapped their arms around each other. He smelled the same and felt the same.

"Mary, look at you, you are so beautiful. I can't believe you are here. It's been so painful not to be with you, and here you are. I can't believe this."

He squeezed her, like he was never going to let her go again, and he kissed the top of her head.

She smiled and laughed as tears of joy filled her eyes. Over a year later, they were together again, and it felt exactly the same. He'd waited patiently for her during her tumultuous journey, but all that was over now.

He kissed her forehead and her nose and her lips as though he was making sure it was really her.

He hugged her, looked upward and quietly spoke.

"Grazie, Dio mio. Grazie."

He returned his attention to kissing her lips, before standing back and looking at her with pure love and adoration, like Mr. Moretti had said he had seen in the photos.

"Let's go home," he said. "You must need a glass of wine. I know I do. We will sit down and I want you to tell me everything that has happened while you've been gone, and I will tell you everything, too. Everything you want to know."

He carried her bags to his car and drove them to the castle.

"You will not recognize this place now, but you will love it," he said as he pulled into the parking area. "It is your new home."

They entered the foyer and went directly to the kitchen. It was beautiful, newly equipped but with an old-world ambiance. Mary especially loved the open fireplace, like the one in Stefania Costa's kitchen. They held and kissed each other before he poured two glasses of wine.

They sat on bar stools at the counter, and Mary told Luca the whole story about Garrett. She had shared some of it over the phone, but now she explained it in detail. She admitted to her confusion about the news of Luca's son, but she confessed she was more upset by her own judgment and thought she'd fallen too fast. She also told Luca she remembered him every day and looked at photos of him often. She explained she couldn't bear to open his letters because she knew it would be difficult, but she kept them.

As she revealed the events of the wedding, it led to one of the many signs – the lavender. She said she knew it was a message, but she didn't know what to do about it.

Luca looked up again and said, "*Grazie, mia madre, grazie.*"

He drank more wine.

"Mary, I've thought of you every hour of every day since you left. Everything I do is for you. Everything. I prayed we would be with each other again, and I never gave up hope. I finished this kitchen for us, and we have a bathroom and a bedroom upstairs. For us. You and me."

He gently brushed her face.

"I love you from the top of my head to the toes of my Uffizi's."

Tears welled up and she hugged him.

"I love you, too."

Mary kissed Luca on the cheek.

"I have a surprise for you," she said.

"But I have a surprise to show you first."

"More than this," she asked, gesturing at the kitchen.

"Yes, more than this."

"You've done so much work. What else could there be?"

"Follow me."

"You didn't say anything about this in the letters."

"It wouldn't be a surprise."

He took her hand. They walked outside to the chapel entrance. He opened the door and said, "Take a look."

She entered and gasped. On the chapel walls hung all the sketches she left at the Ribelli. Luca had framed them.

"This is your art gallery," he said. "After you left, I went to your apartment and picked up the pillow to see if it still smelled of you. I wanted to be with you. Then I went upstairs to the terrace, to remember being there with you, and I found your sketchbook on the table. I knew you were sorry not to have it, but it allowed me to keep you with me. I looked at the art all the time. They are so beautiful, like you. I decided to have prints made and they are in the cabinet in the back."

He pointed to a broad armoire.

"We can post a sign on the road, and you can sell your art right here. It's what you always wanted, isn't it?"

She started to cry again.

"Thank you. I can't tell you how much this means."

"It was easy. This is what you were meant to do, and this is where you were meant to be."

"You don't know how right you are, and I have something that proves it. Are you ready to know more about my surprise?"

"After you kiss me."

Following a long, tender kiss, she buried her face in his neck, a place so familiar. It now felt like they'd never been apart. She inhaled, comforted by his scent. Right here is where she knew she was meant to be. It was time to tell him the rest of the story.

"Let's go back to the kitchen," she said. "I think you should sit down for this."

"Okay," he said, taking her hand.

Chapter 84

IN THE KITCHEN, they refilled their wine glasses. She began by taking off the pocket watch necklace and handing it to him.

"We both know this was an unbelievable discovery, but what I'm about to say might be difficult to comprehend."

She paused.

"I believe this watch originally belonged to your great grandfather."

"What?"

He cocked his head.

"How could you know this? My great grandfather Rusconi?"

"No, not him. Your biological great grandfather."

"I don't know who my real parents are. I'm sorry, I'm confused."

"You're right, it's complicated, but let me show you something that will tell you more about your parents."

"Okay, you have my full attention."

"I found this on the day I left the Ribelli."

Mary pulled out a black velvet drawstring bag where she stored the old diary.

"This was hidden in the armoire in my bedroom, and I accidentally found it."

She carefully removed the small book.

"Mr. Moretti's nephew translated it for me, and I read it only several weeks ago, the first night I called you. If you read it, you'll learn more about your family than you can imagine, including the origin of the Timex watch you're wearing."

He looked at her as though he didn't believe what she was saying because it was so incomprehensible. He put the pocket watch down, took the diary and began to read.

"The writer's name is Anna? You think it's my mother?"

Mary nodded.

"You think this pocket watch was owned by the solider and he knew my mother?"

Mary nodded her head.

He took a slug of wine and continued. Then he stopped, shook his head and ran his fingers through his hair.

"I love you from the top of my head to the toes of my Uffizi's! That's what my mother always said. You know that."

Mary nodded.

"I was as surprised as you when I read it and found it hard to believe it was a coincidence."

"This is unreal."

He focused all his attention on the diary again then blurted out, "You are my moon, my stars and my sun! She always said this, too!"

"I know, you told me and you always thought she meant that you were her son, not the sun in the heavens."

"I can't believe you found this. It was in the armoire?"

"Yes, tucked in the upper front corner, where I hid Garrett's engagement ring. I found it when I reached for the ring, and I think it's possible the armoire was originally in the castle."

"That's entirely possible, but my mother was never here."

"I think she was when she was a young girl. Keep reading," Mary said.

Luca reached the illustration and held the pocket watch next to it.

"They are the same and now I know why it was in the bottom of the tower. The mystery is solved."

"Yes," she said. "The notes are still inside, too."

"Really? I'll have to see them, but let me keep reading."

He reacted the same as she did. He was eager to know the rest of the story.

As he read the final pages and realized he was the illegitimate child of his mother and the American, his eyes filled with tears.

"She was my real mother."

He was shaken, as anyone would be with news like that.

"She never told me any of this."

He looked at the Timex watch he wore, the one formerly owned by Luke Davis.

Mary put her hand on his while he sat thinking through it all.

"It makes sense. My mother and I looked alike, except for my blue eyes. And our interests were the same. In my dreams, I wanted her to be my mother. I wanted no one else to fill her role. I loved her so much."

He kept shaking his head, obviously in shock.

"My father must know, don't you think?"

"I don't know," Mary said. "She may have kept this secret from him, too. He loved you and cared for you like his own child. Maybe she was afraid to tell him?"

"Yes, and he would most likely never admit it if he did know."

Luca read the words again and ran his fingers over the handwriting of the diary.

"I can't stop reading this," he said. "I am so surprised and amazed. It's hard to believe this lost diary contained so much information and harder to believe that you, of all people, found it."

"It's mind boggling," she said.

They both shook their heads in disbelief.

"Do you want to see the notes?" she asked.

"Yes, of course."

He pried open the case with a pocket knife he carried and delicately unrolled the notes and read them in the same careful way she did in her apartment.

She wondered what he was thinking about his real father, and he addressed it without her asking.

"I don't think my mother ever saw Luke Davis again," he said. "She must have lived her life wondering what happened to him, but I think she always loved him. I bet that is why she convinced my father to buy this property. To come back for the pocket watch, to come back to the tower, to come back to the place where I was conceived and where Luke might still try to find her. I don't know."

He stopped for a moment.

"When I was young, she often took me to the Uffizi Gallery on Fridays at ten in the morning. It was a tradition for us."

"We'll never know, unless you try to find him."

"Right now, I don't think I will, but I really don't know. My father who adopted me gave me so much. This is my life, and I don't want to disrespect him. But I may change my mind later. I'm so confused. The only thing I know with certainty is that my mother wants you to be with me. She handpicked *you*. She gave *you* the pocket watch, the diary and the lavender in the wedding bouquet. She didn't give up on you."

He sat quietly for a little while.

"Do you mind if we go to the tower and stand where she stood? It's the place she loved so much and the place I love, too."

They climbed the tower to the lookout facing Terzano and viewed the long, white dusty road leading to it. Luca stood behind Mary with his arms wrapped around her, resting his head on her shoulder. Neither of them said anything, but Mary assumed he was reflecting on the same lost memories as she was. She imagined a blond haired, blue-eyed American soldier rumbling up the hill on a motorcycle to be with his love one last time before returning to Vietnam. They didn't know it would be the last time they saw each other. He didn't know she'd become pregnant or that he had a son. The stories left untold were heartbreaking.

After a long, quiet embrace, Luca stepped back and Mary turned to face him. Their love and attraction was no different than the feeling his mother had described having about Luke.

The blue eyes that haunted Mary's very soul since the day they had met spilled all the love he had to give.

"Thank you," he whispered. "Thank you. Everything makes sense now because of you."

She slowly let her body melt into his. Their limbs wrapped and entwined, like the old knotty grapevines clinging to their posts. Reunited, she knew they would weather time and the elements. They would dig their roots deeply into the rocky soil, reach for the sun, dance with the wind and drink the rain with the same passion as the ancient vines that wove them together.

ITALY

11 Years Later

J ESSIE MORROW LEFT HER FIANCÉ at an internet café in Siena to work, while she decided to retrace their route to the countryside to find an art gallery, *Galleria di Ribelli - Arte di Chianti*. They passed the sign earlier, but Charles said there was no time because he had an urgent e-mail to send. So she went off to the gallery alone while he worked.

She easily found the sign for the *Galleria* and turned right as it directed. In a kilometer, she saw a second sign pointing left, onto a narrow dusty path, similar to the one that led to their property near Castellina in Chianti. Excited for the adventure, she tightly gripped the Fiat's leather steering wheel and turned toward the art gallery.

Another sign - *Galleria 4 km.*

Whether or not she found the gallery, it didn't matter because the drive itself was worth the trip. The narrow road meandered up a gentle hill, and on her right was a field of grazing cows - huge white ones, the biggest she'd ever seen. On her left, there was an orderly vineyard. As the road climbed, it was increasingly flanked by dark green cypress tree soldiers that added formality to the rustic setting. But the most intriguing sight was a medieval castle tower peeking above the distant trees like a fairytale image. She couldn't put her stirred senses into words, but she had a strong feeling that she was meant to make this excursion. Charles was only a short distance away, but she was confident she needed to be here, alone.

The road entered a bristly woodland, and she lost view of the castle tower ahead and the Chianti Highway behind her. She didn't worry, though. Italy felt safe and serene. And she had sufficient street sense to know when things didn't feel right, honed by necessity while growing up in a rough neighborhood outside New Orleans, the only child of a single, working mom. Not only had her father been absent, but she never even knew his name.

She dodged deep ruts and jagged potholes while the little Fiat created a cloud of dust larger than the car itself, slowly turning the royal blue paint a light shade of milky brown, like so many others in Chianti. After one more bend in the road, she passed another large vineyard close to the roadside. The vines showcased their prized gift to mankind - plump and abundant Sangiovese grapes. They were the primary variety in Chianti wine, as she had learned the day before at a wine tasting.

Soon the castle tower peeked above the trees again. It was closer than she'd realized. After one more sweeping curve along an ancient stone wall and through a dense grove of oak trees, she found a duplicate of the simple hand-painted sign - *Galleria di Ribelli - Arte di Chianti.* She turned right, drove up a short, shaded driveway, and almost stalled the car when she arrived in the gravel parking area. She found the gallery and the castle.

She stopped and sat still, surprised by the discovery and a bit in awe. She didn't know why she hadn't considered that the gallery could be in the castle.

She thought about how Charles would like this place and she could try to bring him back later.

She gazed at the historic structure, hundreds and hundreds of years old. It had withstood weather and wars and had been home to countless generations before her. It would be around beyond her lifetime, giving her a sudden feeling of life's brevity.

In a quaint building next to the castle, the gallery was crafted of uneven fieldstone with thick, rugged mortar sealing the gaps. Its recessed entrance was marked by an arch of red brick bordered with thick ivy.

So beautiful and romantic, she thought.

She parked the car, and when she got out, she attempted to straighten her wrinkled sundress, now sticking to her warm body. The tangerine fabric complemented her bright blue eyes and flattered her fit but curvy figure. She threw her messenger bag over her shoulder and strolled toward the entrance in her favorite broken-in cowboy boots, stopping to take photos. She snapped a shot of the pretty entrance and angled it to include an arrangement of decorative pots. One large pot bore a lemon tree and the others overflowed with red geraniums. A thick row of lavender bordered it all.

This shot will be a perfect backdrop for a painting, she thought. What a dream for an artist to have an art gallery here in the middle of scenic, quiet nowhere, and in a castle, no less. She thought she would love to have the same thing.

The fragrance of lavender filled the air as she approached the solid wood door, which was adorned with a heavy wrought-iron knocker. The door was open, so she passed under the arch and entered, unsure of what to expect. She was immediately enchanted.

Not obvious from the outside, the building was a simple chapel. Its shell-shaped apse featured a faded fresco of the Madonna, and this along with two shallow oak pews was the remaining evidence of the sanctuary's history. It was now a charming gallery of sketches, paintings and photography, all mounted against the warm-white stucco walls.

Slowly she looked around, absorbing it all. The simply framed images of Italy triggered emotions buried deep inside, like they were her own memories she'd been storing in dusty old photo albums, just waiting for the perfect moment and place to be opened. She loved this place, and as she took notice of a wine and olive oil display near the front, she heard the warm, friendly voice of a woman.

"*Buongiorno.*"

Jessie rotated.

"Um, *buongiorno.*"

She pictured her English-Italian dictionary in the dusty Fiat's backseat and wished she had it with her now. Her confidence level in speaking Italian was low.

"Are you American?"

The woman spoke American English.

"Yes," Jessie said with relief. "You too?"

"Well, I've live here many years, but yes. I'm Mary."

She extended her hand.

"Pleased to meet you. I'm Jessica or Jessie."

"Where's home?" Mary asked.

"New Orleans."

"I thought I detected a southern lilt to your voice. New Orleans is an incredible city, one of my favorites, but I haven't been for so long. I used to love going to Jazz Fest, and I have a couple of framed posters in the house."

"Some of those posters are really valuable now. You should look online at the prices, and Jazz Fest is still a great event. It survived Katrina."

"Talking about it makes me miss it. Do they still have the buttery crawfish bread?"

Jessie grinned.

"Yes, it hasn't changed."

"Crawfish sacks and meat pies, too?"

"Yeah."

"Yum! I need to go back someday. But welcome to Chianti, it's quite fantastic here, too. Enjoy the gallery and stay as long as you like."

"Thanks, I have about an hour."

She drifted off, picturing Charles engrossed in work at the Internet café.

"The work is my own, so I can tell you anything you want to know about the pieces."

Mary pushed a long, curly strand of dark brown hair behind her ear.

"I'm glad to know that."

Mary wore a long, lightweight cotton shirt over a pair of loosely flowing white cotton pants, with a long silver pendant that looked like an old pocket watch.

She looks so calm and peaceful, thought Jessie. Her skin is radiant, her dark eyes are warm. She's so naturally beautiful. Jessie thought Mary was probably in her late thirties or early forties.

"All the photos, paintings and sketches on the wall to your right feature this property, including the castle and its adjacent farm, which belongs to my family. On the opposite wall, you'll find images of Siena, Florence and Venice. Everything you see is an original, but I have prints for sale."

Mary gestured toward the front of the gallery.

"The wine and olive oil on the table are our own production. Please feel free to try it. I think it's wonderful, but I'm biased."

She laughed and continued.

"They're available for purchase and the prices are printed at the table. And now my sales pitch is over."

"Thank you."

Jessie loved the gallery and castle she had discovered.

The property must be huge if it contains a castle and a working farm, she thought.

Jessie slowly strolled along the wall to her right, enjoying the black-and-white photographs of the property's landscape and architecture. There were shots of the castle from new angles that weren't visible on her drive, and there were more of what looked like the chapel before it became a gallery.

The collection also captured everyday life, which she enjoyed the most. It included grapes and vines in all seasons, farmers' calloused hands pruning the vines, workers on ladders bundled in heavy clothing collecting olives from trees and tired but smiling faces drinking wine from small juice glasses, lit by the noonday sun.

Jessie carefully examined each piece of art as though she were the photographer or artist herself, standing in Mary's place when she captured the image, seeing the same view as Mary. Instead of moving to the opposite wall, she reversed direction to have a second look at these soul-tickling pieces of art.

"These are so beautiful," Jessie said. "And that's quite an understatement. I feel like there's a story with each of these pieces, and I'd love to hear them all."

Mary smiled and gazed out the small window by her desk.

"You're right, Jessie, they tell a story, and it's safe to say they tell the story of my life, or at least its most important chapters."

Mary gave Jessie an appraising look, as if sizing her up.

"Are you an artist, too?"

"Well, yes, a starving artist."

Jessie began to play with her ponytail.

"I work full-time in a coffeehouse where the owner lets me sell my paintings. It's where I met my fiancé, too. His family's law office is next door. But I haven't created much lately."

Jessie told Mary some details of their upcoming wedding.

"Is your fiancé here with you?" Mary asked.

"Yes, but I left him near Siena to work at an Internet café. The WiFi at our rental villa went out and he had something important to send to his father. So he's there and I'm here. It's not such a bad thing."

Jessie giggled a little.

"Too much time together?" Mary asked. "Sometimes traveling can be tough even with the best of friends."

"Oh my gosh, yes. He's making me crazy, and I'm exhausted by his schedules. He wants everything to be planned, and I want to throw away the maps and explore. He's such a taskmaster, and I haven't really been enjoying myself. I'm beginning to wonder if we're right for each other."

Jessie stopped. She couldn't believe she'd said what she'd been thinking for the last several days, especially to a stranger. But maybe it was easier this way. There was nothing to lose by telling Mary how she felt. She and Charles were nothing alike, never had been, never would be. He was an analytical patent attorney and she was a fiery artist. They were complete opposites, but their physical relationship was as hot and steamy as the New Orleans summers. Suddenly, acutely, she became aware this wasn't enough.

"I presume you like Chianti Classico? It sounds like you might need a glass."

"Like it? Who doesn't?"

Both ladies laughed at the comment.

"Sure. Thank you."

"Good," Mary said. "I think it would be worthwhile to talk. You and I have more in common than you might imagine."

Chapter 86

MARY POURED OUT TWO GLASSES of wine and invited Jessie to sit down at her desk, a simple oak table.

"My first trip to Italy was with my boyfriend," Mary began.

In the time it took them to empty one Ribelli Chianti Classico bottle and open a second, Mary recounted how she ended up living in Italy and owning the gallery.

Jessie listened attentively, mesmerized by the life story of this stranger. But now she wasn't a stranger anymore.

"What an incredible story. I can't believe Luca opened the gallery for you. It's so romantic."

"I almost lost Luca by trying to do the 'right thing,'" Mary reminded her.

Jessie nodded, acknowledging the subtle advice coming from Mary, someone who was in a remarkably similar situation only a decade or so earlier.

"Of course the first several months weren't easy," Mary said. "My mom and sister were upset until they finally came here and met Luca. They fell in love with him and Tuscany, too."

"That must have been a relief."

"Yes, but ending the marriage to Garrett took more time than I expected. There were frequent calls to the U.S. and documents sent back and forth for our divorce. He and his manager ultimately served minimal time in a white-collar jail. Garrett's company was lending for commercial real estate developments. In exchange for falsifying loans for some companies with bad reputations, Garrett and his managers were forging documents. In return they were getting money and other incentives, like the condo in L.A."

"Who would've ever guessed he would do that?"

"I know. Some of the signs were there, like his secrecy about work, and I think his uncle was involved, although he was never incriminated. I don't know why, but I wasn't ever suspicious because he was so accomplished and charismatic. I felt really naïve for a while, but I got over it, especially with all the positive changes I was able to make."

"I can imagine. So you quit your job and opened the gallery here?"

"Basically. At first, it was more like a vacation. I explored on my own, and Luca showed me all of his favorite places. When he worked in Florence, I stayed with him and walked all the city's streets, visited museums, churches, parks and piazzas. It was incredible. About a year later, I was feeling sick and wondered if I had the flu, but it was a baby. So Luca and I decided to have our wedding right here in this chapel. Mr. Moretti was at last able to return to Tuscany, and his family came to the wedding, too. He walked me down the aisle this time."

Mary was radiant as she told Jessie about Mr. Moretti.

"He had a long overdue visit with his family, and his sister Stefania shook some sense into his son. Thank goodness, because Mr. Moretti only lived another six months. It seemed he was holding on for one last visit to his homeland and once he made the trip, he let go."

Mary's eyes filled with tears.

"He was an incredible man. I loved him like a father."

"I feel like I know him," Jessie said. "I wish I had someone like him in my life."

"We named our son after him – Enzo. So a day doesn't go by that I don't say his name. And when Enzo was about two, I opened the gallery."

"Your life is amazing, and Luca sounds incredible."

Mary picked up another framed picture on the desk and handed it to Jessie.

"This is him on our first picnic when I could hardly wait to wrap my arms around him. Do you see why?"

Luca sat on his motorcycle in dark brown jeans and a snugly fitting cotton shirt, parked in front of some cypress trees. Mary looked at the picture the way a young bride might.

"Absolutely! He's hot!"

Jessie laughed at her own comment about someone who might be old enough to be her father.

"Do you still have the leather business? I'd love to buy a jacket."

"No, the year after Enzo was born, Luca's father died, and in the following year we sold the factory to a larger leather producer. But I can recommend some stores in Florence."

"What's Luca doing now?"

"Luca and Giovanni negotiated the estate, with Luca honoring the promises he'd made. In the end, Giovanni decided he had worked long enough and with the inherited money, he and Rossana stopped running the *agriturismo*. Now Luca and I own it, but we have a family living full-time on the property to manage the operations. Giovanni and Rossana work limited hours for us during our peak season, and they're much happier."

Mary took a drink of Chianti and continued.

"Luca has grand plans for Ribelli wine. He bought neighboring vineyards, increased production and we just started exporting it to the U.S. That's where he is now. He's working with the distributors, going to wine tastings and visiting stores across the country."

"Didn't you want to go with him?"

"Not on this trip, but I will another time. I sure do miss him now."

Mary picked up the snapshot again.

"Stella will be here in a couple of days. It's been about a year since I saw her last. She still has her boutique and the Internet has allowed her business to grow beyond anything she expected. She married once, but it only lasted 14 months. So she comes here as often as possible 'in search of her Luca,' as she says."

"She sounds like fun."

"She's wonderful. I ship our wine to her periodically since she hasn't been able to buy it there. But that's quickly changing. Do you know what the name 'Ribelli' means?"

"No idea."

Jessie looked at the bottle's label. It featured a sketch of an antique compass and a vintage typeface.

"An old family name?"

"Good guess. Winery names are often derived like that, and I originally thought the same since I didn't know much Italian, but this name is different. Giovanni and Rossana created it when they started the wine production and *agriturismo*. It translates to The Rebels."

"Oh, I like that."

"It's perfect because it's like all of us, full of spirit and passion."

Jessie thought about the struggles she'd faced in life with her family or lack of one. She'd fought for everything she had with a good dose of spirit and passion.

Mary told Jessie more about how her life had unfolded in Italy. She worked diligently to become fluent in Italian and understand the local dialect while meeting new friends and neighbors. She easily adapted to the Tuscan lifestyle and loved participating in the grape and olive harvests, selling the family's products, working in the gallery and openly sharing their home with Luca's son, Alex. It was Mary who pushed Luca to build the relationship.

"Do they see each other often?"

"He lives here with us now."

Mary looked proud.

"That's great. What does he do?"

"He went to the University of Siena and after he graduated, he began giving tours of the area. He often starts the tours here at the gallery."

"That's interesting. And what about that pocket watch? You're wearing it now. Does it still have the notes in it?"

"Of course. The notes belong in it."

"Do you mind if I ask, did Luca meet his American father?"

"He respects his Italian father for adopting him and giving him so many opportunities, and he's never wanted to his biological father."

"Does he wonder?"

"Sometimes, but he didn't want to disrupt the family that Luke Davis might have now."

As Mary was talking to Jessie, they heard a car pull in the gravel lot. One car door closed, followed by another. Mary looked at the time.

"It must be Alex and Enzo. Their timing is good. I'll have Alex give you a ride to pick up Charles, since I've given you too much wine. I'd like you to bring Charles back and stay here for dinner with us. Okay?"

Jessie smiled.

"We'd enjoy that."

At this point, Jessie didn't care if Charles agreed or not. She wanted more time with Mary and her family.

The door opened and Jessie gasped at the adorable young boy who hurried in. It was Mary's son, Enzo, dressed in brightly colored clothes – orange shorts and a yellow-and-red striped shirt. He looked like both his mother and father with his dark skin, dark wavy hair and dimples. And his eyes were dark like his mother's.

"Hi, my little sweetie."

Alex entered next.

Jessie quickly glanced at the photo of his father and back up at him. Alex had all the handsome features of Luca, including blue eyes, but he had dark blond hair. He was stunning and took her breath away.

"Hi, boys. I'd like you to meet my new American friend, Jessie."

Enzo was shy, but Alex politely reached to shake her hand.

"Good to meet you, I'm Alex."

He flashed a warm smile.

Jessie tried to speak, but no words came out. All these people were larger than life.

"Alex, do you mind taking Jessie to Siena to pick up her fiancé? Where did you say he was, Jessie?"

She managed to squeak out a reply.

"Um, the Cybercafé near the north entrance of town."

"I know the place. I've been there. Do you want to go now?"

"Sure, thank you."

She stood up slowly since her legs felt unstable. She looked at Mary, a beautiful and strong woman who was gently talking to her young son. She scanned the gallery again, admiring the photos, sketches and altar where Mary and Luca were married. She could only dream of having a similar life and took a deep breath, committing the inspiring moment to memory, fully recognizing the path hadn't been easy for Mary.

She followed Alex outside, and as he headed to his car, his leg brushed against the lavender, releasing its soothing scent. Jessie stopped, broke off a few lavender sprigs and stuffed them into her bag, planning to put them in her pillowcase later.

Heading down the hill away from the gallery in Alex's car, Jessie gazed at the scenery, spellbound. She wanted to stay and learn more about this magical place and the Rusconis.

"What's your favorite thing about living in Tuscany?" she asked.

"Spaghetti," he said.

His expression was serious, without a hint of a smile.

"Spaghetti?"

She raised her eyebrows, wondering if he was teasing.

"Yeah. I can't eat enough of it."

"Okay."

She was surprised, but didn't comment.

Alex started laughing.

"Seriously, as a kid, spaghetti was my favorite reason for visiting Italy, because I could eat it every day for lunch and dinner. Now, I know everything is fantastic. I love all the food and the wine, of course. Look around. This place is beautiful, and it's a living history book. I can't get enough of it."

"I can see why."

What little she knew of it, she already felt the same.

"It's a special place, but I must warn you that you have to be careful."

She wondered what he could be talking about. It seemed safe to her.

"Be careful? Of what?"

"You may never want to leave."

ACKNOWLEDGMENTS

THIS IS MY FIRST NOVEL and in no way did I start or get to "The End" on my own. Thank you to all my family and friends who were supportive and encouraging, especially to my husband, Craig, who always had good ideas when I didn't, and to my mom who encouraged me every step of the way, like always.

Several friends deserve special recognition: Robert Rodi, a witty, intelligent and creative writer and editor who gave me wise direction and critique and who can edit Italian as well as English (www.robertrodi.com); Dina Wilder, a clever and honest friend who challenged me to think about the story in ways I hadn't considered; Dario Castagno, whose books and tours of Tuscany are inspiring, enlightening and entertaining (www.dariocastagno.com); and Gail Gross and the 10 Day Book Club, where I published my first few chapters, which enabled me to have the courage and confidence to share my writing publicly (www.10daybookclub.com); Grier Ferguson, a fantastic and patient editor and writer.

So many people read (and reread) manuscripts or gave valuable advice, and I cherish every one of them abundantly: Allison, Andy, Brandi, Brenda, Cara, Carol, Cindy, Connie, Dan, David H., David W., Gail, Greg, Jill, Karen, Ken, Laura H., Laura S., Lisabeth, Marisue, Matt M., Matt S., Melissa R., Melissa S., Phyllis, Richard, Rita, Sandy, Stephanie, Steve, Tanya and Tracey.

In loving memory of my two favorite Italians – Giorgio Rondinara (an immigrant who changed his name to an American one, George Egan Ross) and to his son, my father, George Edward Ross.

AUTHOR'S NOTE about ITALY

ITALY IS A PLACE I LOVE and have explored often, especially Tuscany. As I wrote Chianti Souls, I needed the locale to specifically suit the tale, so Terzano is a fictitious hamlet that is modeled after a real one in Tuscany. You won't find it on a map, only in the wilderness of my imagination.

THE SEQUEL:
"Because of Tuscany"

Before I finished writing "Chianti Souls" I had started the sequel. It picks up where the first book ended and features many of the same characters – Mary, Luca and Stella, and new ones. The story moves from Tuscany to New Orleans and visits Ohio, Kentucky and West Virginia. Mary and Luca's love story continues, but Mary has a couple of problems to solve.

The first four chapters are included with this edition.

ABOUT THE AUTHOR

AS A TEENAGER KAREN ROSS read an excerpt from Alan Alda's commencement speech to the Connecticut College class of 1980, and remarkably, his words still inspire her. Mr. Alda said to the young graduates, "You have to leave the city of your comfort and go into the wilderness of your intuition. You can't get there by bus, only by hard work and risk and by not quite knowing what you're doing, but what you'll discover will be wonderful. What you'll discover will be yourself." Since then, Karen has challenged herself personally and professionally to live on that outside edge of comfortable and writing this debut novel did just that. Not a classically trained writer, she had a story to tell about life experiences: Gutsy romantic love (something not easily found and often lost), soul-tickling romantic Italy, delectable food and wine (especially Chianti) and passionate living and traveling. So she put pen to paper, not sure of what she was getting herself into. The experience was sometimes easy and often challenging, but it was always exhilarating and satisfying. She definitely traveled outside of her "city of comfort," but it was undoubtedly worth the hard work and risk.

CONNECT

Facebook Page: www.facebook.com/chiantisouls
Twitter: @ChiantiSoul
Website: www.chiantigirlpublishing.com
Author Email: chianti.souls@yahoo.com

Suggested Reading Group Questions

1) Italy is a living, breathing character in the book? Could this story be set elsewhere and have the same outcome?

2) What places have inspired you and why?

3) Mary is floundering in relationships. What are the reasons this is happening?

4) CHIANTI SOULS is "an Italian love story." In how many ways is it a love story?

5) Could you forgive Mary for "moving on" with Luca and not breaking up with Garrett first? What is your tolerance of infidelity?

6) Do you think CHIANTI SOULS should be told from a first-person point of view? How would the story change?

7) Why do you think Luca never wanted to find his American father?

8) The character of Mr. Moretti is based on the author's father, who was part-Italian and loved to feed people. What kind a character would your father play in a novel?

9) Where have you traveled that it felt like "home" even though you'd never visited before?

10) Do you know anyone like Patrick Sullivan? Why do you think he lied to Mary about Luca?

11) Did you like Garrett, or want Mary to end that relationship sooner?

12) Mary wasn't close to her mother or sister. Should she have tried to strengthen those relationships?

13) Anna's life in the sixties had much less freedom than women of today's generation. Think about and discuss how much women's independence has changed during your lifetime.

14) Which character would you most like to meet?

Because of Tuscany

A Tale of Friendship and Love

Karen Ross

Chianti Girl \kē-'än-tē, gər(-ə)l\

Definition:
- Knows the power of love and friendship
- Lives passionately and wholeheartedly
- Recognizes her imperfections and embraces them
- Resists judgment of herself and others
- Sometimes drinks too much wine (especially Chianti)

To all the Chianti Girls I know

(you know who you are)

I hope you will go out and let stories happen to you, and that you will work them, water them with your blood and tears and laughter til they Bloom, til you yourself burst into BLOOM.

-Clarissa Pinkola Estes

CHAPTER 1

ॐ

Fayetteville, Ohio

LUKE DAVIS PROPPED the black and white photo of Anna against the Jack Daniel's bottle and stared at her beautiful face. He replayed the memories of the magical four days they had shared nearly thirty years earlier during his military leave in Tuscany. Then he imagined the countless possibilities of what could have happened to her.

Coping with painful memories of Vietnam was difficult, but losing contact with Anna was worse.

He ran his thick fingers through his sandy gray hair and let out a big sigh before emptying the bottle of Jack Daniel's into his glass. Straight up was his preferred way to drink it.

Jack was a constant companion. And so was Scout, the 10-year-old hound mix sleeping at his feet under the table.

The phone rang. It was Caroline.

"Sure," Luke said. "I'll be there in a couple of hours, around eight."

He needed time to shower and stop at the liquor store for a new bottle of Jack.

A warm meal and a night under the covers with Caroline would take care of some of his basic human needs, and hers. In the fifteen or so years since they met at his favorite local dive, they had kept each other company and agreed not to complicate their relationship with commitment. He didn't know why her heart was as frozen as his was because they never talked about things like that.

He studied Anna's face for a minute longer then guzzled the Tennessee spirit. It went down warm like sunshine, but it cooled his aching heart. He let out another big sigh. Scout let out a snort.

He wished he had more photos of her, but this was the only one. And he had carried it with him every day since the sixties, then laminated it in the seventies, but by now the laminated edges were frayed and curled.

He carefully put it back in his wallet and removed the credit card-sized calendar his insurance rep had sent with his annual holiday card. Luke needed to figure out when he could take his next trip to New Orleans.

As a retired firefighter and paramedic, his skills had been invaluable during the months following Hurricane Katrina's wrath on New Orleans. And now his carpentry expertise was equally prized as he helped to rebuild the homes lost in the storm. Since 2005, he averaged two month-long trips a year to the Crescent City, and this year was no different. He had already been there a few months earlier in the spring.

He squinted at the tiny calendar. July was almost over, and he ruled out August because of the Mississippi Delta's sweltering heat and humidity. In September and October, he was booked because he had volunteered to be an extra hand at his friend's nursery and landscaping business. Autumn was peak season in Ohio for selling and planting trees.

At 68, he could still perform heavy-duty landscaping tasks because his back was as strong as an ox. His arms and legs were well built, too, attracting second looks from ladies of all ages – especially when they saw his baby blues. No one ever guessed he was over sixty.

The month of November will be best, Luke thought.

He didn't mind hopping into his Ford pick-up he called "Big Blue" and making the 12-hour drive to New Orleans with Scout. But he'd call his friend Tom to find out if he wanted to go, too. Same as Luke, Tom was an excellent carpenter, but he would probably want to be home for Thanksgiving with his kids and grandkids.

As a lifelong bachelor, the holiday didn't matter as much to Luke. In fact, he preferred being out of town and working. Then he'd have a good reason for being alone.

CHAPTER 2

ಋಲಿಂಗ಄ಲ

Terzano, Tuscany

MARY LISTENED AS Luca made calls to U.S. wine distributors to confirm his upcoming appointments in New York City, Newark, Philadelphia, Chicago, Miami and Atlanta.

"I wish I could make this trip with you," she said after his last call.

Luca wrapped his arms around her waist and gazed into her big, dark eyes.

"I know, and I would like to take you with me. But when I return in the winter for the West Coast sales calls and wine expos, you'll be there."

"I know," she said.

Even though it was Ferragosto – a holiday period in August for most Italians– she needed to stay home. She had to take care of their nine-year-old son Enzo, and there was a never-ending list of work for the art gallery, two vacation rental properties, the winery and the fourteenth-century villa they called home. And her adult stepson Alex had limited time to help because he was busy with his thriving Tuscan tour business. So she knew it was impossible to join her husband on this trip.

"Will the boys be home tonight?" Luca asked.

"Enzo is spending the night with his cousin, and Alex is staying with friends in Siena."

"Hmmm, an empty house. Is this on purpose?"

"What do you think?"

Luca smiled and slid his hands up Mary's back, under her long dark wavy hair. He pulled her closer.

"So dinner in the courtyard?" he asked.

"Of course."

"Mm."

He cradled the back of her head in his hands and kissed her.

The open-air courtyard in the center of their home was their *paradiso*. They savored time together in this sacred place as often as possible, giving in to the rhythm of life and love under the night sky.

This was where they made love the first time. On that wildly romantic night surrounded by warm candlelight, ancient castle walls and a twinkling night sky, Luca had told Mary their souls already knew each other, and it was only their bodies that were new.

Twelve years later and now in their mid-forties, their soulful connection was as strong as ever, and they knew each other's every curve and crevice.

This night was not much different than the first one, but this time they started it with a picnic-style dinner in the courtyard.

Mary prepared a simple antipasto plate of meat, cheese and marinated vegetables, a basket full of crusty bread and their winery's own Ribelli Chianti.

Luca piled cotton blankets on the ground and surrounded them with a dozen candles.

They settled in at sunset and the *cucina povera* nourished their bodies while the Chianti wine warmed their souls.

As the sky grew darker, they lit the candles and it didn't take much longer until their clothes were off. Their bodies exquisitely melded together in the way only the bodies of two people who share a deep love can.

After making love, they fell asleep tangled in each other's arms, not waking until just before sunrise on Saturday by the rooster crows of the Tuscan countryside.

Luca was catching the early bus to Rome's Leonardo da Vinci airport for a New York-bound flight. The bus was efficient, and it was the most economical means of transportation to Rome. This, and other sensible decisions, helped them save money to reinvest in their business.

"The two weeks will go fast," Mary said, as Luca got out of her royal blue Fiat at the bus station.

She was trying to convince herself and even nodded her head as though it would help.

"Stella will be here in a week," she said. "And we'll go to the Palio. She's never been so it should be fun."

"And it might be a good time to work on your novel. You will have some quiet time without me trying to steal all your attention."

He winked one of his soft blue eyes.

"What do you think I prefer?" Mary asked. "Being naked with you or writing?"

"Let me think."

He touched his lips with his forefinger.

"Hmmm..."

Then he winked again.

"Stop it," she said. "You look too sexy. It makes me want to take you back to home with me."

"You better not," he said. "I have some wine to sell."

"Like you always say, wine gets better with age. So the wine can wait!"

"You would not do that."

"You're right. I wouldn't because we've worked so hard for this opportunity. And I have a lot to do this morning to get the apartment ready at the Cielo villa for the German couple who get in this afternoon."

"We need more people like them to rent that villa."

"I know," she said. "We're getting too many cancellations. But it's probably a blessing in disguise since we've had our fair share of repairs to make."

Luca didn't say anything else.

The Cielo villa was a delicate topic. On paper, buying the neighboring property five months earlier was a good idea because it doubled their vineyard size and provided four additional apartment rental units in addition to the six they already owned at their other farmhouse called Ribelli.

The price had also been good. They bought it below market value because the recently widowed owner had to leave abruptly. She was older and unable to care for it alone, so she moved in with her younger sister in Florence.

But since purchasing it, Mary and Luca had dealt with endless repairs, so the new venture hadn't gone exactly as planned.

Luca's only brother Giovanni had even warned them against purchasing it. Giovanni strongly believed a local rumor that there was a hex on the villa by Sardinian ghosts, or the Sardi, as everyone referred to them.

Luca thought it was nonsense and didn't listen to Giovanni because he rarely agreed with his older brother. Luca only saw the villa's potential value to expand their business, and he still stood by his decision.

Mary wasn't sure yet.

"Hopefully, this week will be better," she said.

Luca barely nodded.

Mary held him closely before saying goodbye. Then she watched the love of her life walk toward the bus in his dark tee and faded jeans, pulling a suitcase. He had a black blazer draped over his tanned arm, and carried a weathered saddle brown leather briefcase. The bag was at least twenty years old and was made in the family leather factory they once owned.

Mary never tired of this backside view. His long, dark hair hit the top of his tee, which stretched across his solid shoulders, and his jeans snuggly wrapped his muscular legs.

He was more than a dream-come-true. Her life with him had blended as perfectly as the Tuscan sun and soil do to make wine. And like wine, Luca got better with age, too.

CHAPTER 3

❧❧❦❦

MARY VISITED HER 92-year-old friend Dorotea Turchi every Saturday morning, traveling the kilometer or so to get there either by car or on foot, depending upon the weather.

She decided to stop in today on her way home from the bus station. It was earlier than her usual visits, but she knew Dorotea would be awake. Mary knocked on her front door and Dorotea answered and invited her into the kitchen.

"*Caffé e crostata?*" Dorotea asked.

"Sure," Mary said. "You know I can never turn down a slice of your homemade tart."

Dorotea loved baking cookies, cakes, tarts and bread, and everyone in the hamlet of Terzano benefitted from her incredible cooking skills. Since she couldn't eat everything she made, she always shared her homemade goods with friends and neighbors – even the ones she didn't like – because the delivery of a homemade treat was the best way to keep up with the local gossip.

"It is a peach tart today," Dorotea said.

As Mary was finishing the heavenly slice of tart, Dorotea got a funny look on her face.

"I'm getting a strong message for you. I need your hands."

Dorotea had psychic abilities, but very few people knew this. In fact, Mary was possibly the only living person with this knowledge because Dorotea had outlived many of her friends and family members. She had asked Mary to keep her ability as a secret, because she didn't want people asking her to tell their fortunes. Dorotea only shared very important visions, as deemed by her.

Dorotea placed her hands over Mary's palms and was silent for a minute.

"I have never had such a powerful premonition. Maybe it is because you are in the room with me."

She paused for another half minute or so.

"You are about to have some new people come into your life," Dorotea said. "There is a lady who will come soon, very soon. She is smart, but a devil rides on one shoulder. A powerful angel is on the other. But she needs your help. She is lucky, because she will have you to play a critical role. I must add, you are the only person who can do this for her."

Mary waited for Dorotea to say more, but she didn't.

"What will I need to do for her?" Mary asked.

"Chase away her devil."

Mary raised an eyebrow.

"What? How will I do that?"

"It is for you to figure out. Your heart and soul will guide you, as always."

The answer was vague, but Mary knew Dorotea never said more than she wanted to say.

"There is one more thing I am seeing," Dorotea said. "You can rest your worries. Luca is going to have much prosperity on his trip in the United States."

"I'm happy to hear that."

Mary wasn't surprised, though, because Luca was determined to make their wine a global success. And he worked hard every day to make it happen.

"Can you tell me anything more about the lady?"

"I can only say it is your destiny, too. By fulfilling your role, you will be rewarded as greatly as she will be."

Mary had many more questions, but she knew it was useless to keep probing once Dorotea had decided she had said enough.

"Well, I better head to the grocery store," Mary said, standing up. "Do you have your list ready?"

"Of course. Here it is."

Dorotea gave Mary a small piece of paper with her grocery items scrawled on it and several Euros.

"I'll be back soon."

Mary hopped into her car and rolled down the windows. She headed to the nearest Coop grocery store, enjoying the fresh air before the sun rose in the sky and it got too hot. Mary didn't mind making the trip to the grocery for Dorotea. Her older friend had never driven a car before, so she needed help getting her groceries.

Of all the people Mary had met in Italy, it was Dorotea who had become her closest friend. Dorotea was a lot like an older Italian friend she had known in Philadelphia named Enzo Moretti. He had owned a deli near her apartment and was from Tuscany. Warm and nurturing, Mr. Moretti had become a surrogate father to Mary and shared his love for Italy with her. She even named her son after him.

Mary kept thinking about "the lady with the devil on her shoulder." She had no idea what it could mean, but she wasn't surprised about the premonition that she would meet someone new. In the seven years she had operated her art gallery deep in the heart of Tuscany, a cast of interesting characters had sought out the small haven perched high upon a hilltop.

But this was the first time Dorotea had ever predicted she would meet a stranger who needed help. So Mary knew to be on the lookout, because Dorotea's premonitions had proven to be accurate time and time again.

In fact, Mary often asked Dorotea for guidance about their business decisions, but she hadn't told Luca she did this. He wouldn't have put much credibility in it. The main reason Mary still had some confidence about buying Cielo was because Dorotea wholeheartedly gave her approval of the purchase.

Yet Mary couldn't help wonder if there was more to the story. The problems with the villa were so frequent it didn't seem right. It was time to ask Dorotea about it, but today she was short on time. She'd ask another day.

CHAPTER 4

᪥᪥᪥᪥

BY WEDNESDAY, Mary missed Luca like crazy. Minutes felt like days and hours like weeks. Their daily lives were so intertwined with running the business together and taking care of their family – and Mary loved it.

She started writing an email message to Luca, but had only typed a few sentences when a solo female traveler walked into the gallery.

The woman wore broken-in cowboy boots and a tangerine sundress that looked like it was from the seventies. A weathered canvas messenger bag was thrown across her five-foot-eight, curvy body. She had long dark hair pulled into a ponytail and bright blue eyes.

It wasn't often young women came in the gallery alone, and if they did they weren't dressed like this. Most tourists wore practical no-iron shorts and shirts in neutral colors. And Mary was pretty sure this was her first visitor to wear cowboy boots, especially with an above-the-knee length dress. She liked this lady's style, and Mary suddenly suspected she was the lady who Dorotea predicted would arrive.

"*Buongiorno,*" Mary said.

"Um, *buongiorno,*" the visitor said.

"Are you American?"

"Yes. Thank God, you speak English. My Italian is horrible. Are you an American, too?"

"Well, I've lived here many years, but yes. I'm Mary."

She extended her hand.

"Pleased to meet you. I'm Jessica or Jessie."

"Where's home?" Mary asked.

"New Orleans."

"I thought I detected a Southern lilt to your voice. New Orleans is an incredible city, one of my favorites, but I haven't been for so long. I used to love going to Jazz Fest, and I have a couple of framed posters in the house. I need to go back there someday. But welcome to Chianti - it's quite fantastic here, too. Enjoy the gallery and stay as long as you like."

"Thanks, I have about an hour."

Jessie slowly strolled along one wall of photos and then turned back to look at them again.

"These are so beautiful," Jessie said. "And that's quite an understatement. I feel like there's a story with each of these pieces. I'd love to hear them all."

Mary smiled and gazed out the small window by her desk.

"You're right, Jessie, they do tell a story, and it's safe to say they tell the story of my life, or at least its most important chapters."

Mary gave Jessie an appraising look, as if sizing her up.

"Are you an artist, too?"

"Well, yes, a starving artist," Jessie said. "I don't sell enough to make a living at it."

Jessie began to play with her ponytail.

"I work full-time in a coffeehouse where the owner lets me sell my paintings. It's where I met my fiancé, too. His family's law office is next door. But I haven't created much lately."

"Is your fiancé here in Italy with you?" Mary asked.

"Yes, but I left him near Siena to work at an Internet café. The WiFi at our rental villa went out and he had something important to send to his father, who is also his boss. So he's there and I'm here. It's not such a bad thing."

Jessie giggled a little.

"Too much time together?" Mary asked. "Sometimes traveling can be tough even with the best of friends."

"Oh my gosh, yes. He's making me crazy, and I'm exhausted by his schedules. He wants everything to be planned, and I want to throw away the maps and explore. He's such a taskmaster, and I haven't really been enjoying myself. I'm really beginning to wonder if we're right for each other."

Mary's heart skipped a few beats when she heard this last bit about Jessie's fiancé. The story was eerily familiar. Twelve years earlier her own boyfriend Garrett had brought her to Tuscany promising the romantic vacation of her dreams. But he went home after three days to manage an office crisis. Mary chose to finish the vacation alone and this opened the door for her to spend time with Luca who added the romantic part of her Tuscan vacation. This hadn't been Mary's intention at all, especially since Garrett proposed to her before leaving Italy.

She has to be the lady Dorotea told me about, Mary thought. Perhaps her hardworking fiancé is her devil, just like Garrett had turned out to be a devil.

"You and I have more in common than you can imagine," Mary said.

She offered Jessie a glass of Chianti because it seemed like she needed one – and because it would give them time to talk.

An hour later, the two ladies had drowned themselves in conversation and a bottle and a half of wine. Drinking this much in the middle of the day wasn't typical for Mary, but she had to know more about Jessie. And she couldn't help but give her some advice. She wanted to make sure Jessie knew she shouldn't have to talk herself into marrying anyone.

Mary did this subtly by telling Jessie about the difficult relationship with Garrett that led to living in Tuscany with Luca.

By the time Jessie had to leave, Mary was almost convinced that Jessie was Dorotea's lady, but she wanted more time to get to know her. So she invited Jessie and her fiancé, Charles, to return for dinner, and Jessie accepted.